IN THE BLOOD

Lisa Unger

SIMON & SCHUSTER

London · New York · Sydney · Toronto · New Delhi

A CBS COMPANY

D0100421

First published in the US by Simon & Schuster, Inc., 2014
First published in Great Britain by Simon & Schuster UK Ltd, 2014
A CBS COMPANY

1 3 5 7 9 10 8 6 4 2

Simon & Schuster UK Ltd
1st Floor
222 Gray's Inn Road
London WC1X 8HB

www.simonandschuster.co.uk

Simon & Schuster Australia, Sydney
Simon & Schuster India, New Delhi

A CIP catalogue record for this book is available
from the British Library

HB ISBN: 978-1-47111-143-3
TPB ISBN: 978-1-47111-144-0
PB ISBN: 978-1-47111-145-7
EBOOK ISBN: 978-1-47111-146-4

Typeset by M Rules
Printed and bound by CPI Group (UK) Ltd, Croydon, CR0 4YY

For
Ocean Rae

I love you like the cherry blossom loves the wind.

Tiger, tiger, burning bright
In the forests of the night,
What immortal hand or eye
Could frame thy fearful symmetry?
In what distant deeps or skies
Burnt the fire of thine eyes?
On what wings dare he aspire?
What the hand dare seize the fire?
And what shoulder and what art
Could twist the sinews of thy heart?

William Blake, "The Tiger"

prologue

There are twelve slats of wood under my bed. I know this because I count them over and over. *Onetwothreefourfivesix-seveneightnineteneleventwelve*. I whisper the numbers to myself and the sound of it comforts me as I'm sure a prayer would comfort someone who believes in God. It's amazing how loud a whisper can be. Surrounded down there by the white glow of my bed skirt, the sound of my own voice in my ears, I can almost block out the screaming, the horrible keening. And then there's the silence, which is so much worse.

In the quiet, which falls like a sudden night, I can hear the beating of my own heart, feel it thudding in my chest. I lie very still, willing myself to sink into the pile of the carpet lower and lower until I don't exist at all. There is movement downstairs. I hear the sound of something heavy scraping across the dining room floor. *What is he doing?*

I have come to this place before. Here, I have hidden from the frequent and terrible storms of my parents' miserable marriage. And I have listened as their voices break through the thick walls and the heavy, closed doors.

1

But usually I can only hear the angry cadence of their voices, and very rarely their words, which I know to be hateful and spiked with old hurts and bitter resentments. It is a poison in the air, a toxic cloud. *Onetwothreefourfivesixseveneight-nineteneleventwelve.* Sticks and stones can break your bones, but words can break your heart.

Tonight it is different. My palms feel hot and sticky. I lift them up and look to see they are covered in blood, the lines on my hands in stark white relief against the red black. I am overcome by a panicked confusion. What happened? Already, it's slipping from my grasp, the last few hours. I have a kind of amnesia when it comes to my parents' battles. I try to forget them and often succeed. *Everything okay at home?* my teacher asked recently. *Great,* I said. *Fine.* And the surface me meant it, even though the deep and buried part knew it wasn't true. I should have been sending up flares, instead I was offering smiles. I just wanted so badly for things to be normal. I had worked so hard for that.

Downstairs, my father issues a grunt of effort. *What happened?* I push hard into my own memory, but a big part of me is shutting down. I can see my own hand (clean) reaching for the front door, hear the hiss of the school bus moving away, and my friend Joelle knocking on her bus window. I turned to wave; she motioned for me to call her.

I had the familiar stone of dread in my chest as I pushed inside. My dad has been out of work, a journalist in the age of digital media. His department got smaller and smaller and smaller, until he, too, was called into the editor's office. He kept a good outlook at first. But as the months turned into a year, his attitude grew ever more sour. And my parents were home together, all day long. I never knew what I was going to come home to, as they swung between poles of giddy optimism and bleak despair.

But when I open that door in my memory, it's only a black tunnel that I see. *Onetwothreefourfivesixseveneight-nineteneleventwelve.* And now I hear my father's footsteps. He is walking from the dining room, slow and steady down the hall. He pauses, as he always does, at the mirror. I hear the familiar creak on the bottom stair and then he's climbing up, his footsteps heavy and weary. Halfway up, he stops. He says my name but I don't answer. My whole body is quivering. I am in the tunnel, falling and falling, swirling and tumbling like when they put that anesthesia mask over your face and tell you to count backward from one hundred and you can't make it even to ninety-eight.

He's on the upstairs landing and walking toward my room. He says my name again, but I still don't answer.

We have to talk. Don't hide from me. There's nowhere to hide from this.

And then he's in my doorway. I can hear him breathing; it sounds like the ocean or the way my mother breathes when she's practicing yoga on the back porch, or the wind through the leaves outside my window.

And then the screaming starts again, it slices through me.

3

It takes me a second to realize that it's not my mother screaming, it's me, loud and long in all my fear and misery. My father drops to his knees and I see his face made strange and unrecognizable by all that has passed. Then he reaches under the bed for me.

PART ONE: **lana**

1

The winter day was gray and cool, not frigid as it had been. But still it was a very typical January day in upstate New York—barren, chill, flat. I rode my bike around the small, deserted campus, reveling in a quiet that is at its most total right before everyone returns from winter break. The trees were bare, twisted fingers reaching up into the thick, low cloud cover.

I had just returned to school from an unbearable holiday spent with my unbearable aunt and unbearable cousins. (And I know for a fact that they feel exactly the same way about me.) But we *did* bear up, because that's what family does, isn't it? We bear up, together, like it or not.

And so they tolerated the dark-haired, dark-eyed sulking interloper, a wraith in their sunny, golden-haired midst. And I tolerated their terrible happy togetherness. But I knew, and so did they, that I had not quite been folded in. I was a cockroach in the batter of their sweet lives. Too polite to remove me, they ate around me.

I can't fault them, really. Because they are kind and good, and they took me in against all advice and good sense. And I do try to be polite, and they do, as well. And we are all very good at enduring unhappiness, especially my aunt, who had a great deal of practice early on.

"I have created my life," she said, in one of the torturous heart-to-hearts she tried to have with me. "And you're smart enough to do the same."

She believes that, she really does. She thinks that we are made and not born, that it is the power of choice that forms our lives. With enough positive energy and good feng shui we can overcome almost anything. She's one of those, the magical thinkers. I think I envy her, even if I can hardly suppress my disdain.

It was *that* time, with graduation right around the corner, when people wanted to know what you were going to do with your life. Graduate school seemed like a good bet, if for no other reason than it delayed my emergence from the freedom and indulgence of academics into the world of alarm clocks and ambition, and nine-to-five. I couldn't see myself sitting in a cube somewhere—file cabinets and ringing phones, office birthday cakes and paper cuts. What was a psychology major fit for, if not for more education? The human mind, with all its mystery, bears endless study. Doesn't it?

But if I hadn't quite made any decisions on that front, I knew one thing. I needed a job. There was money for everything—for school and housing, for books and extras.

My parents, whatever their failings, had made sure of it. There was an account, and I had a lawyer whom I called if I needed something: Skylar Lawrence, the man with the checkbook. He always sounded young on the phone, like a teenage girl. But he was old, ancient even—stooped and bald, draped in expensive suits, sporting gold-rimmed spectacles. He had known my parents for many years, and was the executor of my mother's estate and manager of my trust. We'd met a couple of times over the years—solemn visits in his office, where he droned on about the status of my mother's investments, budgets, conditions of the trust. I would sit, nodding sagely, with no idea what he was talking about, too shy to ask many questions.

When I thought of him, which was really only when I needed money, I always envisioned him dwarfed in his huge leather chair, with his stunning view of Manhattan spread about him like a glittering carpet. With a gnarled hand, he'd press a button and money would appear in my checking account. I know: a trust-fund baby, how annoying. Believe it, you wouldn't want to be me.

During my last conversation with Sky, he suggested that I might find some work since my class schedule was light.

"It would be a good thing for you," he said. I heard a sharp inhale and slow exhale. He was a smoker; there was an occasional edge to his otherwise youthful voice, sudden bursts of wet, rattling coughs. "To earn something of your own."

9

"Okay," I said. I always said that. It was my stock response when I didn't know what to say.

"Because you're an adult now," he went on, as though I'd put up an argument. "And you need to decide what you are going to make of your life. Earning your own way is part of that."

"You sound like Aunt Bridgette."

I heard the hiss of a match lighting, and he drew in another breath sharply. I suppose it wasn't a stretch to think that this was a scheme they'd hatched together. *We choose who we are*, she'd said over break, certainly not for the first time. And I could tell that it was important to her that I believe that. We don't inherit everything.

"Am I out of money or something?" I asked.

"Not yet," he said. "But as you know, there is a period of diminished support after graduation. You won't come into your trust until you're thirty. It was your mother's wish that you find your calling, and earn your own way."

"Right," I said. Of course, I knew this. Both Sky and Bridgette had mentioned it repeatedly. But somehow it had always seemed so very far away, that time when I'd spread my wings and fly on my own. Here I was, on the edge of the academic nest and looking down. I had no idea whether I'd take to the air or crash into a pile of bones.

"So, when you say 'diminished support,' you mean … ?"

He told me the small yearly sum I would receive, just to help make ends meet and to provide for some extras should

I have a low-paying job. "Your mother wanted you to follow your dreams, make a difference. It was her hope that you'd help people. She didn't want you to choose your career based on how much it paid, but she did want you to do something."

Of course, no one ever mentioned my father or what he wanted from me.

"I know," I said. "I will."

So, that first day back after my winding, solitary bike ride around campus, I walked to the office of student affairs to gaze at the job board. I was weirdly excited. I liked the idea of doing something other than studying, which I had been doing diligently for years. I had been the valedictorian of my high school class. I had a perfect 4.0 average at university. Knowledge and the regurgitation of such in the form of essay and exam came very easily to me. It was everything else that came hard.

Dog walker? Coffeehouse waitress? Bookstore clerk? Librarian assistant? Math tutor? The board was a colorful riot of help-wanted notices, and the possibilities seemed endless. The office assistant was typing behind me. Beside me the phone rang three times, went silent, then started ringing again. I ripped off little paper tags with phone numbers on them. I imagined myself tugged down the street by five dogs with bladders about to burst, or rushing between bistro tables delivering espressos to the undercaffeinated, or quietly filing homeless books,

11

putting them in proper order. Is that what my mom would have wanted for me? Did these jobs qualify as helping people?

"What about this one?"

Startled from my reverie, I saw my psychology professor lingering nearby. He was looking at yet another board brimming with offers. So many people with menial needs, offering positions to those of us desperate for pocket money. It was a sub-economy: easy jobs for overprivileged youth. It seemed like an inside joke. While the larger economy faltered and the working poor labored tirelessly only to make ends meet, some of us drifted on a silly cloud, only asking to receive. Or maybe that's just me being cynical.

I walked over to stand beside him. He was squinting through his glasses as he pulled a notice off the board and handed it to me.

"'Single mother looking for afternoon help with her eleven-year-old son,'" I read. "'After school through dinner, some overnights.'"

"Should work with your schedule," he said easily. I had mentioned to him my need for a job before break and he'd promised to be on the lookout for something suitable.

In addition to being my teacher, he was also my school counselor. He'd come to the university shortly after I started. And we'd always walked the line of friendship, which was easier now that I was older.

Langdon Hewes was a study in propriety. We had only met in public places, or with the door to his office wide open. He was too young to be so cautious, but he hinted at having had some kind of negative past experience. And I didn't pry—because I certainly didn't want to talk about my past either. He ran a hand through the perpetual tousle of his dark hair, and looked down at me from his towering height.

"Nanny?" I said, skeptical.

"More like babysitter," he said.

"What's the difference?"

He shrugged, looked up. He had this way of searching the sky or the ceiling for his answers. He'd tilt his head up and squint into nothingness, as if it were all there in the ether, just waiting to be found.

"Nannies are for little kids," he said finally. "It's more of a full-time position. Babysitting is, like, more casual, more as needed."

He said this with a firm nod that brooked no questioning. Even though he surely knew nothing about nannies or babysitters, I took him at his word. He *did* have a Ph.D. in child psychology, was the known expert in childhood psychopathy. He'd published several articles in major consumer magazines—including the *New York Times Magazine, Psychology Today, Vanity Fair,* as well as the ever-important academic journals. Publish or perish; it was no joke at this school. He was currently at work on a book, a collection of case studies that was, he hoped, a blend between a text and something more mainstream. So maybe his opinion on this topic counted for something. At least that's what I told myself.

I held the ad in my hand. Unlike the other pink and green and yellow sheets, with their fun or fancy typefaces, this was just a plain white paper, with centered Times New Roman text. It offered nothing but its own simplicity. A need in black and white, waiting to be filled.

"You only have three classes this term," he said. "Mine, criminal psychology, and art. Light load. Never a good idea to have too much time on your hands."

I wouldn't call him handsome, but there was something pleasant about his aspect. Even his slouch, his perfectly pressed oxfords and chinos (sometimes jeans), those Merrell cross-training shoes, had a kind of comforting predictability. With Langdon, there were never any surprises. My own inner life was always chaotic, churning. I wondered what it was like to be so even, so measured. His presence never failed to calm me.

"I'll be your reference."

"I don't have any babysitting experience."

"You're a psych major," he said. "There was your internship at Fieldcrest. You were fabulous with the kids." He said this with a smile, as though it was a little private joke. "You got an A in my class."

My work at Fieldcrest, a school associated with the university for troubled and emotionally challenged young people, had been intense, to say the least. I was pleased that he thought I'd done a good job there. It was the first time he'd said so out loud, even though the internship evaluation he'd written had been glowing. I shifted forward, closer to him, feeling a little jolt of excitement. There was something about the paper in my hand, about his being there, about the prospect of something new in my life.

I fished my phone from my backpack and dialed the number as we walked into his office. I sat across from his desk and he sat, spun to face his computer, and started typing.

"My name is Lana Granger," I said when a woman answered. "I'm answering your ad."

"Oh, great," she said. She sounded slightly breathless. I heard paper rustling in the background. "Can you come for an interview today?"

Outside the window, it seemed like a ray of sun had broken through the cloud cover and I saw a little bit of blue in the sky for what seemed like the first time in months.

"Uh," I said stupidly. I hadn't expected things to progress so quickly. But why not? I guess when you needed a sitter, you really needed a sitter. I looked at my wrist only to realize that I wasn't wearing a watch. I didn't even own a watch. And I knew that I had nothing whatsoever to do that day anyway. "Sure."

"Perfect," she said. She sounded bright and cheerful; nice, I guess. "After lunch, say two-ish?"

We made all the arrangements, exchanged necessary information like her address (just a quick bike ride away from campus), her name (Rachel Kahn, son Luke), my phone number. After I hung up, Langdon turned to look at me. He had an odd expression on his face, something I couldn't read. But he was like that, a total brain, his mind always working, figuring, developing theories.

"Good work," he said.

"I didn't do anything," I answered. "It was just a phone call."

"Today is the beginning of your real life," he said. "This could be your first *actual* job."

I couldn't tell if he was making fun of me in that sweet, gentle way that he had. But I found myself smiling at him. It did feel like kind of a big deal, and my stomach was a little fluttery with happiness. And I was glad I had him to share it with.

"I'll take you out to lunch to celebrate," he said. "Let's go get some pizza."

I thought about my aunt Bridgette, who is not really so unbearable. Seriously. It's only that she's not my mother. Though I know she cares for me, she doesn't love me. Only a child who has lost a mother knows how yawning and uncrossable is the space between those two things. *Just because horrible things have happened to you doesn't mean you can't have a happy, normal life*, she'd said to me once. I had felt sorry for her, only because I suspected that she might be wrong. I was marked, wasn't I? Forever? But for whatever silly reason as we left Langdon's office, I let myself wonder if maybe she was right after all.

2

I could have gone to college anywhere. My grades and test scores, essays and recommendations, garnered me admissions to Harvard, Columbia, and Stanford. I'm not bragging. It's totally true. But I just couldn't see myself in any of those places. They seemed big and impersonal, and I imagined myself wandering in crowds of people, sitting in the back of stadium-size classrooms. I saw myself moving dark and small, unwanted, out of place among the world's financial and intellectual elite like a raisin in the sun.

"But a degree from one of these schools is your ticket to *anything*," said my uncle in dismay. "Your mother would have been so *proud* of you."

What he didn't understand was that, at that point, I didn't actually *want* to do anything. I just wanted to hide. I wanted to find a safe place and disappear inside it. I didn't want to Achieve Great Things or Make Everyone Proud or Prove Them All Wrong. I just wanted to be left alone.

I chose Sacred Heart College in The Hollows, New York.

And if everyone was disappointed that I had decided on a tiny but well-regarded liberal arts college in the middle of nowhere, no one was surprised. Everyone expected bad decisions and unpleasant outcomes from my side of the family, and this was the least of them.

The minute I stepped on the campus, small and isolated on 132 acres of land, I felt ensconced, secreted away. I wouldn't be asked to do anything special here, I thought with relief. It wouldn't be expected that I distinguish myself. This town, The Hollows, this school, would wrap themselves around me, and keep me safe. Just like I wanted. I was immediately accepted and I enrolled right away without a second thought.

New, gleaming buildings stood shoulder to shoulder with historic structures. A tall Norman tower stood at the center of the campus and loomed high as you pulled down the long, tree-lined drive up to campus. One was greeted on arrival by a rambling five-story colonial, which housed the president's office and her staff. Students and faculty assembled there, in the grand foyer, for all parties and gatherings. There was a stone chapel where services were held. Alongside that, in the spring and summer, was an elaborate herb and vegetable garden. Because of the competitive equestrian team, there was also a stable of horses, as well as a small barn of animals—including laying hens and three milking cows.

Winding running paths laced through the acres of woods

populated by oak and maple, sycamore and birch. The dormitory buildings—Evangeline, Dominica, Marianna, and Angelica—were four renovated Victorian-era mansions with barely a right angle between them. It was my dream of a college dorm, with curved baluster staircases, bay windows, restored woodwork. Imagine towers of bookshelves packed with leather-bound volumes, secret attic rooms, and tiny, winding back staircases. And yet we had high-speed wireless, cable, and laundry in the basement, all the modern conveniences.

The classroom buildings and library, science center, gymnasium, and a newer dorm building were all gleaming glass and stone. Built to coordinate in essence with the older buildings, they seemed to mesh with rather than oppose the existing structures.

There was a part of me that hoped never to leave the safety and isolation of a school campus. Certainly, I knew it was possible; Langdon never had. He'd done his undergraduate work at Boston University. Then went on to get his master's and his Ph.D. in childhood psychology, as well as his postdoctoral certificate in psychoanalysis and psychotherapy. Now, he was a full tenured professor here at Sacred Heart.

"It's a life sentence," he always joked.

He also worked as a clinical psychologist at the nearby hospital, and with troubled children at Fieldcrest. Fieldcrest was a school where children went when no one else would take them anymore—bring me your bipolar, your ADHD, your raging, your callous-unemotional.

I'd done several internships with Langdon at the school—art therapy, some poetry with the least disturbed of the kids. I could see myself following his path. I could see myself helping people in a significant way doing something like that. And I made the mistake of saying so over Christmas break. The leaden silence that followed was almost a scream.

"Oh, but," said my aunt with that strained smile she always seemed to wear when I was around. "There are so many other things you could do."

I felt myself bristle. My cousin Rose was at FIT; she wanted to be a fashion designer. My other cousin Lily (I know. My aunt is *really* into gardening) was studying film at NYU's Tisch School of the Arts. They were bright and creative and gorgeous, both of them, full of life and energy and promise. Maybe that was because my aunt had *created* her life, as she was so fond of saying, and my mother had most certainly not created hers. But I wasn't Bridgette's child, was I?

"I want to help people," I said weakly. "My mother wanted me to help people."

"Your mother wanted you to be happy and free and safe," said Bridgette with uncommon passion. She was usually so *careful* with me, so *gentle*. I always wondered if she wasn't a little afraid of me, of what she might see if she pushed me too hard.

"I don't know what that means," I said.

My uncle and my two cousins had drifted from the room, presumably to play with their new iPads. We'd all gotten one from Santa.

"It *means* that you don't spend your whole life with *psychopaths*," she said. This time she nearly shouted. And then she covered her mouth and bowed her head, blond waves bouncing, diamonds glittering. "I'm sorry."

The Christmas tree was glimmering, the fire crackling (even though we were in *Florida* with the a/c cranking—I mean, come on, the *planet*, people!). A low strain of classical music—Mozart, Beethoven, who knows?—was coming from the mounted speakers. We sat on chintz sofas, leaning against perfectly coordinated throw pillows. I caught sight of myself in the mirror, a slim black line with folded hands and furrowed brow, an ink stain on cream silk.

"But what if …" I started to say. I hadn't voiced this thought to anyone. And I almost didn't want to. She stared at me expectantly, eyes wide open and caring.

"What if?" she said. She was eager to make a connection to me, always had been. It was I who pushed her away, rebuffing her with chilly politeness and icy platitudes.

"What if I *could* help someone?" I said. "What if I could keep someone from doing something horrible?"

We locked eyes—hers a deep blue, mine coal black. Each of us had endured horrors most people don't allow themselves to imagine. And so when we looked at each other, we

23

could hardly see through all of it. But I saw her that afternoon. I saw how frightened and sad she was at her core, and that all the prettiness with which she surrounded herself was a kind of armor. Behind it, a little girl's heart beat fast with terror and grief.

"Then you're a stronger person than I am."

We both knew it was true, so I didn't bother to argue. When I saw her start to cry, I moved beside her and put my arms around her and she kissed my head. We stayed like that for a while with nothing resolved between us.

Come with a purpose and find your path. That was the school motto, and I'd had it ringing in my ears since I'd returned from break. Not that babysitting was exactly my path. But, for whatever reason, as I rode my bike through the crisp air down the winding road that led out of the school, and onto the street that would take me to town, I felt infused with a new forward momentum.

Skylar was right; it felt good to seek to do something, whatever it was. If not for the job interview, I'd have been buried in a book or at the gym, killing time until classes started. My suite mates weren't back yet, so I didn't even have their various girl dramas to entertain me—boys, and who said what on Facebook, and Lana, can you write my essay for me?

*

The Kahns' house stood white and pretty, a small colonial just off the square. People in The Hollows called this area Soho, short for south Hollows. There were wreaths with white lights and red bows in each window—the remnants of Christmas past—black shutters and a shiny, red door. My aunt would have no doubt reminded me that red was an auspicious color and that a red door meant opportunity in the world of feng shui. I thought about texting her, just to be nice. But then, of course, I didn't. I walked up the gray-painted steps to the front door and used the brushed gold knocker in absence of a bell.

I waited a moment and listened to a lone bird singing in the tree above me. I looked up at him, a gray-and-black sparrow sitting on a branch.

"What happened?" I asked him. "Why didn't you fly south for the winter?"

He whistled at me long and low, annoyed as if I'd asked an embarrassing question that he would be compelled to answer out of politeness. We count so much on politeness, those of us who are hiding things. We count on people not staring too long, or asking too many questions. Finally, after a brief standoff, he flew away.

Thirty seconds passed, then a minute. Wondering if I'd gotten the time wrong, I knocked again. Then I heard the staccato rhythm of heels on hardwood, and the door flew open. She was tiny and powerful, like a ballerina, with dark hair pulled back into a tight bun. Her pale face was a spotlight and I felt the sear of her assessing gaze just briefly before she smiled. Unconsciously, my shoulders slouched a little, arching my body away from her gaze, as I am prone to do under too much scrutiny.

"Lana." She was breathless again, a woman always on the move. "I love that name. It's so—*romantic*."

"Thank you," I said. I hadn't heard that before and it made me blush idiotically.

"Rachel," she said. She offered me her tiny hand in a hard and steely grip. "Rachel Kahn."

Did it sound familiar? I thought, not for the first time since she gave it. Every time I reached for it, it slipped away. I liked her name; one could do great things with a name like that: run companies, compete in triathlons, conquer nations. It was all hard sounds, three abrupt syllables. My name was all loops and whispers, the name of a dreamer, a procrastinator, someone who slept in. I bet Ms. Kahn was up no later than 5 a.m., whether she had to be or not.

She ushered me inside, apologizing for the unpacked boxes that stood in the hallway, next to the exquisite cream sectional, beneath the large Pollockesque oil which hung over the fireplace mantel and reached almost to the tall ceiling.

"I thought I'd have accomplished more by now," she said, lifting a veined hand to her forehead. She released a frustrated sigh. "But the days just seem to race by, don't they?"

Not my days, no. My days were long and winding, filled

with big, empty blocks of time to fill with nothing but studies, books, films, pub crawls with my friends and roommates, weekend parties that lasted into the night, occasionally some Internet shopping. My days didn't race by, not at all.

"They do," I said, just to be sociable. The best way not to call attention to yourself is to agree with what other people say. Even silence attracts attention.

I followed her to a cavernous dining room and we sat at a long table fit for a king's feast. It was one of *those* tables, the kind you see in design magazines and never anywhere else. It was basic, rustic even with the natural lines of the tree, and a surface with lots of knots and eyes and shades of color. But I could tell just by the feel of it that it cost more than a car. A simple piece of black wood, lined with three perfect green apples, served as a tasteful centerpiece.

From her crisp gray shift and her silver flats to the simple black-framed glasses she unfolded as slowly and carefully as one might a piece of origami, she exuded the kind of style that could not be bought. I slid my hastily cobbled-together résumé across to her. And while she looked it over I gazed around. Even in the disorder of unpacking, there was beauty. Even the dishrag folded by the sink looked like a gorgeous accident, coolness caught off guard.

"So," she said after a minute. "Do you have any child-care experience?"

She placed her palm on the résumé, and pushed it away toward the middle table, where it lay looking inadequate.

Not sure whether she hadn't really read the document, or just wanted to hear it from me, I told her about my various internships which involved working with troubled kids in various capacities. But actually picking someone up from school and hanging out, making peanut butter and jelly sandwiches? No, I admitted.

She put her hand to the back of her neck and rubbed. I figured we'd chat for a few more minutes and then she'd ask me to leave. She'd want someone who knew what they were doing, of course. This had been a silly exercise and I felt bad for wasting her time, of which she clearly had too little already.

"Interestingly enough," she said, "your experience might better prepare you for Luke than I could have hoped."

She took off her glasses, and I saw something in her eyes that I recognized—a deep and fearsome sadness.

"You see," she said, "we moved here from the city so that Luke could attend Fieldcrest during the school year and over the summer as well."

"Oh," I said. "I see."

Okay, so he was troubled. No problem. Who wasn't? I mean, *I* had been classified as a troubled kid and I hadn't set things on fire. Much. Just kidding.

"At his age, another kind of boy might be approaching the point where he could spend some afternoons at home alone. But I don't feel comfortable leaving Luke to his own devices. He's quite smart, and certainly capable of taking care of himself. But he needs someone—" She stopped short of finishing the sentence.

"To keep him out of trouble?" I said.

She looked relieved. "Yes."

I searched for a tactful way to ask what his problem was, but she asked me if I wanted some tea and I said yes. She motioned for me to follow her into the kitchen. I took a seat in a breakfast nook that looked out onto a trim backyard— a square of lawn, a single bare tree, a lonely bistro table and two chairs. Beyond that, there was a thick wooded area. I knew there were more houses on the other side, but I couldn't see them.

"Luke has had a lot of different diagnoses," said Rachel, reading my mind. She flipped on the electric kettle. "But none of them quite fit. We thought at first that it was ADHD. One doctor thought it was clinical depression, which runs in my family." Here a kind of darkness fell over her features, but then was gone. "Another said that Luke was bipolar. He's been in therapy, taken various medications."

She took tea bags from a box by the kettle and poured the water into two mugs. She went on about how she'd reached the end of her rope with having to change schools, doctors, how her work (she didn't mention what this was) was suffering, Luke was growing ever more difficult and hard for her to manage on her own.

Then she'd read about Dr. Charles Welsh and the work he was doing at Fieldcrest. I knew Dr. Welsh; he was

Langdon's direct supervisor, a warm and disheveled man whom everyone adored and held in the highest regard. His work with troubled children and his theories on childhood psychopathy were groundbreaking. When Luke was accepted to Dr. Welsh's program, Rachel and Luke moved here to The Hollows.

"We left family and friends behind," she said. She sat down at the table, putting a cup in front of me. The scent of peppermint and honey rose up to greet me. She hadn't asked what kind of tea I wanted or how I liked it, but it was perfect. "But to be honest, those relationships were becoming very strained. Luke's behavior. It's—well, it *can* be—appalling. Even my family, what little I have, wasn't equipped to handle him."

I took a sip of my tea. She wasn't exactly selling the position.

"I just want to be honest," she said, maybe reading my expression. "There's no point in your taking the job if you're going to be overwhelmed by him."

For whatever reason, maybe it was hubris, or the naïveté of youth, or just a general lack of foresight, but I wasn't discouraged. In fact, I felt a bit proud of myself for wanting a job that probably no one else would want. Or maybe it was because, when I was young, my behavior could have been called appalling, and many people had difficulty "handling" me. Or maybe it was this idea I had twisting deep in my psyche about helping people.

She went on to talk a little bit about his behavior, his unnatural attachment to her, his rages, his silences, his manipulations. As she went on, she seemed to get more and more tired, her shoulders drooping, head bowing. I waited to say something about Luke's father. But she didn't.

"Things have been—challenging," she said. I couldn't see her face at all.

I'd known plenty of kids like Luke at Fieldcrest, and had spent time helping them during the summer program. Often, they did better without the parents around. Those relationships were so complicated, the grooves of manipulation dug so deep, so twisted around each other. Sometimes, not always, troubled kids were more relaxed in an environment that wasn't controlled by their whims and tempers.

"So maybe I should meet Luke and see if we can get along at all?" I said.

She looked up from her teacup, her eyebrows lifted in surprise. "Okay?" she said. "Yes. That would be great. Maybe you'd like to come back for dinner?"

"I could do that," I said.

"Or," she said, looking around, "I could pay you for the afternoon and you could help me with some unpacking. And you'll be here when he gets home in a couple of hours. Are you free?"

I didn't wonder if she'd interviewed anyone else, or why she didn't seem to have checked my single reference. To be honest, I just liked her. I sensed she needed someone, and I wanted to be that person. I couldn't have told you why. These things are so complicated, every decision under-pinned by reasons conscious and subconscious. What we think of as our "gut instincts" are really a very complex mosaic of past experiences, deep-seated hopes, fears, desires. But that feeling, a kind of giddy, hopeful *yes!*, came from deep inside. I wouldn't have thought that I wanted or needed anything as badly as I must have to so enthusiasti-cally sign on for the jobs of unpacking boxes and caring for a disturbed child. But there I was.

So, we passed the afternoon, chatting and unpacking, shelving books and unwrapping glasses. I skirted questions about my family in a way that had become second nature to me, offering vague half answers. Most people don't press early on.

Where's your family from? she asked casually.

South Florida, I answered.

Do you see them often? She wanted to know, clearly just making conversation. *Well, I was just home for Christmas. You mentioned your family was still in the city?* I tossed back.

It wasn't lost on me that she changed the subject just as quickly when the focus shifted to her family. The relation-ships were strained, she'd said. No one ever really wanted to talk about that. But then we fell into an easy rapport, chat-ting about school, my suite mates, her years at NYU, how we both hated Hemingway and distrusted people who lauded his work, were fools for *The Sound of Music* (the hills are alive!). There was a definite love connection. She reminded me of someone. But I wouldn't have been able to tell you who, not then.

We were laughing at something, I don't remember what now, when we heard the front door. Her smile quickly faded and a tension settled into her shoulders. She moved away from me quickly.

"I'm home," came a voice down the hall. "Mom? I'm hungry."

"One of the other mothers picked him up today. We carpool," she whispered. She looked guilty, as if she'd done something wrong and was hoping I'd cover for her. "I lost track of time."

"In the kitchen, Luke," she called. "I want you to meet someone."

There was a pause, where she turned to me and offered a tight smile. Then I heard slow, careful steps approach. I don't know what I was expecting, but certainly not the slim, handsome boy who stepped into the room. He was her younger, male double, the same creamy, pinched beauty. His eyes were dark like hers, intense and smart. His hair was a tousle, his eyes heavily lidded. I hesitate to say that there was a reptilian beauty to him, because that wouldn't quite capture the flush to his skin, the shine to his eyes.

"Luke," said Rachel. She moved over to him and gave him a peck on the head, then dropped an arm around him. "This is Lana. She's going to be helping us out."

He regarded me shyly, with the shade of a smile, and leaned in tight to his mother. I returned the smile, trying to keep the wattage down. I sensed a strange skittishness in him. I worried if I approached him too quickly, he'd retreat.

"Hi, Luke," I said. "Nice to meet you."

"Can you say hello?" she prodded, when he didn't say anything. She cast me an apologetic look. Finally, he took a step forward and offered me his hand. It was soft and hot in mine.

"Nice to meet you," he said.

What was there between us in that very first moment that would have told, if observed, everything that would follow? Nothing. I am sure of it. Not anything, not a twinge of instinct, not an internal shudder. He was that good.

"You're pretty," he said.

I felt the heat rush to my cheeks, even as I saw Rachel visibly relax. A broad smile crept across her face and it was unmistakable as relief. I, on the other hand, felt my tension ratchet as he kept his eyes on me. Inside I squirmed as I always do when someone looks at me too long. I thought he'd break his gaze, but he didn't, and my face was burning. Still, I didn't lower my own eyes either. It was some kind of strange, subtle standoff that I didn't like, but from which something inside me refused to back down.

As I look back now, it was really the first move in the game we'd already started playing. There was something about him, about our chemistry, that immediately hooked us

34

into each other. But it was all so brief, just a second. Finally, it was Rachel who broke the moment, lightly, as if she hadn't noticed anything passing between us. And maybe nothing had, I thought then—just a curious boy unsettling a person who was too self-conscious at the best of times.

"Why don't you change out of your school clothes, and I'll get you a snack?" Rachel said.

He nodded and bounded off like any other eleven-year-old boy. And I felt silly as he galloped away.

I'd expected someone different. Someone obviously hyperactive, or disturbed like some of the kids I'd worked with at Fieldcrest. Not just from the way Rachel had described him, but from the way she *acted* as she described him. She was as nervous, as wary, as an abused woman, as if wondering when the next blow might be delivered and forever scheming as to how she might avoid it. As he pounded up the steps, I actually found myself wondering a little about what might be wrong with *her*.

She walked over to the steps and peered up, as if she was concerned that he might be listening. Then she returned to the kitchen, and grabbed my arm, smiling giddily. She leaned in close. I'm not sure if she noticed me shrink from her touch.

"He likes you," she whispered, as if I'd just won a fabulous prize.

3

Is the prey complicit in its own demise? Are we not seduced in some small way by the beauty, the grace, even the dangerous soul of the predator? Do we not look into its eyes and see something that excites us, that entices, even hypnotizes us? Yes, in some sense, I think we are seduced by danger. When we stand on the edge of a precipice and look down at the deadly fall, who among us doesn't imagine tipping his weight over and plummeting to a bone-shattering death? And it's not just terror that we feel at the thought. There's a thrill there, too, isn't there? Or maybe that's just me.

"So, how did it go?" Langdon asked the next day as I entered his classroom. I was the first to arrive, as I usually am to all my classes but especially to his.

"I got the job," I said.

He looked up from his notes and pushed his glasses up, gave me a nerdy smile.

"Hey! Good for you."

"Yeah," I said. "I'm excited."

He looked back down at the text on his desk. "Awesome," he said distractedly.

"The kid's a student at Fieldcrest."

I put my bag under my seat on the far left of the front row. Langdon usually kept the lighting dim and the room cool. The bright fluorescent lights hurt his eyes and made everyone look hungover, he'd said when I'd asked why. That's because everyone *is* hungover, I'd answered. He'd found that funny.

"Oh," he said. He wore a frown now. "Who is it?"

"Luke; Lucas, I think. Lucas Kahn?" I said, hating that everything I said sounded like a question. It was a verbal tic I couldn't seem to master.

He looked up at the ceiling with a little scholarly squint.

"I haven't worked with him," he said after a moment.

This was hopeful news. Langdon generally worked one-on-one with the most difficult cases, the callous-unemotional kids, a term they used a lot at Fieldcrest. These children—who display a total lack of empathy, disregard for others, and a severely deficient affect—are those whom certain experts now believe will evolve into psychopaths. But a 2008 review of this diagnosis found that there was not sufficient evidence for it to be included in *The Diagnostic and Statistical Manual of Mental Disorders*. Even so, most child psychiatrists recognized these early warning signs of very bad things to come. Of course, the mind is a mysterious thing and the mind of a child even more mysterious still. So everyone in the field was pretty careful about what kind of diagnoses they threw around. Some children grow out of their disorders, rather than grow in. (I was living proof of that. Sort of.) If Langdon wasn't working with Luke, maybe Luke wasn't that bad.

I told him about the interview, the unpacking, the pleasant dinner that had followed with all of us chattering and laughing as if we'd known each other forever. It was actually a little strange. It had stayed with me, the feeling that I had known Rachel and Luke for a very long time. I was more comfortable at their table on our first night of knowing each other than I had ever been with my own family.

"Well, good," he said. "It sounds like you're all going to get something out of this. I'll ask around about him."

I almost said, *Don't!* I don't even know why, maybe I didn't want anything to break the charm. Instead I said, "How did you know?" Because it had been he who found the ad and insisted that I call.

"Just a feeling," he said. He flashed that funny smile he had, and I felt a familiar flutter in my belly, which I immediately quashed. In our closest moments, I had this sense that he'd always been around to advise me and listen to my problems. And I hoped he always would be, in one way or another. But I refused to be the cliché. I was not and would never be the student who had a hopeless crush on a professor.

The rest of the students started to file in, and Langdon

turned back to his notes. It was the first day of my final class with him, abnormal psychology. Of course, I already knew more about the subject than I wanted.

You see, I am a person with secrets. And I guard them carefully, keep them locked in a box inside myself. I rarely opened the lid of my psyche to look inside. Almost no one, except the doctor I saw in town, knew the truth about who I was, or my history. There was very little I wouldn't have done to keep it that way. Shame was a thick cloak that I wrapped around myself and hid beneath. It was dark and lonely, but at least it was safe.

I opened my notebook as Langdon took the podium.

"Where is the line between normal and abnormal? At best, it is faint and nebulous, isn't it? We've talked in your earlier classes about the difficulty of drawing that line in some cases, about the various criteria used to make diagnoses in our field and design appropriate and effective treatment. In this class, we'll discuss the types of cases that are undeniably over the line into abnormal. Over the last decade, new research in the areas of genetics and neuroscience has us thinking about mental illness in an entirely new way. How much of it is environment, how much biology? How much the union of those two things? And what other elements contribute? What, if any, power do we have in the most extreme cases to be of service?"

He went on and on in the dim room, and I bowed my head dutifully scribbling notes, wondering if he had anything to teach me about mental illness that I didn't already know.

I found the keys in the planter, just as Rachel had promised, and let myself in. It was a carpool day and Luke would be home at three.

"Just, you know," she said on the phone, "just let him do what he wants. Make him a snack, let him watch television or play a video game. I'll supervise his homework after dinner."

She sounded nervous.

"Don't worry," I told her.

"And if anything, just call," she said. "I'm minutes away."

She was opening a bookstore in town, which impressed me as being nothing short of suicidal in the electronic-book age. But she had leased a spot on the square and was waist-deep in renovations. It was to be a bookstore and café, a gathering space with a wireless Internet service. She was planning discussion groups and open-mike poetry nights, free coffee for study groups. She had a thousand ideas for the space and the passion of a zealot—parties, author visits, story time, a small play space in the kids' section. I simultaneously admired and felt sorry for her.

"Don't worry," I said again. "We'll be fine."

"Stroll down if you two feel like getting out for a while," she said.

"We will."

We, that magic word, that syllable of belonging. Its sound tells others that you are a part of something instead of *apart* from everything, which is how I have always felt.

The house had the special hush of emptiness, where all the sounds we don't hear—the heat, the refrigerator, the settling and creaks—create a quiet symphony. Rachel had cleared some more boxes and the place was looking more settled. There was a pile of newspaper on the table, an empty coffee cup, rinsed and sitting in the dish rack. I found myself compelled to walk around. As I climbed the stairs, I heard some cubes drop in the icemaker and it made me jump a little.

Her room was at the top of the stairs, the master suite. Light washed in through a big bay window where there was a cozy seat with chenille throw pillows and a folded blanket. A low bed was covered all in white with crisp linens and a down comforter. Silk pajamas were tossed over a dove-gray chair. A hardcover book by an author whose name I didn't recognize sat askew on the bedside table. On the cover a slim girl walked into a stand of trees.

I walked down the hall. Two other bedrooms were totally empty except for a few unopened boxes. Rachel had mentioned that she planned to use one of them for her office. She said that she used to write and had plans to start a new novel after they had settled in. She'd said it with a certain wistfulness, as though she were not at all sure that they *would* settle in. I had been curious enough to Google her name, to see what she might have written. But nothing turned up. Actually, nothing at all turned up. Similarly, nothing came up for Lucas Kahn. So, he hadn't been in any real trouble—which was comforting.

Luke's room was the expected disaster area. Boxes half unpacked, clothes in piles, books stacked beside the shelves. There was a huge computer screen on his desk, which was part of a wall unit of shelves and cubbies. He had his own television. Cable box and video-game system lay on the floor; long, black umbilicals led back to the large flat-screen mounted on the wall. A wireless game controller sat on the beanbag seat.

It would be another half hour before he got home. So I started shelving the piles of books on the floor. I didn't want to just sit around doing my reading when I was being paid fifteen dollars an hour.

I got immersed in the project, as I am prone to do, organizing books by subject and size, and I lost track of time. I must not have heard him come in.

"What are you doing?"

I spun, startled, to see him standing there. Backpack slung over one shoulder, coat in his hand. He had some kind of blue paint on his shirt, and a warrior stripe of it on his right cheek.

I felt guilty, as if I'd been caught stealing.

"Oh, Luke," I said. "I'm sorry. I didn't hear you come in."

"Obviously," he said. There was no trace of the shy, sweet boy I'd met the other day. He was icy, his face slack and eyes dead. He walked into the room and put his backpack down. He stood blocking the door, and looked at me with unmistakable menace. I found myself thinking of Rachel, and how skittish she was around him.

"I was helping your mother unpack the other day," I said. I lifted my chin and squared my shoulders to him, kept my voice low and easy. He wasn't going to cow me as he had his mother; that was for sure. "So I thought I'd help you start shelving your books."

"I don't want your help," he said. "Get out."

Gut-punched by the quiet ugliness of his tone, I let the book drop from my hand to the floor with a thud, rather than move to put it on the shelf. I kept his gaze as I moved past him toward the door. I am not a large person. Always the smallest kid at school, as an adult I stood just over five foot four inches, with a slight build. He was only eleven but he did not seem that much smaller than I was. We were nearly the same height. My arm brushed his on the way out. My face must have been scarlet, as it always got when I was angry or embarrassed.

"My mother told you to make me a snack and then let me do what I wanted, right?"

"Uh," I said. I turned to face him. I wasn't going to let him talk to my back as if I were the help, which maybe I was. But fuck that. "Yes, that's right."

"Then do that," he said. Again, we locked eyes.

He followed me as I exited the room and closed the door behind me. I turned around, considered knocking and apologizing, trying to get off on a better foot. But then I noticed that there was a lock on the outside of the door. Did she lock him in there sometimes? I don't know how long I stood there, looking at the lock. It seemed so odd, so incongruous with the woman I met. It wasn't reasonable, was it, under any circumstance to have a lock on the outside of your child's door? A dead bolt? But, then again, maybe it was already there when they moved in. Maybe she hadn't put it there at all.

I went downstairs and called Rachel, told her what happened. She sighed heavily when I was done, and I felt like a failure. I could hear the sound of someone hammering in the background.

"I'm sorry," I said. "I was just trying to help you out. Like the other day."

She sighed again. I expected her to tell me that it was okay and not to worry. But she didn't.

"Just make him a ham sandwich with apple slices," she said. "And put it outside his door. He'll get it after you've gone back downstairs. Just stay away from him. He might get over it and come down. If not, I'll be home by six."

"Okay," I said. I thought I heard her disconnect the call, and I was about to hang up.

Then, "Lana?"

45

"Yes," I said. I was childishly eager that she not be mad at me, that she would offer some words of support.

"You're a tattletale."

I realized that it was Luke, not Rachel. He'd obviously been listening in on the line upstairs, chiming in now that his mother was off the phone.

Embarrassment and a flash of anger got the better of me. "Luke?" I said.

"Yes," he answered, mimicking me with annoying accuracy.

"You're a brat."

I heard him gasp, then start to laugh. He hung up the phone, but I still heard him laughing upstairs. I instantly regretted it and figured I would be fired on my very first day as a working adult. Fine, I thought. Whatever. He *was* a brat and someone needed to tell him that. He was obviously running the show around here and had been for a while.

Even though I didn't want to, I made the snack and brought it upstairs with a bottle of water, then placed it on the floor outside the door and departed with a little knock. Once I was down, I heard the door open and close. I could hear the sound of whatever video game he was playing, gunshots and screeching tires. Bad choice for a problem kid, I thought. If anyone shouldn't be playing games like that, it was a boy with emotional issues. But what did I know?

In the kitchen, I opened my textbook and pulled out my notebook. I made myself a cup of tea and sat at the table, and tried to focus on my reading. I wasn't going to touch any-thing else unbidden. It was just before four in the afternoon.

The sun had nearly set, and the kitchen was dark except for the light I had on over the table, when I heard the door upstairs open, then Luke on the stairs. He appeared in the doorway with his empty plate and spent bottle of water. I looked up at him and he paused for a minute, then went to the sink and washed his plate. He tossed his bottle into the recycle bin under the sink, put the dish in the rack.

I watched him for a minute and then went back to my reading. I felt him come over and stand behind me; the hairs went up on the back of my neck.

"You'll probably find my picture in there," he said.

I was reading my abnormal psychology text.

"Do you consider yourself abnormal?" I asked him. He walked around and sat across from me. He offered a shrug. In the light, he looked like exactly what he was—a boy, trou-bled maybe, but just a kid. I felt an unwanted tug of empathy.

"Everyone else does," he said. He pulled a sad face, which didn't seem quite sincere.

"Through no fault of your own, I'm sure." Was he old enough to detect sarcasm?

A bright smile crossed his face, and his eyes glittered. He was truly beautiful, and I found myself mesmerized by the almond-shaped pools of his eyes, the milk of his skin, his perfect Cupid's-bow mouth, even the spate of freckles across his nose.

"Maybe," he said, drawing out the word, "we got off on the wrong foot."

"Maybe we did," I said. I closed my reading and notes and put them in my bag. "I'm sorry I touched your books. I was just trying to help."

He gave me a princely nod. "You did a pretty good job, actually."

"Oh," I said. "Thanks so much."

"You're not like other grown-ups," he said. He was tracing a finger on the wood of the table, back and forth slowly. "There's something really different about you."

I didn't know what to say to that, so I said nothing. I wasn't sure I wanted to tell him that I didn't feel quite grown up, yet. That a big part of me still felt like a kid most of the time, which was why it was so easy for me to sink to his level when he called me a tattletale. Or had he already intuited that, and now he was sinking to mine? It was something I wouldn't consider until much later.

"You didn't lock the door," he said. He leveled that challenging gaze, which I knew I had to hold.

"Why would I?" I asked. "I'm not afraid of you."

Again, he issued that spritely laugh. It managed to sound innocent and vaguely menacing all at once.

"Want to play chess?" he asked. It sounded like a dare, one I was happy to take.

"Sure," I said. "I'm warning you, though. I'm really good at it. I hope you're not a sore loser." I strongly suspected that he was a terribly sore loser, and I was already planning to throw the game.

He bolted upstairs and returned with a chess set in a wooden case, which he unpacked and assembled with unsettling speed and dexterity. He then proceeded to destroy me, game after game, until his mother came home and found us there, heads bent over the board. She let us be as she prepared dinner. And we all shared a lovely meal of grocery-store rotisserie chicken, salad, and macaroni and cheese.

"Lana's a terrible chess player," Luke told his mother. His eyes glittered, watching carefully to see if it bugged me. It did. Could I hide it from him?

"It's not that I'm bad," I said. "It's just that Luke's so good. Who taught you to play like that?"

He was too young and too spoiled to be gracious in accepting the compliment, too arrogant to then make some kind of concession that I wasn't that bad after all.

"I taught myself," he said. He pulled back his shoulders, gave me a heavily lidded look. "Who taught you? A monkey?"

"Luke," said Rachel. She put her fork down heavily. "That's not nice. Apologize."

"Actually," I said, "my father taught me."

Luke's face went suddenly pale, and his posture grew rigid.

49

The father button, I knew it well. The absence of a male presence in the home was notable by the fact that no one had mentioned it. I took a small, dark victory inside for hitting him where it hurt. Mature, I know.

"Well, he must have been a shitty player," said Luke. Rachel had gone very still, too, I noticed, and bowed her head. She was bracing herself for I don't know what kind of emotional storm. A stronger mother would have punished him and sent him from the table, would have done so long ago. But I found I couldn't judge her. I felt sorry for her more than anything.

I offered a little laugh to soften the energy, and they both looked at me. "He really wasn't very good, to tell the truth. He was awful."

There was a moment, a held breath. Then everybody laughed, and any tension disappeared like mist.

"Who wants ice cream?" asked Rachel, giddy, it seemed, with relief.

We both did.

4

Dear Diary,

I am not much of a journal keeper. I've never felt the need to record my thoughts. In spite of some early hardships, I have always been a happy person, free from angst. And I used to pity the poor souls who needed to record their pain on the page—the misfits, the outcasts, the wallflowers. The pretty one, the cheerleader, the prom queen didn't need to do that, did she? She had no secret pain to share with a Moleskine. I have been the girl cruising in a convertible along the beach drive, my golden hair flowing. I am the one who is envied, who is desired. I am not sure when that changed. But it has changed.

If, a year ago, you had told me where I'd be today, I wouldn't have believed you. Since then, a gray and gauzy film has settled over my life. My limbs ache with fatigue; I can barely pull myself from bed. When I look in the mirror, my golden hair has gone mousy, my eyes sunken, my skin gray. My hands shake from a constant throb of anxiety. And my days and nights are filled with the incessant crying of my newborn child. The keening, inconsolable wailing fills every nook and cranny of my consciousness. It's possible that each of us sleeps a few hours a day. But I still hear his misery in my brief and troubled dreams.

I am being punished. I know that. There is no other explanation. Somewhere during a past life, I must have done something horrible. Maybe I suffocated my baby, or perpetrated a mass shooting, or stabbed a homeless person in a dark alley. Somehow I escaped punishment in that life, and so now, lifetimes later, a very special kind of hell is being rained down on me, the full rage of karmic justice.

And if you think I'm being overly dramatic, consider this: sleep deprivation is a sanctioned form of torture, as is piping into a closed room the sound of a baby wailing. In its pitch, every human recognizes the notes of accusation and judgment—it is the very sound of failure, a veritable siren of misery.

Right now, as my son screams, I am sitting in my walk-in closet, with classical music blaring outside in the bedroom. But I can still hear it, a single ugly note that never ceases. In case you think I am a depraved and mentally ill mother, which maybe I am, it is my mother's turn to walk and walk and walk him. We take shifts—my mother, my husband, and I. We walk and walk and walk and walk, and soothe and croon and shush and rock and rock and rock. We never stop moving; we have crossed miles, oceans, and traveled into space walking our boy.

Colic, the pediatrician says. Whatever the hell that means. It should stop at eight weeks. The digestive system should mature by then.

The Baby Whisperer. The Happiest Baby on the Block. What to Expect When You're Expecting. Touchstones. T. Berry Brazelton. Dr. Spock. Ferber. Attachment parenting. Nurse on demand. Set a routine. Baby slings. Baby swings. Vacuum cleaner. Car rides into eternity. There is no book, no expert, no contraption we have not tried. And still, he cries.

When there is a blessed time of silence, we all sit waiting, holding our breaths, keeping our bodies very still. Once he slept for three hours. And me, my husband, and mother whispered giddily to each other in the kitchen. What was it? I had given up wheat, dairy, broccoli, coffee, and citrus— any one of those things might have been passing to him through my breast milk and causing him an allergy. Maybe that was it, finally, after a week of eating nothing but (gluten-free) chicken soup? Was it the new Sleep Sheep, which issued soothing white noise? Was it the swaddling, the classical music, the new pink lightbulbs? But then it started again.

Tomorrow, my husband has to go back to work. And soon my mother will have to return to her own life. Only I will remain with the boy who I want more than anything to love but who screams every time I touch him. I have never cried so much; I didn't even know I had so many tears.

I hear my husband knocking softly on the door. But I don't

53

want him to come in, so I don't answer. He will leave me alone; he knows I need the silence. I can feel him linger, waiting. But I feel dark inside, mean and selfish. There is almost nothing left of me, and I need to hold to every cell.

I am angry. I have been robbed. There is a fantasy we are sold. I can see it even now, the nestling mom and newborn. The blissed-out hours of just lying and looking, sucking on little toes, eliciting smiles, dangling colorful toys. The cooing, fat, pink baby in adorable onesies, lying beneath soft blankies and cuddling plush ducks. I didn't get any of that.

My baby cut a bloody swath through me. Labor and delivery was a grueling, twenty-six-hour ordeal that ended in an emergency C-section necessary to save both our lives. I remember, though I was addled and racked with pain, wondering why my child was trying to kill me. I could feel that something was wrong. The pain, the consciousness-altering waves of agony that rolled through my body, did not feel productive. There was a darkness to it, the pull of death. Had he been born in the Middle Ages, certainly we would not have survived, neither of us. It was that bad.

But luckily, it's the modern first world, where white-coated, scalpel-wielding, trained professionals zip us into sterile rooms and save the day. In my darkest moments, I wonder if it was a cheat, an escape from that cosmic yawning. Maybe there is an angry god somewhere, raging. He wanted us, almost had us. We were nearly washed to him on a rushing river of my blood, pulled back just as he closed his hands around our hearts. Maybe in my baby's incessant crying, this god is making himself known.

My husband, my beautiful, kind, loving husband, is still out there. I can feel him hovering, wondering whether to knock again or drift away. Since the hospital, he treats me so gently, as though he is afraid that I might shatter into a million little pieces and all the king's horses and all the king's men wouldn't be able to put me together again.

I want to lean on him, to cry to him, to let him hold and comfort me. But it's as if I can't access the person inside me who wants that. I can't wrap my arms around him and weep into his chest. I want to comfort him because I know he is suffering, too. But I am as stiff and cold as a corpse, limp in his embrace.

We used to have heat, so much heat. But we are a lifetime away from the hot, humid, stormy summer night in Key West when we first met. I had come down for a long weekend with my girlfriends. God, we were young, my girlfriends and I. We were all just out of college, all working seemingly glamorous but poorly paid jobs in New York City. We were all edgy, hungry. We wanted big things, and had no reason to believe we wouldn't get them. We were privileged, well educated— we didn't know anything about the world yet and how it conspired against you and your dreams.

When I saw him, standing on the edge of the dance floor, I watched. He was dressed in black in a sea of colorfully patterned dresses and shirts. He was cool and composed, while everyone was rowdy and writhing around him. The music was terrible, deafening and discordant. People were wasted, living it up. It was a messy, ugly scene that everyone seemed to be enjoying except for him and me.

I saw him watching, as I was. I am not one to always participate. More often than not, I stand on the sidelines observing, taking in details. I don't want to be inside the crowd, being carried along in its current. I don't do well at parties, though you'd never know it to look at me. I blend— laughing, dancing, chitchatting. But inside, I hold myself apart. He knew that about me intuitively, knew it right away. There was pain there, he said. I saw it right away. Something about it made him feel tender, he said. He wanted to care for me, protect me from whatever it was that made me so sad.

"It's a bit of a mess, isn't it?" he asked. Actually, he yelled this at me because it was the only way I could hear him over the music.

"It really is," I said. And I couldn't help but smile. Because he had dark pools for eyes, and a long, full mouth. He had a jaw of stubble, and close-cropped brown hair. His shoulders were wide and defined, pressing against the black of his T-shirt. I found myself thinking that he would have been gorgeous even if he were a woman.

Maybe it was the full moon, he always says when he tells our story, or the booze. (He always gets laughs for that one.) But I leaned in and kissed her, he'll say. When she didn't slap me, I knew it was love. He makes light, but it's true. From that night onward, we were never really apart again. Until now, when we are worlds away. The floor of my life has turned to quicksand, and I am sinking, sinking, sinking down. He is reaching out his hand to me, trying to pull me back. But I don't even have the strength to help myself be saved.

Sweetie, my mom crooned when my head was in her lap this morning. It will get better, I promise. One day, he'll just stop. And he'll be the beautiful little boy that he is inside. And you'll all be fine. This will be a distant memory.

I didn't believe her. It doesn't seem possible that our lives won't be lived under the incessant siren of my son's unhappiness. But I pray that she's right. And I pray for silence.

5

"He sounds like a *nightmare*," said Rebecca (or Beck, as we called her). She peered at me over her notebook. She was the only one I knew who didn't type her notes into a laptop. "Don't you just want to work at Starbucks or something? Less baggage. Free lattes for your best friend, maybe?"

She also didn't text, e-mailed only when absolutely necessary, and would rather "lose two fingers on her left hand" than create a *Fake*book page. She could sometimes be convinced to watch a movie, if it was suitably obscure. But as soon as the television went on in the common room, Beck left. *I'm an artist. Garbage in, garbage out. We are what we watch.* I am not sure what she considered herself an artist of, precisely. She neither painted nor wrote. *I am an artist of living.* Okay. Whatever.

Twice already, the librarian had reprimanded us for laughing, and now we had our heads pressed close over the table as we whispered.

"I think I want to help them," I said.

"Not this again." She clicked the piercing in her tongue against her teeth, which was such an unsettling habit she had. "You can't help anyone yet. You're still a kid."

"I *can* help them," I said. I was a little surprised at the rush of defensiveness I felt. I softened my voice. "They need it."

She lifted her eyebrow (also pierced) and her palms (lotus flower tattooed on the right hand). "Hey, you want to babysit for the bad seed? Go for it."

A lash of anger heated the skin on my cheeks, but I quashed it. I'm good at that, hiding my feelings. I bury them deep and you wouldn't want them to start clawing their way up through the dirt. People were so quick to judge, referencing their own prejudice to prove themselves right. That idea of the "bad seed" is something that pervades our culture like any other of the myriad acceptable bigotries. The idea that a person might be born bad, be a lost cause, better off dead—it was something that I railed against for all sorts of reasons.

"Don't go quiet on me," she said. She was peering at me over her book again, looking sheepish. "I'm just teasing you."

I issued a little laugh. "I know," I said. I wrinkled up my face to show her that I was in on the joke. But I couldn't soften the prickle I had inside.

"I'm sorry," she said. She fingered a little gold star that she wore around her neck. I'd given it to her before Christmas break. On the back there was a carved inscription in impossibly small print: *Stars are like good friends. You can't always see them, but you know they're always there.* "For real. I'm sure he's great."

I went back to my reading and so did she. We had these little dustups, Beck and I, always had since freshman year. There was an essential difference between us. She was very loudly and fearlessly herself. She held back nothing—not her political or religious views, not her laughter or her tears, not her sneezes or farts. She was a hurricane of emotions, ideas, brazen sexuality.

"So, how's it going with *Long Dong*?" she asked. She shot me a mischievous grin, which I did not return. She was baiting me, wanted a reaction. She thought I had a crush, a serious soul-destroying case of lovesickness over Langdon. (See how clever she is? Langdon, Long Dong, get it?) She'd never accepted that the only personal element to my relationship with Langdon was friendship. Above all else, he was my mentor, my professor and adviser; that was all it was or ever will be.

"I heard he has a boyfriend in the city," she said. "Goes to see him on the weekends."

She had a pen in her mouth. She was alternately chewing it and clicking it with her tongue piercing. I wanted to knock it out of her glossy, pouty, cherry-red lips.

"That's bullshit," I said. Was it? I had no idea what Langdon did with his spare time. It wasn't my business, and I really didn't care.

"I don't think so." She licked her lips and I had to avert my eyes. "I've heard the rumor more than once."

"Oh, well, that proves it."

"Time to face it," she said. "Your crush is a queer."

Something hot and nasty pulsed inside me.

She'd kissed me once. We were both hammered, at a party in the common room at one of the three fraternity houses that sat on the edge of the school property. We were dancing on the makeshift dance floor framed by old, stained couches. The music was some kind of warped electronica. There were strobe lights and a disco ball twirled overhead, casting fragments of light. I was on the wrong side of the line, where being drunk is just about to not be fun anymore. I was watching her, the way her body turned lithe and graceful. And she saw me looking. We were drawn together, a line of energy between us taut and growing shorter, pulling us nearer and nearer. I was powerless to move away, which under other circumstances I surely would have done.

"Come here," she whispered in my ear, boozy and sexy. Our bodies were touching, hand to hand, thigh to thigh. Then she put her fingers in my hair. "I want to show you something."

She led me up the stairs, and the room around us wobbled and warped. The music was so loud, a throbbing presence pulsating through the thin walls. I could feel it in the floor beneath my feet. I was dizzy, the stairs tilting. (I would later be so ill that to this day I can't even say the words *Fuzzy Navel* without feeling a rise of bile in my throat.)

"Where are we going?" I asked. But I didn't even know if she heard me.

She didn't say anything, just led me up the staircase to the darkened hall. The second level was for lovers—on the chaise, on the floor, on the bed in a room where the door stood open. It was a little quieter here, but my heart started thundering.

Virginity was just one of my secret shames. I'd never been touched in that way by another person. I'd never even been kissed. All around us couples were groping and thrusting in the dim smoky air, awakening a host of unpleasant, uncomfortable feelings in me. I started pulling her back toward the stairs.

"Beck," I said, feeling the first wave of nausea hit. "I want to go. I have to go."

But she kept tugging at me, until we were in a room by ourselves. She pushed me against a wall, and a framed picture tumbled from the cheap particleboard dresser beside us. She touched my hair, my face, moved in and sucked lightly on my earlobe. My whole body froze as I started to tremble with desire, terror, and shame.

"It's okay," she said. "It's okay to feel good."

And she did feel good. Her lips were hot and soft as she

pressed her mouth to mine, tasting of whiskey and cigarettes. I stood rigid, unmoving, even as she put her hand inside my shirt. She ran her hand over my belly, and up to my chest. Here, she paused and looked at me, a deep, knowing, penetrating gaze. I almost reached for her, pulled her to me. I wanted to. I wanted her. Bad.

But then I was on my knees puking up more fluid than I knew my body could hold. And it never ended. We spent the next hour in the bathroom, where I heaved and heaved into the toilet, while she sat beside me, rubbing my back until we both passed out.

We woke up the next morning, her hanging over the rim of the tub, me with my face pressed against the cool tile floor. We opened our eyes at the same moment, and if we hadn't been so poisoned by alcohol, so sick, so muddled by drink and fatigue and what had passed between us, we might have laughed. We were ridiculous. When I looked in the mirror, the right side of my face held the small, square impressions of the tile floor.

We stumbled home in the cold, milky-gray light of morning and slept for the rest of the day. We never, ever spoke of that night again. She'd gone on to suck and fuck girls and boys all over campus, while I remained as chaste as a nun. But there was an undeniable tension, a wondering, a building resentment. It was a current that had threaded its way through our friendship; it was part of who we were together.

After that night, there was suddenly constant fighting in my relationship with Beck. Spats could spring up over anything—maybe she took one of the million black button-down shirts I had. (That was my uniform—jeans, a button shirt, a pair of chunky shoes, some kind of black coat in winter.) Or she'd steal my class notes and then get mad at me if she didn't do well on a quiz. She'd say my music was keeping her up. It could be anything that got us going at it. But it wasn't any of those things.

"Why don't you two just fuck and get it over with," our other suite mate, Ainsley, complained the last time we argued over who had done the dishes last.

We both stopped mid-bitch and looked at her, then at each other. Then we each marched off for our separate rooms. Our doors slammed in unison. I pressed myself against the wall, my heart doing the dance of shame I knew so well. I could smell the whiskey and cigarette smoke on her breath the night she kissed me.

My anger at her in the library had me thinking about all of these things. Suddenly I couldn't stand to be near her another second. I hated that smug look she had on her face, as though she had discovered things about me, as though she knew me. Which she didn't. Not at all.

I slammed my book shut so hard that a girl from the next table looked over at us. I started stuffing things into my bag—my iPad, my journal, my textbooks. I clutched my little pen case covered with smiling matryoshka dolls. The nesting doll, a self inside a self inside a self, my own personal symbolism.

"Really?" she said, pulling an annoyed grimace. But I could see she felt bad. She knew she'd pushed me too far. In fact, she'd been pushing and pushing and pushing me all year in little ways like this. And I was finished with it. I slung my bag over my shoulder and walked out.

"Grow up," she called after me, causing everybody in the library to look at her (just like she liked it). But I was already walking out the door.

Around 2 a.m., there was a soft knock at my door. It roused me immediately from sleep, but I lay there for a minute listening. My first thought was that it was Beck, come to apologize. But no, that was impossible. Beck was not hardwired to apologize. She clung to her own rightness. Anyway, maybe I was the one who needed to apologize to her. And I wasn't hardwired for that any more than she.

Another knock, then: "It's me, Ainsley."

I got up and walked over to the door, which I had locked upon returning home, and opened it. She stood there shivering in an oversize sweatshirt and leggings, her hair a tumble of curls pulled up high on her head.

"Beck didn't come home."

"So," I said. I moved past her and sat on the plush couch in the common room. She followed and sat beside me. I handed her the blanket that hung over the arm, and she wrapped it around herself. The old dormitory buildings, built from stone, were freezing in the winter, almost impossible to heat adequately, as though the walls soaked up all the warmth and kept it for themselves. We all walked around in robes and big slippers, wrapped in blankets in the cooler months.

"So," said Ainsley, "she should be home by now. The library closed at midnight. Weren't you there with her?"

"I was," I said. "But I left first."

"Oh," she said.

"What's the big deal?" I asked. "She could be in someone's room somewhere. You know Beck."

She stared off out the window, where the wind was tossing the branches of the tall, bare oak.

"You know," she said.

Her hazel eyes were growing wide. I knew what she was thinking about. Two years ago when we were sophomores, a girl, a friend of ours, disappeared from the campus. Elizabeth Barnett left a party we'd all been attending, but none of us had seen her leave. She'd had a fight with her boyfriend and left in tears, according to someone who'd seen her and let her stumble off into the night drunk and hysterical.

Before her disappearance, we had all thought of the

campus as an idyll of safety. Nothing bad had ever happened here, and it seemed as if nothing ever could. With its rolling grounds and close-knit buildings, its well-lit paths and roaming security guards, we strolled about at all hours, in all conditions, without a worry in our heads. Some people said the woods were haunted, but we all knew that was just a ghost story we told ourselves, something that was cool and entertaining rather than frightening.

It was days of pandemonium, the campus crawling with police, Elizabeth's parents running a command center from the gym. All of us stunned and crying, huddling, participating in searches through those haunted woods, gathering together at night to comfort each other. Theories and rumors abounded, and accusations were thick in the air. Elizabeth's boyfriend was questioned, but not arrested. It was revealed that Elizabeth's swim coach had been fired from his previous university job for having an inappropriate relationship with one of his students. He was suspended, questioned seriously by police, and by day four he was considered the prime suspect.

On day seven, Elizabeth's body was found. She'd fallen down a flight of concrete stairs, one of those staircases on the outside of a building that led down into a cellar. It was a building on the far side of campus that was used for storage—desks, file cabinets, computers—with a workshop in the basement where the janitorial staff made repairs. What had she been doing there, far from any place she would need to be? She'd have had to walk a long winding path through the woods, away from the main campus buildings. We all knew she wouldn't have done that without a reason.

She'd broken her neck in the fall. It was unclear how long she'd lived while she lay there, how much she had suffered. The incident was suspicious, but there was no physical evidence to link anyone else to the scene. We were all shattered in ways big and small, and a pall was cast over the rest of our year. It was a small college, and Elizabeth was missed. And we were all afraid. Had it been an accident or foul play? No one was ever sure.

I could see it all on Ainsley's face; she'd taken it hard. And last year, we'd started calling her "Captain Safety." She was always reminding us to not walk home alone, to call if we were going to be very late or spend the night away from the room. And last year, we'd been good about it. But memories fade, and that fear we all felt grew dull and distant. We all wanted to believe that we were safe, and so we let ourselves feel that way again.

"I thought we weren't going to let each other walk home alone," she said. She wasn't one to be sullen or accusatory. She just sounded disappointed in me.

"I know," I said. "But . . ."

I didn't want to tell her that Beck and I had had a fight. I just didn't want to get into it with her. "I wasn't feeling well," I said instead. "And she wanted to stay and study."

"What's wrong?" she asked. She reached out a hand and

put it to my forehead. Beck and I were selfish and lazy. Ainsley was the nurturer, the mother among us. We counted on that from her, took her for granted at times. But we loved her for it, too. "You feel warm."

But it was just that her hands were icy cold. "I don't know," I said. "I was just feeling super tired."

Ainsley nodded slowly and looked back toward the door, as if she expected Beck to come charging through. Beck always entered the room like a gladiator, swinging the door open and tossing her bag to the floor, announcing that she was *Exhausted!* or *Starving!* or *Pissed off!* about whatever.

"She'll be home by breakfast at the latest, I'm sure. Get some rest," I told Ainsley. And she nodded uncertainly, shuffled off to her bedroom.

But the next morning when I left for class, I peeked into Beck's room and her bed hadn't been slept in. I felt a rush of guilt and regret, but I quickly quashed it. Beck had picked a fight, and I was only guilty of rising to the bait.

Over our afternoon chess game, I caught Luke staring at me. When I looked up at him, he didn't avert his eyes.

"You're getting better," he said.

I *was* getting better—because I'd been studying chess on the Internet. The kid was destroying me day after day. And even though I bore it with a smile, it was grating on me—and not a little. He was *eleven*. But he was confident, crafty, always five moves ahead. He was aggressive, backed me into corners. Even when I came armed with strategies, he seemed to know what I was going to do before I did it, made the most stunning evasive maneuvers. I mean, he wasn't just beating me. Game after game, I never even had a chance.

I'd been studying chess blogs, playing online. I'd even downloaded a book called *Practical Chess Exercises*. I still couldn't beat him, but I'd seen him pause a few times and look up at me. It was pathetic, I know. But the urge to compete with him and win was a fire in my belly. Beck's voice rang in my ears: *Grow up*.

"Do you like other games?" Luke asked. The corners of his mouth turned up in a grin that wasn't quite a smile, not quite a sneer.

"What kind of games?" I asked.

"Checkmate," he said. There was something unpleasant on his face. It took me a second to realize that it was pity. He pitied me, knew that I could never beat him, and was sorry for me that I kept trying.

"What?" I said, looking down at the board in dismay. "No."

He didn't say anything, just let me examine the pieces until I saw that his knight was threatening my king, and that the placement of his queen and his bishop made escape or evasion impossible.

"Wow," I said. There was literally a taste in my mouth, a thick oatmeal of annoyance. "You're amazing."

He gave me that nod he seemed to have perfected, a princely acknowledgment of his own greatness. *He's a genius*, his mother had told me. *They call it "profoundly gifted" when your IQ score is over a hundred and eighty. And his levels are right around there.*

It irked me because I, too, prided myself on my superior intelligence, had been classified as profoundly gifted in my youth. But he seemed smarter, had better focus, was more creative or something. But it was childish for me to care, wasn't it? It wasn't a competition. Why did it feel like one?

But his intellect works against him because of his other challenges, Rachel had qualified. *He outsmarts the people trying to help him.*

But what was wrong with him exactly? After that first afternoon, our time together had been relatively peaceful and even enjoyable. Of course, it had only been a short time. I didn't doubt Rachel, and I knew they wouldn't have taken him into Fieldcrest without good reason. But I hadn't seen any evidence of behavior problems. He was a little arrogant, kind of obnoxiously sure of himself. There was something deeply unsettling about his cool, adult gaze, his often grown-up word choice and phrasing. I was smart enough to know that his charm was a bit superficial, put on. But there'd been none of the rages Rachel warned me about. *If it happens, just sit very still and let him burn himself out. Don't attempt to subdue him.*

"You didn't answer me," he said.

He was packing up the board. *Why bother playing again, really?* his aura said. There was even something smug about the way he packed the soapstone pieces into their foam slots, placing them precisely then snapping closed the wooden case.

"Do I like other games?" I said. "You didn't answer *my* question. What kind of games?"

"Games that you can win," he said.

"Nice," I said. I reached over to give him a playful push on the shoulder. My touch, though very gentle, elicited a wince.

"What?" I said.

He pulled down the neck of his striped oxford and I saw that on his shoulder was an enormous bruise, a black-and-purple rose against the snow of his skin. It sent a wave of concern through me.

"How did that happen?" I asked.

"I fell down the stairs last night," he said. But he looked down at his cuticles. And I found myself thinking of that lock on the door. I was silent for a second, waiting for him to go on.

"My mom put ice on it," he said. "But I got in a fight at school today and it got hurt again."

There were lots of physical altercations at Fieldcrest. So many troubled kids in such close quarters, and violence was sure to erupt. In fact, it was one of the biggest criticisms of the place leveled by skeptics of Dr. Welsh's work.

The children were violent with each other, manipulated each other, the stronger sometimes preyed upon the weaker. Last year, after an article ran in the *New York Times Magazine* about the school, some parents had pulled their children from the program. They'd then gone on to form a group lobbying to close the school. *All these kids in one place? Aren't they just learning from each other, forming alliances?* one parent railed in an online discussion about the school. *Some of these kids*, parents complained, *are getting worse instead of better.*

My internships there had been brief, just a semester each. But it wasn't a happy place and I wasn't sad to leave when they were over. My art therapy class had been an unmitigated failure (Langdon thought differently, but I knew it was bad). My sessions generally devolving into pandemonium with paint being thrown, or someone raging on the floor, or tears shed after cruel words were tossed about. Once, a particularly violent boy tried to stab me in the eye with his brush. Luckily, Langdon had been there to subdue him.

"So," said Luke. "Games."

"Sure," I said. He seemed eager to change the subject, so I went along. I was going to bring some of this up with Langdon, ask his advice. "I like other games. Scrabble?"

"What about scavenger hunts?"

I thought about this. I wasn't sure I'd ever participated in a scavenger hunt. I didn't have that kind of childhood.

I didn't remember games, and family vacations, summer camps, and school field trips. I didn't spend time with my cousins at the beach. My parents didn't plan activities and playdates. So none of the places where scavenger hunts might have taken place even existed in my life.

"I don't think I've ever done one," I admitted.

His eyes went wide, and he leaned forward almost halfway across the table. "Never?"

"Nope," I said. I had that feeling again, the uncomfortable buzz I get when I accidentally reveal how different my life was from almost everybody else's. Not that Luke's childhood was all fun and games. But I held my ground, didn't backpedal with a *Well, maybe, a long time ago*. Luke was way too smart for that. "Never."

"Wanna do one with me?" I remember thinking that he looked so childishly eager, so happy. I thought about the bruise on his shoulder, that lock on his door, his days spent at Fieldcrest. And I thought: *It's harmless. Why not?*

But maybe, even then, it was more than that. He was leveling a dare, and I was childish enough, competitive enough, to take it. I wanted to play his games. But more than that, I wanted to win. No. I wanted to beat Luke. I know. It's sad and terribly irresponsible when the adults act like children. But we're not so far from that place, most of us. Most of us grow up very slowly.

"Sure," I said. "When do we start?"

"Soon," he said. And then he did something strange.

He walked around the table and hugged me. It was soft and sweet, but I sat frozen a minute, not sure of what to do. I wouldn't say I'm the most affectionate person in the world. In fact, physical contact makes me pretty uncomfortable. I fought not to pull back, and then finally closed my arms awkwardly around him.

6

When I got back to the dorm, I knew something was wrong before I entered my room. The door stood ajar, and I could hear voices within. There had been a lot of chatter around the espresso machine when I entered the lobby—which was normal. But a silence seemed to fall as I entered. And girls who ordinarily wouldn't have given me a second glance looked at me strangely.

Standing inside our suite, there were two uniformed officers, and two other official-looking adults standing near the fireplace. Ainsley was sitting on the couch, crying. Our dorm mom, Margie, who had been responsible for taking care of Evangeline girls for twenty-five years, was there. *I've seen it all, girls*, she said every year at orientation. *So don't bother trying to pull one over. No room parties. No overnight guests in your room. No booze. No pot. There's no curfew, but if you're expected, it wouldn't be the worst thing in the world to let someone know where you are. We all like to*

77

think we're safe here, and usually we are. But things happen, as we all know.

Margie, fit, lean, and pushing sixty, wore a deep scowl. Elizabeth had been an Evangeline girl. Some people said that she wasn't over Elizabeth's death, was in therapy in order to move on from the responsibility she felt. Of course, we all knew there was nothing Margie could have done. It was an accident, a terrible accident. Or so it had been ruled, nearly a year after Elizabeth's death.

"What's up?" I said.

Everyone turned to look at me, and then Ainsley looked away. I recognized the heavyset, balding man as one of the detectives who had worked Elizabeth's case. He had a bear-ish quality, a warm smile, but bright, analytical eyes. Everyone thinks bears are so cute, but their claws can easily dismantle a human body. They were always watching, those eyes, drinking in details, making connections.

"Beck didn't show up for class today," Ainsley said into her tissues. I sank onto the couch beside her. "She hasn't come back to the room."

I offered a slow shrug. "Beck has skipped class before," I said. I ignored a rise of worry, of guilt. I shouldn't have left her. "This is not a new thing."

"We found her bag in the trees by the path that leads from the library," said the detective. He walked over to me and offered me his hand, which I took. His grip was hard and firm—I mean, of course it was. It wouldn't be wet and limp, would it? Not this guy. Even though he was balding and had an impressive paunch, there was still a kind of power that radiated from him.

"Detective Chuck Ferrigno," he said. "Lead detective for The Hollows PD. Maybe you remember me? You're Lana Granger, right?"

"That's right," I said. "I do remember you, sir."

He gave me a warm smile. "Are you okay?"

"You found her bag?" I asked.

He nodded. "What time did you leave the library?"

"Around nine or ten," I said. I thought hard, trying to remember the exact time. "Nine-thirty, I guess."

"And where did you go after that?" I felt the heat of everybody's eyes on me. It was the thing I hated most, being the center of attention. I wanted to sink down into myself and I realized that I was slouching horribly. I forced myself to sit up straight.

"You went together and were supposed to leave together, though. That's what Ainsley told us."

"Right. But I wasn't feeling well." I really didn't want to lie, but I had already lied to Ainsley.

"And where did you go after that?"

"I came right home and got into bed." I felt Ainsley turn her head to look at me.

"What time was that?" he asked.

"About nine forty-five."

"Is that about right, Ainsley?" asked the detective.

"I was in my room studying, and I had my headphones on," said Ainsley. I saw her foot start to twitch. I saw the detective notice it, too. "I didn't hear her come in."

The detective was scribbling in a little notepad, which struck me as kind of old school and made me think of Beck. Some people just don't want to give up the pen and paper thing, the analog experience.

There were a few more questions, which I heard through a kind of mental fog. Was Beck seeing anyone? *Not that we knew of.* Was she having a problem with anyone? *No.* Had she mentioned being afraid of anyone? Had she seemed depressed? *No. Nothing more than the typical angst.*

"Her parents are divorcing," Ainsley chimed in. "She's pretty upset about that."

But that was news to me. It was kind of a big deal. That she hadn't confided in me underscored the space that had opened between us lately. She'd told Ainsley but not me. A little flame of jealousy flickered inside.

I thought about Beck's bag sitting out there all night, my mind searching for some logical, harmless reason that her bag with all her notebooks, her laptop, probably her cell phone, would have been cast to the side of the path. I couldn't come up with one.

When he was done with his questions, the detective and the other officers in the room left. But not before he paused in the doorway and said, "So, Lana, how are you feeling now?"

"Better," I said. "I think I was just overtired."

"Good," he said as he closed the door.

When they'd gone, I turned to look at Ainsley, who was watching me strangely.

"What?" I asked.

"Nothing," she said. And then she started to cry. I should have moved over to her and held on tight. I could have stroked her hair, telling her that it was all right, a big nothing. Beck would be home by dinner, I could have said. Ainsley was my friend, and it would have been right for me to comfort her. It was the expected thing. But I didn't do that. I moved away from her instead, and she wrapped her arms around herself. I stood awkwardly for a moment.

"Don't worry about it, okay," I said as I moved toward my bedroom. "She's fine."

I saw her nod, but she didn't say anything.

I saw a shrink in town, Dr. Maggie Cooper, and I had been seeing her my entire time at school. I had sessions once a week, sometimes every other week. It depended largely on the time of year, how heavy was the burden of my past in any given season, if I was especially stressed or sad.

I think it would be safe to say that Dr. Cooper knew me better than almost anyone alive who was not related to me, and even she didn't know everything. But I liked her and trusted her, had never felt safer or less judged than I did on the couch in her office. Luckily, I had an appointment that afternoon.

I told her about the things Beck had said—about Luke, about Langdon. And how I had left Beck in the library, both of us angry. And how Beck hadn't come home. Dr. Cooper listened in that careful way she had, nodding, issuing affirming noises. In her office, the real world always seemed so distant and far away, infinitely manageable. I could sink into the plush couch, hug one of the overstuffed throw pillows to my middle, and just *be*, while everything waited swirling and chaotic outside her door.

"I'm so sorry to hear this, Lana. It must be so frightening for you," said Dr. Cooper. She reached over and handed me a box of tissues, even though I wasn't crying.

"A missing girl is always cause for alarm," she went on. "But it's important for you not to get catastrophic in your thinking. It could yet be a false alarm. The police are reacting quickly, which is as it should be. But, for you personally, try not to imagine the worst-case scenario."

"But her bag," I said. That was really the thing that got to me. "She'd never leave that anywhere, not for any reason."

Dr. Cooper made an affirming noise. "That is troubling, I admit."

It wasn't possible for me not to get catastrophic in my thinking, not to imagine the worst-case scenario. I told her as much.

"It's a process," she said. "To change the way we think. And you have unique challenges. But it is possible."

The good doctor was so far out of her depth, she didn't even know. Like a weak swimmer congratulating herself for treading water while a school of sharks circled her below the surface.

"I'll work on it," I said.

She gave me a smile that didn't quite reach her eyes. I'd noticed a change in Dr. Cooper the last couple of sessions. Was it that some of her warmth had faded? Or was she holding something back, or sensing that I was? I tried to think back, wondered if I'd said anything I shouldn't have. It was true that I was getting very comfortable here, had even started to look forward to the sessions that I had agreed to initially only to appease my aunt. *You have to talk to someone regularly about the things you're dealing with. You need someone to help you narrate the past in a healthy way.* She was a big believer in talk therapy. She was also the joint manager with Sky of my trust. Not that she ever used it to manipulate me, but it always just seemed like a good idea to do what she wanted.

Then, to have a place to talk about some (not all) of the things that haunted me, that leaked into my dreams, that kept me feeling distant and separate from the world that went on around me, had actually been a big relief. The doctor had never once seemed rattled, never recoiled or looked shocked by what I told her.

Of course, there are some disturbing blank spaces in my memory, places where things are foggy or black altogether. They rise up at me sometimes, white noise in my dreams, or startling flashes in my waking life. And Dr. Cooper says that it is the psyche's nature to protect itself. She does not recommend prying into the dark places, crowbarring open the locked boxes. *When you are ready to deal with those memories, they will come back, and we'll work through it then. And they may never come back—which might not be a bad thing.*

I'm not into navel-gazing, and I am not especially curious. In fact, I'd rather avoid all unpleasantness inside myself and without. Which might explain my lack of desire for any kind of relationship, my lily-white virginity. My parents kept their wedding photo on their dresser. In it my mother is a vision of loveliness with her blond hair pulled back tight and crowned with white roses, her blue eyes shining. My father is her contrast, his dark hair long and wild, his black eyes intense and staring. The look of love on their faces, so passionate, so desirous, so joyful—it was almost an embarrassment to behold. They went from that day of ice-cream-white love to a day that ended with my mother lying in a pool of her own ink-black blood. Every couple starts off loving each other, don't they? It's how a relationship ends that really defines its nature.

We talked a little more about my new job, about my classes. But my heart wasn't really in it. My mind was on Beck, and her bag sitting out there in the night.

"Lana?"

"Sorry."

"It's okay," she said. "I get it. It's impossible not to be concerned about Beck."

I liked how she never offered any physical comfort. I appreciate people who have a healthy respect for personal boundaries. Our culture is too touchy-feely; everyone wants a hug these days. But Dr. Cooper just sat and was present. She would let me rant and rave at her, just sat and waited as one might wait for a storm to pass. Maybe she sensed that I was uncomfortable with physical contact. Or maybe she just felt it best to establish and keep boundaries—for herself as well as for her patients.

"There's something I've been wanting to discuss," she said. "And honestly I've been struggling with how to bring it up, or whether I should at all."

That didn't sound good. "Okay," I said. "Go for it."

"Your father has reached out to me via e-mail."

My whole body froze, and I felt my stomach go hollow and wobbly. I liked to pretend that my father was dead. In fact, I was quite good at convincing myself of it. That's what I told those people who pushed their way into my past, that my parents died in a car accident when I was sixteen. (People usually backed way off after that, except for Beck, who had only moved in closer. Tragedy turned her on.)

So, the doctor might as well have told me that she'd conducted a séance and was communicating with my father

85

from beyond the grave. That's the kind of jolt her news sent through me.

We sat in silence for a moment, then: "Should I go on?" she asked.

I nodded, even though I wanted to get up and run from the office.

"Am I wrong in thinking that you have a right to know about this? We can end this discussion right now. I can let your father know that I will not be reading his messages, and that you have no desire to hear from him. If that's what you want, that's what we'll do."

It was tempting to tell her that yes, that's what I wanted. But wasn't there a nagging curiosity, a tidal pull I still felt to him? One would think that after what he did, any bond we shared might be severed like an umbilical cord—a harsh, irrevocable cut, two parts of the same whole that would never knit back together. But that's just not how it works.

"What does he want?"

I could see the blood on the floor, the perfect red hand-print on the white of the wall. It was all still so vivid, if I closed my eyes I could go back and live in that house, in that moment, forever.

"He wants to talk to you," she said. "He loves you and there are things he wants you to know. That's what his message says. The date of his execution is drawing near, and all of his appeals have been denied. He can only hope for a stay, but that doesn't seem likely."

I didn't have a voice to answer with. I wondered how much worse this day was going to get.

"How does he know about you?" I asked finally. Outside the sky had gone a gunmetal gray and the dead branches outside her window quivered in a sheath of ice.

"I have no idea," she said, with a slow shake of her head. "Who have you told about our sessions?"

"My aunt, my lawyer," I said. "That's it. Oh, and Langdon, my student adviser."

"Do any of those people have contact with your father?"

"Sky Lawrence," I said. "But he doesn't mention it. We don't discuss my father."

She pushed herself up in her seat, and uncrossed and crossed her legs again. She kept her eyes on me in that gentle way she had. I usually didn't like it when people looked at me for too long, but with her I didn't mind. There was never any judgment on her face, only intelligent concern.

"I need to think about this. Okay?" I said. I knew I seemed calm and level on the outside, but there were sirens blaring inside my head. I'm good at hiding my feelings. Really good.

"Of course," she said. "And if you need to talk before our next session, give me a call."

When I left her office, I looked at my phone and realized if I didn't hurry, I'd be late getting to Luke's house and he'd have to go into the house alone. I was worried that it looked like snow, but I hopped on my bike anyway and rode through the frigid air toward town. My face and fingers were burning with cold, and I wondered, if I had actually been capable of shedding tears, would they freeze on my face and form a mask of ice.

7

Dear Diary,

Then it did stop, just like they promised. And a strange
silence has settled like a pall. You would think I'd be
overjoyed—my husband and my mother certainly are. They
are giddy with relief, hand slapping and embracing when the
baby sleeps. Even my sister was so happy for me that I could
hear the relief in her voice. She has always been deeply
empathetic, so much so that I have leaned too heavily on her.
Yes, they are all so happy. The worst is over.

Magically, he is sleeping for six-hour stretches and so are
we all. The mental fog has lifted somewhat, and I am starting
to remember what it was like to be me. I stare at him for the
first time, as he lies quiet in his crib. We swaddle him in a
fuzzy blue wrap, which we think might have been part of the
solution. His pink face is wrinkled like an old man's and his jet-
black hair is a funny little helmet. I recognize his beauty, now
that he has stopped screaming like a siren. He smells like a
clean, powdery gift from the gods.

But when I hold him in my arms, and when he takes my nipple in his mouth and sucks, I feel nothing, just a strange emptiness. He looks up at me with those intelligent, shining eyes—and he knows it. He squirms in my arms, takes no comfort in my body, which feels brittle and too bony. He doesn't nuzzle and coo. He is an animatronic baby—he looks real, makes all the appropriate noises. But he doesn't live. His stare is as flat and glittering as a doll's, as though his eyes were made from glass.

I have made the mistake of sharing this with my husband.

"There's something wrong with him," I say.

It is a rare, quiet moment. My mother, who extended her stay out of concern for all of us, has turned in early. The baby is sleeping soundly in his crib, his room filled with the sound of white noise from the humidifier. And the ceiling is a field of blue and green stars from his turtle nightlight.

In our first shared moment in a quiet house, we are sitting on the couch trying to remember how to be alone together. But it feels awkward. He looks different, thin and pale with dark circles under his eyes. I am different in about a hundred different ways, jumpy and nervous, quick to snap. We are both waiting for the noises on the monitor that will send one of us up the stairs.

But when I looked at my husband, I didn't see the mirror of my own despair. He didn't seem shattered the way I felt. But, of course, he left for the office every day. Our front door was his portal back to the normal world where people work, and went out to lunch, and surfed the Web at their desks in the afternoon, and met for drinks. People laughed and had thoughts, important thoughts that didn't fly out of their heads like owls delivering secret messages.

He disappears through the portal by seven in the morning (before the baby, he never left until eight-thirty at the earliest). Sometimes he comes home as late as eight. He says he has to work more now, because of the baby, because I have decided not to go back to work and to stay home with our child. I felt the first trickle of resentment the minute he walked out the door his first day back, clutching his little book of photos. Six weeks later, my resentment has bloomed into a full-blown rage. But I bury it, deep inside. I know it is wrong. I wasn't really angry with him, was I? After all, he was supporting us now. And it was I who had pushed for a baby.

"We had a hard few weeks," he says. "But he's doing a lot better, isn't he?"

I don't say anything. There's a glass of wine for me on the table, but I don't want it. If I drink it, I'll have to pump and dump. I hate hooking myself up to that machine, sitting and listening to it sigh and whir as it drains the milk from my breasts.

"The crying," he says. "That was so hard. But it's stopped, other than what's probably normal. And he's sleeping a lot."

"He doesn't seem right," I say. It sounds weak and a little whiny. I can't put into words what I feel in my body.

My husband stares at me in that way that he has, so present, so earnest. He has his hand on my leg.

"The labor, the C-section, the colic," I say into the thick, expectant silence. "Maybe it hurt him."

He is tender, tries to talk it through with me. (He's just a baby. We'll all adjust, because everyone does, don't they? Maybe we got all the hard stuff out of the way, maybe we'll sail through the terrible twos and adolescence, he joked.) But I had a feeling that we wouldn't be sailing through anything ever again.

"My father," I say. And I hate the words before they've even tumbled out of my mouth.

"No," he says, horrified, as though the thought has never crossed his mind. "Don't."

"He looks just like my father."

So much for "date night."

The next day, he calls in sick to work. Appointments are made—not for the baby, but for me.

My ob-gyn quickly diagnoses me with postpartum depression. And my husband and I sit in her pink, sunlit office while she explains how the massive hormonal shifts that occur after pregnancy don't regulate right away for everyone. She kept calling it the baby blues, which I think she did to take the edge off of it. Because while "baby blues" sounds soft and pastel-colored, easily managed, postpartum depression is black and red, with thick, hard edges; it bludgeons. It was likely, said the doctor, that my traumatic labor, the emergency

C-section, followed by the colic, have contributed to my descent into PPD.

"It all feeds into each other," said my doctor patiently. "And—P.S.—none of this is a walk in the park under the best of circumstances. More women suffer PPD in a given year than will sprain an ankle or be diagnosed with diabetes. So, you're not alone."

To my husband: "Let's make sure Mom is getting plenty of rest. Can you take the nighttime feedings?"

"Of course," he says. "Of course."

And for me, a low-dose antidepressant, the decision to go to formula and stop breast-feeding—which was already on the table because the baby was gaining weight too slowly.

Another failure for me: drugs during labor, emergency C-section, colic, unable to nurse beyond two months. No wonder my baby hates me. I have failed him in every single way and he's not even three months old.

In the mirror, there's no trace of the happy pregnant person I was. My ripe bosom, my glowing hair, my round belly—it's all gone flat. I am dull and deflated, abandoned by life and joy and expectancy. I am flabby and gray.

I have started taking the pills and I pray that everyone is right, that I have been sabotaged by my own brain chemicals. And that the little blue pill is going to put things right again.

"All the hard stuff just goes away—the pain, the stress, the sleep deprivation," my mom soothed in the car. "You just don't remember any of it later on."

93

Please, please, please, let them all be right. Let it be me. Let there be something wrong with me. Something normal that can be fixed quickly and easily. Please let there be something wrong with me, and let it not be something wrong with him.

8

Luke was waiting for me on the porch when I arrived. A light snow had started to fall, and I'd wiped out twice on the slick roads. I was going to need a ride home from Luke's mom. He was sitting on the porch swing, emitting a sullen and self-pitying energy.

"You're late," he said as I swung off my bike. My pants were ripped, and my knee was bleeding from the second fall.

"She left you?" I said. A red Volvo usually dropped him off, waiting in the street until I opened the door. Whoever it was, a slight woman with a wild frizz of red hair, she'd never gotten out of the car. Her name and phone number were scribbled on the chalkboard in the kitchen. But it was not information I had committed to memory.

"She didn't wait," he said. "By the time I realized that you weren't there, she was gone."

"You have a key," I said, climbing the steps.

He pumped his legs lightly and the swing emitted an irritating squeak as it moved back and forth. Something about the noise, about his pouty face, sent a skein of irritation through me. What a baby.

"I was afraid to go in alone," he said. I didn't buy it. I'd been spending time with Luke for about three weeks. He was lots of things—a scaredy-cat wasn't one of them.

"Afraid of what?" I asked. I stood in front of him and gave him a light tap on his foot with my toe.

He shrugged and looked up at me. His eyes were a little damp but he wasn't crying.

"I just didn't want to be alone in there."

I remembered coming home from school alone when I was a kid. Occasionally, I had to let myself in, make my own snack, and do my homework until my mother came back from wherever she was. When the school day had gone well, it was heaven. I'd eat anything I wanted, lie on the couch and watch television, giddy with my own personal freedom.

But when the day had been bad—if I'd done poorly on a test, or been bullied in gym class, which I often was, or if there had been some "incident," or I hadn't eaten my lunch because of some kind of cafeteria torture, I'd hate that empty house. I'd hate the way it echoed and was dark when I entered. I hated how no lights were on, and nothing was cooking in the kitchen, no music, no television sound. No mom to metabolize the events of the day.

"I'm sorry," I said. "For real."

I held the door open for him, and he walked inside. He went straight up to his room, where I knew he'd drop his backpack and change his clothes. And I made his snack—apples and graham crackers with peanut butter and a glass of milk. My hands were shaking as the knife sank into the white flesh of the apple. I was trying to keep it all at bay—Beck, my father. But I was shaky and fragile, ready to shatter.

As I put his snack on the table my phone chimed. It was a text from Ainsley:

Still no sign of Beck. Her parents are here. Can u come back? I'm losing it.

"What's wrong?" Luke stood in the doorway, watching.

"Nothing," I said. "Just some problem with my roommates."

I didn't know what was okay to say to him. Even though I hadn't wanted him to, Langdon had apparently asked around about Luke.

"He's very smart," Langdon had told me. He'd held me after class. "His IQ is higher than most of the doctors on staff, including mine. He has a history of violence with other children, teachers. He is disruptive in the classroom, a wild and incorrigible liar."

"I haven't seen any of this," I'd told him.

I'd sat back at my desk in the front row. The room was a windowless space with plush stadium seating. It was in one of the more modern buildings. There were power outlets every few feet on the floor. The seats were generous and comfortable, the half-moon desktops polished wood.

No expense was ever spared at Sacred Heart, no corners ever cut. We had a chef in our kitchen, Chef Bruce, and the restaurant served things like Chilean sea bass with lentils and saffron rice accompanied by a vegetable medley, as well as staples like free-range chicken sandwiches (with apple-wood bacon and white cheddar), or all-beef hot dogs with hand-cut fries, fresh-mozzarella Margherita personal pizzas, and organic beef hamburgers.

"He was a little prickly that first day," I said. "But since then, we've gotten along fine."

"There were other incidents. A fire in a wastepaper basket—though no one could prove conclusively that it was Luke. Playground fights, which might or might not have been his fault. In second grade, he was so viciously unkind to an overweight girl, such an unrelenting bully, drawing support from other bad personalities in the classroom, that her parents moved her to another school. Luke was reprimanded, but his abuse was only verbal, so no real action was taken. It was almost as if he was already learning how to work the system. He had already learned how to pick on people who were vulnerable, and do it in such a way that he couldn't quite be punished. He was a natural leader, mainly because children feared him."

"I have to be honest," I said. "I can't reconcile any of that with the boy I know."

But Langdon went on.

"In fourth grade, he developed an unhealthy attachment

to his teacher, a young married woman in her late twenties. When he learned she was pregnant, he turned hostile, verbally abusive. He called her a whore, told her that he hoped she miscarried her baby. Finally, he tripped her as she was walking through the aisles during an independent work period. He was expelled."

"Expelled?"

"Yeah," said Langdon. "Kind of a big deal for an eight-year-old. But it was the total lack of remorse that really unsettled the headmaster. He wrote that Luke didn't seem to care, or even to understand, what he had done. He maliciously tripped a pregnant woman; lots of kids saw him do it. When asked if he'd like to draft a letter of apology to his teacher, he refused. 'She should apologize to me,' he allegedly said. 'She said she loved me.'"

I involuntarily shuddered as a sudden chill settled over the room.

"His mother homeschooled him after that," he said. "Finally, she enrolled him in Fieldcrest. We only have her account of the last two years, which she describes as 'challenging.' But since he began at Fieldcrest this fall, he has been a model of good behavior, and is well beyond his age as far as academics are concerned. So she obviously did something right. Or he's very motivated to stay at Fieldcrest for some reason."

"There are locks on the outside of his door," I said.

Langdon raised an eyebrow at that. "Is that so?"

"I don't know if they were already there when they moved in," I qualified.

"And?" He seemed to know I had something else I wanted to say.

"He had a terrible bruise on his shoulder," I said reluctantly. I really liked Rachel, and I knew that saying things like this was raising a red flag. "He claimed to have fallen down the stairs."

"Children like Luke tend to elicit a lot of anger from their parents," said Langdon. "But by all accounts, she's a present and concerned mother. She cares and is doing everything she can for a boy who, quite honestly, is exhibiting all the signs of a callous-unemotional. You know— a childhood psychopath."

He must have read something on my face. "Of course, that's not a diagnosis," he continued. "Just a conclusion from what I've read. He's not my patient."

"He's been fine."

"Just be careful with him," said Langdon. He leaned back, ran a large hand through his hair. "Make sure he's not running an agenda with you. And don't forget that he's way smarter than you are."

"I'll remind you that this was your idea," I said.

"So it was," he said. He issued a little cough. "Maybe I should have done my homework before encouraging you."

*

"You look upset," Luke said now. He sat at the table and started eating.

"I'm fine," I said. I knew I should call his mother and tell her I had to go. I really should get back to Ainsley and to Beck's parents. But I didn't want to. I didn't want to face what might be happening. I was still hoping it would all go away.

"I heard there's someone missing at your school," said Luke. "Is that true?"

There was an expression on his face that I didn't like at all, as if he were hungry for drama, for news of mayhem. I worked not to react. How could he have heard that? I asked.

"I heard some teachers talking in the lounge, on my way back from the bathroom."

I didn't think there were unsupervised walks to and from the bathroom at Fieldcrest, nor did I think anyone would be discussing Beck in the faculty room, not yet. I didn't say so. But how else could he have known?

"I wouldn't say she was missing," I said. "She hasn't come home since yesterday."

"And that's not missing?" The gaze he held me with was open and inquiring. But there was something swimming beneath those black pools.

"Well," I said. How much could you really say to a kid? I couldn't offer my various theories: she might be on a bender, sleeping around? "She might be with a friend."

"Or playing a joke," he said. "Messing with you?"

It was a really odd thing for him to say, but I shrugged. "Maybe."

"Why would she do that?" Again, his face was a mask of innocence. Was he goading me? I was rankling as if he was.

"I don't know," I said. "Our relationship is complicated."

"Like ours?"

"Our relationship is not that complicated," I said. This elicited a little frown. "You're a kid. I'm your babysitter."

"If you say so," he said. He offered a shrug. "So where would your friend go, if she was messing around with you?"

"A bunch of places," I said. "She could have gone anywhere."

"But you don't think she did," he said. He was chewing his apple loudly. "You look really scared."

"Let's talk about something else," I said.

There was a flash of something on his face—delight. As though he'd discovered something about me, a weakness, and would squirrel away the knowledge for his future use. But maybe Langdon had just made me paranoid about him.

That's what they do, psychopaths. They figure out your language, your currency, your needs, your dreams and fears. Then they figure out how to use those things to get what they want from you. Most of us wear it all on our faces. We telegraph our inner lives with what we choose to eat, how we eat it, what we wear, how we carry ourselves, the words we use and don't use. We tell about ourselves in a million small and large ways. And most people don't even notice, because they're so busy telling about *themselves*, listening to the symphony of their own inner lives. But the psychopath doesn't have an inner life—no attachments, no feelings, no self-doubt, no regrets. Psychopaths just have their own desires, and a single-minded focus to achieve those desires— whatever they happen to be. So they have a lot of attention to direct at their chosen quarry, figuring, testing, planning, exploiting. But that wasn't Luke, was it? It couldn't be.

"So," he said. "Let's start our game."

There it was again, that sweetly mischievous grin.

"Sure," I said. "Why not?"

I was happy for the distraction. There was only an hour before Rachel had said she'd be home. After that, I'd have to reenter the real world, face the ugliness of it all.

"So this hunt will be like a history lesson," said Luke. "How much do you know about The Hollows?"

"Some," I said. I knew quite a bit about the sleepy, spooky little burg in which my college nestled. But I didn't want Luke to know how much I knew. I figured that would give me a much-needed leg up.

He took something from his pocket and clicked it on the table. It was a rusty old key. Tied to it with a piece of red yarn was a blue-lined index card.

"What's this?" I said with a smile. I held up the key and looked at it. It was warm from his pocket, with a heart-shaped bow and a long stem. He watched me intently as I turned it in my hand.

"Where did you get it?"

"Read," he said.

I turned the card toward the light. It read:

> *Within its walls,*
> *For a hundred years,*
> *People have learned and prayed and died.*
> *Now, some believe, a tortured soul is trapped inside.*

> *On a winter's night when the moon was full,*
> *A broken man decided that his life wasn't much fun.*
> *So he drank a bottle of whiskey*
> *And ate the barrel of his gun.*

> *Why did he do it?*
> *What secret did he hide?*
> *What led him to end his life*
> *While his children cried and cried?*

I stared at it a moment. It was written in the careful print letters of a child's hand. When I raised my eyes to Luke, he was staring at me with an odd and unsettling grin.

"I'm a poet," he said. "And you didn't know it."

Just then, we heard a key in the door and we turned to see his mother walk through, brushing snowflakes from her coat. I couldn't help but notice her shoes, a practical but decidedly unstylish pair of boots. They seemed not to belong to her, and I found myself hyperfocusing on them for reasons I couldn't explain. But I guess when it came to snow boots, it was function over form, even for the most fashion-conscious. The snow outside was falling heavily now, and the sky was turning black. I shoved the note and the key in my pocket.

"Lana," she said. Her face was flushed with cold, and she looked pretty in her red wool hat. "I tried to call but got a strange busy signal. I closed up early because I was worried that you'd be on your bike. I wanted to drive you back to the dorm before the storm gets too bad."

Luke wore an expression of unmasked annoyance. She'd broken the spell he was weaving and he was pissed about it.

"Oh," I said. "Thanks."

Luke helped me get my bike into their garage (Rachel had too much stuff in her trunk to fit it in the car), neither one of us looking at the other. Like a little man, he took the bike from me and rolled it down the path and up the driveway. As he leaned it against the wall, I noticed a kid's dirt bike stood on a kickstand just over to the left. The wheels were caked with mud. I wondered when he had time to ride it. There wasn't another adult bike in the garage, and I couldn't see Rachel letting Luke ride around by himself.

"Do you still want to play the game?" he asked.

I was already puzzling over that odd poem, tumbling its

words around in my brain. Of course I wanted to play, more than any adult reasonably should. In fact, thinking about the poem was the first moment that I wasn't thinking about everything else. Here was a puzzle I could reasonably solve. Not like my life, which seemed like an endless series of questions with no answers. But I didn't want him to see how creepy and bizarre I thought it was, how anxious I was to figure it out. Somehow I thought if I did, Luke would have the upper hand. And I couldn't let him get that.

"Definitely," I said. "Yeah, I'm looking forward to it. I mean, I've got some stuff going on. But I'll think about it."

I turned away from the dark look he gave me. He expected more from me. I had disappointed him. Inside I smiled.

We all hopped into the Range Rover, Luke in the backseat, me up front with Rachel. There was a very faint scent of cigarette smoke, covered by some kind of artificial cherry smell. I could see her as a secret smoker. It was something she tried to give up over and over, I guessed. But she just couldn't kick it. She hid it from everyone, sneaking smokes on the deck after Luke was asleep, or as she drove home with all the windows open. Her breath always smelled like peppermint, candy she was probably sucking on to hide the smell. She didn't smoke enough that it permeated the fabric of her clothes.

"You two are awfully quiet," she said after a few minutes. Her tone was light and playful. The windshield wipers were scraping against the glass, the icy bits of snow crunching softly. "Are you up to something?"

"Lana's upset," Luke chimed from the backseat.

"Oh?" said Rachel.

"Her friend is missing."

"Oh!" she said, giving me a sideways glance of concern. "Is that true?"

"Why do you always think I'm a fucking liar?" said Luke, his tone slicing and bitter.

"Watch your tongue," she said, just as sharply.

"*Watch your tongue*," he mimicked nastily. "A physical impossibility, by the way."

He was mad that we'd been interrupted, that she'd come home early and ruined his game. I just knew it; I don't even know how. An awkward silence swelled, and I could hear him tapping on something in the backseat.

"She didn't come home from the library last night," I said, addressing Rachel. I was eager to move on from the uncomfortable vibe in the car. I could see how things might quickly heat up between them and I didn't need that. "But that's happened before."

"I hope she's okay," said Rachel. "Wasn't there an incident a couple of years back?"

"Yes," I said. "There was. Another friend of mine fell down some stairs and she was missing for a few days before—" Rachel glanced at me and I clamped my mouth shut. It wasn't really appropriate to be talking about this in front of Luke. I certainly wouldn't have brought it up if they hadn't.

"Before what?" said Luke. He was straining forward in his seat.

"Before they found her."

"She was dead, wasn't she?" In the light of the passing streetlamps, he seemed like he was grinning. But when I turned to look at him, he was pale and grim-faced. I didn't answer him.

"I'm sorry," said Rachel. She shook her head sadly. "That's awful."

"It's a statistical anomaly, isn't it?" said Luke. "To have two friends go missing like that. Especially at your age?"

"Luke," said Rachel. "What a thing to say."

"I really don't know," I said stiffly.

He made some kind of noise in the backseat; it sounded like a derisive snort of laughter. But when I turned to look at him, he just stared ahead blankly. He was a super weird kid.

I was relieved to see the dorm ahead of us. But my relief only lasted for a minute. There were also two squad cars, and an SUV with Pennsylvania plates, which was where Beck was from.

"Oh, dear," said Rachel.

"Thanks for the ride," I said.

But I could barely hear over the sound of blood rushing in my ears, the pulse throbbing in my neck. I tried to remember what the doctor said, not to get catastrophic in my thinking. But I was water going down the drain, twirling, getting sucked into the void.

"See you tomorrow!" Luke was yelling from the rolled-down window of the backseat as they pulled away. "Don't forget about our game!"

I turned to look at him, lifted my hand in an absent-minded wave, and headed inside.

9

Detective Ferrigno and I were sitting at the bistro table in the tiny suite kitchen. Ainsley, and Beck's parents, Lynne and Frank, were outside in the living room, each of them on a cell phone, calling literally everyone Beck knew.

There was an aura of urgency, certainly. But it hadn't yet descended into the terror of a missing girl, mainly because Beck had run away three times before.

As a teenager, she'd left home at sixteen because she wanted to go to Cuba to experience the burgeoning art scene. With the help of her ex-stepfather, she'd purchased a ticket to Toronto, then took a flight from there to Havana, where she was apprehended in the airport and returned to her parents. (Her ex-stepfather realized he'd screwed up and came clean pretty quickly.)

I am the product of my parents' misery, she claimed often. Her parents had divorced when she was eleven, each married other people and then got divorced from those people to marry each other again when Beck was fifteen. Now her

111

parents were about to divorce for the second time. They were the kind of people who thought that they could call their toxic, shitty relationship "tempestuous" and make it cool. They often framed their vicious, violent fights and passionate makeups as "romantic." *I don't even know what a real marriage looks like,* Beck said to me once. *Do you know how much pain they've caused each other, and every other person unlucky enough to get involved with them? They make me sick.* I could relate. She knew I could, because I'd told her some about my parents, even though she didn't know everything. Our shared horror of our parents' terrible marriages was what initially bonded us.

She'd disappeared briefly during the summer between freshman and sophomore year because she didn't want to live with her parents again. She hitchhiked across the country, dropping e-mails along the way—just to let everyone know she wasn't dead. She ran out of money in Albuquerque, and asked me to wire her seven hundred dollars for a ticket back home, which I did. She paid me back (even though I told her she didn't have to) in increments of twenty and fifty dollars whenever she had extra cash. I loved her for that, that she was crazy and irresponsible, but totally ethical. It was a rare quality in a person.

"So the librarian said you two were arguing," said Detective Ferrigno.

"I guess," I said. "Nothing serious."

"Serious enough for you to storm out."

"I didn't *storm* out," I said. "I wasn't feeling well, so I was impatient with her. I didn't want to talk about what she wanted to talk about."

"Which was?" He didn't have his notebook. He was doing the we're-cool-just-hanging-out thing. But he'd obviously been walking around campus asking a bunch of questions.

"First, she was giving me a hard time about my new job," I said. "I'm babysitting for a difficult kid. She thought it was a stupid thing to do."

If you want to babysit for the bad seed, go for it. I wondered what she would say about Luke's poem. She would probably be really fascinated, would really dig the whole scavenger hunt thing. I couldn't wait to tell her about it. Then I remembered and my heart sank. We wouldn't be sharing things like that anymore. I was on my own.

"And what else?"

"I'm sorry?" I said.

"You said 'first,' as though there was more than one topic you hadn't wanted to discuss."

"Oh," I said. I picked at a string on my sleeve to communicate my nonchalance on the topic. "She thinks I have a crush on my student adviser, and she likes to give me shit about it. I just wasn't in the mood."

I heard Lynne's voice in the other room, an easy conversational pitch that ebbed and flowed. Who was she talking to? I wondered. What would she learn about Beck from the cast of characters in her phone book? Some of it might not be pretty.

"*Do* you have a crush on him?" the detective asked. There was a smile in his voice, a friendly tease.

I realized I'd hiked my shoulders up high, and I consciously pushed them down. "No," I said. "I don't. He's a lot older than me. He's also my professor."

He shifted in his seat and it groaned under his weight. It was cheap furniture from IKEA, the kind that you put together with one of those torturous little metal L-shaped tools. Did those things have a name?

"It's not like it doesn't happen," he said. He gave me an understanding smile. "You're both consenting adults."

"It's inappropriate and unethical." Was I really such a prude? Beck was always accusing me of being too stiff, too uptight. *Loosen up, my friend. Let go.*

"Who is it?"

"Professor Langdon Hewes," I said. He nodded as though the name meant something to him. He got internal for a second, maybe searching his memory for a connection. Of course, he'd be looking for connections now that two girls had gone missing in two years. Elizabeth's death was ruled an accident, but no one had ever felt good about it. There were too many unanswered questions. Her parents had been back to town twice, trying to get the case reopened. So far, that hadn't happened.

"Why didn't you tell me before that you two had argued?" he asked.

"I don't know," I said. I blew out a breath, brought a hand to my forehead. There were a couple of ways I could play it. Finally, I said: "It didn't seem important."

He cracked some tension out of his neck and leaned toward me.

"But being mad at you would be a decent reason for her not to come back to the room." He sounded cool and reasonable, like he was looking for a reason that Beck would be fucking with us.

"I guess," I said. "Honestly, it just wasn't that heated, you know." It hadn't been, really. Not for us.

The third time she disappeared was after our encounter at the frat party, our kiss. She didn't come back to the room for three days after we slept off our hangovers. She'd met a guy in town a few days before the party, and she'd been yammering on about him in that kind of goading way she had—as though she was trying to elicit some response from me. He was a construction worker or something, but he was into raves. *He's as dumb as a thumbtack*, she said. *But even thumbtacks have their application.*

She made a point of saying she was meeting him for coffee the day after, then spent the next three days at his place— blowing off classes, not returning calls. Her parents had come down that time, too. When she wasn't getting enough attention, she still regaled me with tales of her sexual exploits that week; he was the best she'd ever had, she claimed. Which—coming from a nineteen-year-old—sounded pretty silly.

I suppose she was trying to make me jealous, imagining her with someone else. She was a child, always looking for attention and drama to keep herself entertained. And she never heard from that guy again.

"Someone said you were in tears." The detective held me in his gaze; I could tell he wasn't sure whether I was being honest or not.

"I wasn't," I said with a little laugh. "Really."

"So after the library, where did you go?"

"I came back here," I said.

"You left the library at around eight, according to witnesses," said the detective. "And you came here around nine-thirty? But the library is only a ten-minute walk at most."

I didn't say anything right away. I remember this from my father: *Don't say too much. Talk as little as possible.*

Finally, "I just walked around a bit."

"But you weren't feeling well."

"I thought some air might do me good."

"Witnesses say that she left a few minutes after you did."

Witnesses say, witnesses say, witnesses say. If I had a dime for every time I'd heard that phrase. People, it seemed, were always watching, taking measure, issuing judgments. They couldn't wait to start running their mouths off. But did you know that eyewitness testimony is often totally unreliable? The human memory only records events through the filter of its own frame of reference. We try to fit the information we receive into schemas, units of knowledge that we possess about the world that correspond with frequently encountered situations, individuals, ideas, and situations. In other words, we often see things as we expect to see them, or want to see them, and not always as they are.

When I didn't say anything: "So you didn't see Rebecca again that night?"

"No," I said. "I didn't. I walked around, maybe longer than I thought. And then I came back to my room."

"It seems like she might have caught up with you on the path."

"But she didn't," I said. *Don't get defensive. Don't let them rattle you.*

"Okay," he said. He gave a quick nod, as though everything had been settled. He made to stand up, then seemed to change his mind.

"If you don't mind my asking," he said. "What is your relationship to Rebecca? Or—you call her Beck, right?"

"We're friends, roommates. Good friends," I said.

"More than that?" He'd lowered his voice to a whisper.

I started to quiver inside, a kind of shocked and angry shaking that started in my core and radiated out. It took my voice away. I looked toward the other room. Had anyone heard him?

"No," I breathed. I wanted to scream at him. *Who said that? Who would say something like that? Ainsley?*

He could see that he'd upset me, held up both his palms in a gesture of surrender. "Okay," he said. "I'm sorry. I have to ask all of these questions, Miss Granger. It's my job to look at all the angles."

I didn't say anything else, just looked down at the table between us. He slid his card under my gaze. "Call if you think of anything you want to discuss, no matter how small."

"Okay," I managed. When I looked up at him, I wore a polite smile. "I will."

He stood, and I felt a wave of relief that the conversation was over.

Then he stopped. "I was going through the files of the case a couple of years back—Elizabeth Barnett?"

"She fell down the stairs," I said. "It was an accident."

"Right," he said. "It was ruled an accident. There was no evidence of foul play and she had been drinking heavily."

I nodded, felt myself choke up a little at the memory of those horrible days, the searching, the waiting. Why did this keep happening?

"You were with Elizabeth the night she disappeared, weren't you? You and Rebecca?"

"We were at a party together," I said. What was he implying? "There were lots of people there. Half the school."

"But the three of you went to the party together, isn't that right?"

"Yes," I said. "We did."

We'd all gone together, but Elizabeth had been meeting her boyfriend there. It had taken us a long time to get ready. We'd been drinking before we left, trying on different out-fits. They'd been giving me a hard time because I went into the bathroom to change, didn't want to parade around in my underwear like they did. But it was good-natured enough. We were mainly focused on Elizabeth, how she thought it was going to be her first time with Gregg. She'd shopped for the occasion, and showed us her black-and-pink lace panties and matching bra. Her body was perfect; it looked like molded plastic. I found myself staring at the swell of her hips, her lush and pretty breasts, the lovely hollow of her belly button.

"God, who looks like that?" said Beck. "You're perfect."

Elizabeth just giggled and pulled on her clothes. "Yeah, right."

She wasn't a girl who knew her own beauty. And she was more beautiful for it. The three of us left together, giddy and happy, and ready for a good time. But when we walked through the door together, Gregg was waiting, looking smitten. I still remember how he enfolded her, and how she looked at him with a wide smile and glistening eyes. *Love, a promise delivered already broken.* Who said that?

But the rest of the night is a bit of a haze. We drank too much, all of us. But maybe especially me. When I drank, I found such a delightful state of blissful numbness, something about the way it mingled with the meds I was on. Naturally, I wasn't supposed to drink. But I did anyway. When I wake up after those nights, all I can remember usually is some blend of music, voices, light, a weird collage of my encounters. The same is true of that night. I sometimes dream of Elizabeth crying, but I don't know if that happened or not. I dream of being angry with her, but I don't know why.

"There was a fight that night, too," the detective said.

"With her boyfriend," I said. "She fought with her boyfriend."

I thought about Gregg and how he had never looked the same after Elizabeth died. Even now, he looks thinner and less golden than he used to. That's what happens when tragedy touches us. It fades out the colors, takes off the shine. Of course, we all know that the world tends toward destruction, that everything withers and falls to pieces. But we imagine that there's so much time. When someone we love dies suddenly and tragically, it's like seeing the curvature of the earth. You always knew it was round, a contained sphere floating in space. But when you see the bend in the horizon line, it changes your perspective on everything else.

I sat silent, waiting for the detective to go on. But he didn't. He stood in the doorway a second and then walked out. I sensed he was trying to make a point, but I didn't know what it was. I heard him talking to Lynne and Frank, and I sat there, shaking, until Ainsley walked in.

She had dark rings under her eyes, and her hair was wild.

She sat where the detective was sitting and reached out for my hand. Mine looked big and ugly next to hers.

"I can't go through this again," she said. "I think I might go home. My parents are coming tomorrow."

"No," I said. I didn't want to be alone here in the room without either of them. "It's fine. You'll see. She'll come back."

"I can't sleep," she said. She put her head down on our clasped hands and started to cry. She was the most sensitive of the three of us. She freaked out at exam time, got edgy when she'd had too much caffeine, cried at sad movies. Ainsley was a delicate spirit, gentle and easily upset. I moved around to her this time and put my arms around her. We sank together to the floor, the chair scraping back. I could hear the low rumble of voices in the other room.

"It's going to be fine," I said. "You'll see."

She didn't say anything for a minute. Then she stood, ran her hands through her hair, and wiped her eyes. I grabbed a paper towel from the roll and handed it to her; she blew her nose. Her cheeks were flushed, and her eyes rimmed red. She came back over and moved in close to me.

"I didn't tell them how late you really came in," she whispered. "But where were you all that time?"

I couldn't tell her where I'd been. I couldn't tell anyone.

10

Dear Diary,

He is an unnatural little boy. But I love him, I really do. He is as pale and beautiful as a doll, with inky hair and eyes. He is quiet, unsmiling, watchful. He doesn't cuddle really, and I haven't yet heard him laugh. Still, he belongs to me and I to him. We are rarely apart; he can't stand to be away from me. And other than my husband and my mother, there is not a babysitter in town who will stay with him. He rages and cries inconsolably until my return, when he goes silent again. Through no choice of my own, he has become my whole world.

After those difficult early months, the rocky road of early parenthood smoothed out some. We normalized, or at least we settled into the new normal of our lives. My mother rented out her house and took an apartment nearer us here. It was clear early on that I could not handle him on my own. With the postpartum depression and his diagnosis as a "high demand" infant, everyone was anxious for us. There had been too many frightening stories in the news that year, women who snap and sink their car into a lake, or drown their babies one by one in the bath. Did they think I was one of those women? I don't know. But I was rarely unsupported in the first year.

I feel the worst for my mother, who had a lovely life on the beach, and who has given it up for us.

"I'm sorry," I told her after a particularly challenging afternoon with the baby. Both of us collapsed in a heap after we finally got him down for the night. "I'm sorry we did this to you."

She put her hand on mine. "Don't be silly," she said. "A mother doesn't stop being a mother when her children are grown."

"You were so happy," I said. I thought of her bustling life of tennis clinics and book clubs, days at the beach. "Finally."

She just shook her head, her blond bob bouncing.

"A mom doesn't get to be happy when her child is unhappy," she said. "That's just the way it is."

It was the first time she'd ever looked old to me.

But as the baby grew, and I left the pall of depression behind me, things got easier. Was motherhood what I expected? No. Was he the kind of baby I imagined—fat and happy, cooing and nuzzling? No. But that's life. As parents, we must accept that our children are who they are. We can't make them into something we want, or be disappointed in them because they don't meet our artificial expectations.

At least that's what my shrink tells me. *Not every child is affectionate,* she said. *And that's hard to accept, but accept it you must.*

Now my mother lives with us up north in the late spring and summer, and in the winter months near my sister (who, of course, never needs any help because she is perfect in every way). I try not to let her know that every time she leaves, I count the days until she returns. Without her, we are housebound.

When she's here, my husband and I steal out for secret dates. We go for walks and have romantic dinners where no talk of the baby is permitted. Sometimes we play tennis, or just go to the gym together. And in those stolen hours, we remember how much we love each other, how much fun we've always had together. When my mother is away, we have "home dates." We build fires, and open a bottle of wine. But we talk in whispers, always afraid of waking him. Sometimes it seems like if we enjoy ourselves too much, he wakes up wailing. And then it will be hours of me in his room, walking and rocking until he goes back to sleep.

I know it's my fault. He is traumatized by his early life, by the fact that it took me a long time to warm to him, to bond with him. And I believe (though my husband disagrees, thinks that I'm being dramatic) it has impacted him in ways that I might never be able to mend. I think about the violence of his entry into this life, a journey that almost killed us both—the drugs, the eventual surgery. It damaged us.

But I will try to repair what has been broken; I will spend my life trying to be a better mother than I was the first few months of his life.

My husband wants another baby. He says it's time. And, of course, that's all anyone ever says. "Time for another one!" Everyone says this . . . relatives, friends, grocery-store checkout clerks. It's like a conspiracy, as though all people who have borne multiple children have had a chip implanted in their brains. Whenever a mother with only one child approaches, this preprogrammed message emits from their open mouths. *Have 'em close, or they'll never be friends.* And I always smile shyly and say, "We're trying!"

But we are not trying. At least I'm not. I am on the birth control pill and I will stay on it for the rest of my childbearing years. Because there is not enough of me for this child and another one. He wants all of me; I can see that. There is no room inside of me for anyone else.

I am being dishonest with my husband. He doesn't know about the pills. He thinks I'm tracking my ovulation and that we are both hoping for another child soon. There's something nice about it, the idea that we might be like normal people, excited and happy to bring another person into the world. That we are making love and hoping that the act is one of creation, and not just pleasure. I can almost feel the tug toward that.

But the thought of another child now only fills me with dread. The day when I see that dark red bloom on my

126

underpants is the happiest day of the month. Isn't that awful? Everybody hates a woman who doesn't want another child, as if you're in some way shirking your biological imperative. I love my child, more than my own life. And more even than that, I love the child I will not bear. I love that child too much to bring him or her into this family with its poisoned gene pool.

I keep this to myself. If my mother sees it, she has not said so. My husband, even while exhausted by our child's ceaseless demands, seems to think our boy is the sun and the moon. If the baby doesn't smile, doesn't cuddle, and has only just a few words—"no," "mama," "bunny," and "more"—my husband always has a ready excuse. *He's the strong and silent type,* he'll quip. Or: *Not everyone is a snuggle bunny like you, baby.* Or: *He's a serious guy, an old soul.*

He doesn't want to see, I know that. I understand. I don't want to either. So I go along and pretend it's all right. Only the baby's pediatrician seems to register concern. *Is he always so watchful? Do you find that he smiles much? If he doesn't have more words at his next visit, we'll need to address that with a specialist.* I just nod and say that we'll keep an eye on it.

"So," the doctor always says before we leave. "Are you thinking about another one?"

Before my son was born, I always believed that love was enough to overcome any obstacle. I believed in nurture over

127

nature. But now I know. When I look at my boy, I see my father. My father who was put to death for the murder of five teenage girls. He is long dead, lives on only as the star of my nightmares, and in my child's eyes.

11

"Hey! Wait up!" Beck's voice rang out, bouncing around the night. I kept walking, my head down.

"Come on," she yelled. "Give me a break."

I kept moving faster and faster, digging in deep. I had my headphones on, so I could pretend that I didn't hear her, that she wasn't behind me.

I walked along the path that led away from campus. It brought you up to the edge of The Hollows Wood, where the school had created and maintained paths through some of the state-owned acreage. There was a two-mile, four-mile, and eight-mile loop that wound through the woods or down along the banks of the Black River, or up to the highest elevation in The Hollows, a scenic lookout over a steep drop into the river below called Bird's Eye Rock.

Up there, you could see the whole town of The Hollows and into the foothills of the Adirondack Mountains. I had watched brilliant sunsets and soaring eagles, a fire that raged through a warehouse on the edge of town. I had smoked dope up there with Beck. But usually I went up there alone when the world was pressing in and the weight of all my secrets was crushing me.

It was the one place in the whole world where I could just be myself, with no eyes watching. And that's where I was headed, even though it was dark and cold. It was where I wanted—no, *needed*—to be. Beck would never follow me there, I thought. But she did.

After the detective left, and Lynne and Frank returned to their hotel, I was more than a little grateful for the distraction of Luke's poem. Otherwise, I'd have just lain there staring out the window at the moon and ruminating on all the dread possibilities. The doctor had warned me about too much down time, where that catastrophic thinking of mine had room to grow, expand, wrap around me like a strangling vine.

So I took the card and key from my jacket pocket and reread the poem, held the old key in my hand. I was surprised to find myself hoping for a challenge, something to occupy my busy brain, but it didn't take me very long to figure out Luke's poem. After all, mad genius or not, he was still an eleven-year-old boy who would sit in his room and play video games all day if he could. How creative could he really be?

I opened my laptop and started searching: "Hollows,

New York, Suicide." The first listing on the search engine was for The Hollows Historical Society Web site.

I already knew that there were lots of supposedly haunted places in The Hollows. So many that the historical society offered a "haunted tour" in the weeks leading up to Halloween as a fund-raiser for preserving some of the town's oldest buildings. And people came from all over to creep themselves out.

For weeks, there were small white buses carting people around the town. There were walking tours, Segway tours (oh my God, really?), and kiddie tours that ended with hot cider and pumpkin muffins at the Old Mill. There was even a stop on our campus. (Naturally, the fraternity boys *lived* for this tour.) Once upon a time, our college used to be a convent, and our dorms were the cloisters where the nuns had lived.

In the early 1900s, one of the young novices managed to get pregnant. She was apparently able to hide it for the duration, and then died trying to give birth by herself. The baby was given away for adoption. Residents of the Marianna dormitory had, for decades, claimed to see her wandering the halls, looking for her lost child. It's the last stop on the tour. As the guide dutifully tells the sad tale, the Delta Phi boys inevitably turn up draped in sheets and smelling of beer, and walk by, moaning. It's usually good for a big laugh from the tour group, who are apparently quite aware of the silly nature of the whole thing but enjoy it anyway.

I scrolled through The Hollows Historical Society Web site, scanning their list of haunted sites—complete with an album of photos, creepy music, and a well-written history of each location. It took me about five minutes of reading to find the place on which Luke had based his lousy poem.

Within its walls,
For a hundred years,
People have learned and prayed and died.
Now, some believe, a tortured soul is trapped inside.

I read about a small, dilapidated building, erected in 1901, that sat sad and abandoned in the old cemetery down by the high school. It had lived several lives, first as one of the original schoolhouses in The Hollows, later as an Episcopal church, then finally as the office of the cemetery caretaker and a storage facility for the equipment needed to keep the grounds.

During the 1918 influenza pandemic, it had been used as a makeshift hospital, and five people died there. There was a colorful description of each of the five ghosts—a man, a woman, and three children. They wandered about at night: the children who happily play among the tilting headstones, the woman who is searching for something, forever looking behind trees, and the man who stands stock-still always beside the same grave.

But there was only one brief sentence about the caretaker

who in 1995, as Luke so eloquently put it, drank a bottle of whiskey and ate the barrel of his gun. Another caretaker had never been found, and now it was the people of the historical society who through volunteer efforts maintained the graveyard.

Of course, the Web site had an agenda to run, to make things sound scary enough to attract but not frightening enough to repel. So the mention of the relatively recent suicide was brief and underplayed. It was as if only old ghosts were permitted to wander The Hollows, harmless shades who passed hundreds of years ago. The spirits wandering around The Hollows were just harmless tricks of light, and the wind through the trees, and the idea that maybe, maybe there might have been something moving in the dark. Certainly nothing real or terrifying, nothing horrible enough to keep people away, only enough to draw the curiosity seekers in. A suicide, the ghost of the man who in terrible psychic pain committed suicide, is not among the featured, harmless Hollows shades.

Why did he do it?

What secret did he hide?

But, of course, there are no secrets anymore. Not in the electronic age, where we lay everything bare or it is laid bare for us. Every ugly thing on earth is just a few keystrokes away. That's why you must be so careful.

As I continued to move through the listings on the search page, I found a news item about the man who committed suicide in the graveyard shack, Harvey Greenwald.

He was a wretched man, a crooked golem with a deeply lined face, and wet, wide blue eyes lashed thick like a girl's. It would be easy to say he was a convicted pedophile, a porn addict, facing yet another accusation, because according to the newspaper article I found online, he was all of those things.

But he was also a husband, a father of two young girls. I know, from bitter personal experience, that there is always so much more to people than what is written about them in police reports and newspaper articles. They never get it quite right, as if the retelling of a life makes it less than what it is—or was. *He was a good man*, his wife was quoted as saying. *What they say about him, it isn't true. It can't be.* He left a note with a brief single sentence: *I'm sorry*.

In the articles about the investigation, a familiar name kept popping up: Detective Jones Cooper. He was Dr. Cooper's husband, and he'd also been the lead investigator on Elizabeth's disappearance. It was odd to see his name. I remembered him; he'd made me nervous. He'd asked a lot of questions of me, seemed to think I was hiding something. Of course I had been.

Ainsley had taken an Ambien, turned on her whale sounds, and donned her lavender-scented eye mask in a hale effort to get some sleep. It had been hours since Lynne and Frank had left, both of them looking dazed and worried. I didn't see any of the vitriol between them that Beck had so often described. They seemed to share a sad and tender connection. He kept a hand on the small of her back as they left the room. I'd seen him take a strand of her silken blond hair, she touch his tattooed arm. Beck's name was tattooed around one of Frank's wrists, in linked letters that looked more like a tribal pattern than anything else; *Lynne* on the other. They didn't seem like people about to get divorced. I could see why Beck found them so confusing. We hate our parents for having their own lives, don't we, for making decisions for themselves that don't seem to take us into account. They're not people, not really. They're parents; how dare they live and love and die without us?

I looked out the window to see that the snow, which had fallen earlier, had all melted away, and the precipitation had stopped. But I didn't have my bike to ride over to the cemetery. That's what you were supposed to do, right? Go to the place and find the next clue? I kept looking for the key with my fingertips, feeling the warm metal now and again like a touchstone. What would that key unlock? What was the secret that Harvey Greenwald hid? What kind of an agenda was Luke running? And why did I care?

My friend was missing. My homicidal father wanted to talk. I had big problems that needed attention. Still, I felt that same urgency to play Luke's game that I had when we were playing chess. Maybe, like in the chess games we played, he was way ahead of me—his moves already planned, and my demise already assured. Still I couldn't keep myself from playing. I *wanted* to know what Harvey

Greenwald's secret was. I *wanted* to find that next clue. In that moment I wouldn't have been able to tell you why. Maybe I just wanted to win. Or maybe, really, I was just looking for a distraction, a temporary escape from the ugly things looming. Or maybe, even then, I sensed that this scavenger hunt was more than just a child's game.

I thought a moment about how I could get there, since my bike was still at Luke's. I could use Beck's bike; she wouldn't care. I went into her room, which I knew had been tossed by the cops and her parents. Her mother had found her weed and confiscated it. Her dad found a pack of condoms in her makeup bag. *Jesus Christ*, he'd said softly. *At least she's being safe*, Lynne said, and then started to cry. *The only time we ever learn anything about our daughter is when she disappears.* Really, I thought. Is it news to you that Beck sleeps around?

I felt bad for them. But I couldn't answer any of their questions. Was she seeing anyone? Where would she go if she was angry or upset or trying to get even with them? She'd been talking about California over the summer, they said. She was thinking about looking for an internship at a movie studio. Might she have taken off for L.A.?

Our relationship had been strained this year; the truth was, we hadn't been talking very much except to argue. And the first conversation we'd had since break was a fight. I had no idea what was in her head. I told them as much. Only Lynne didn't quite seem to accept this. There was something narrow and untrusting about her gaze. I avoided her eyes.

Most people don't see me. But there are always those that do, usually mothers. They see what I am trying to hide, even if they're not quite sure what it is they're seeing. I can tell by the way they can't pry their eyes away. With my innocuous, androgynous wardrobe, my slight frame, my plain face, I usually just blend. Neither boys nor girls usually give me a second look. But sometimes, the sensitive, the keenly observant . . . they see me.

I slid open the narrow drawer in Beck's desk and found the bike-lock key in the little corner pocket. I was slipping it out when something else in there caught my eye. I tugged on the corner of a piece of paper, a printout of a news story she'd obviously found online. I read the headline and I literally felt a pain in my chest. I thought of that bag of hers, which was now in the hands of the police, along with her laptop, journal, cell phone. What else was in there?

I folded up the piece of paper and shoved it angrily in my pocket. I could still smell her in that room, her perfume and hair gel. Why did she have to search and pry? Why did she want to know me so badly that she had to dig up the past? How was it possible to love someone and hate her at the same time? I was thinking this as I bundled up and headed outside. It was stupid; I knew this. But I had to get out of that room, out of my head. The scavenger hunt was the only thing I actually wanted to think about. Sad, I know. Maybe more than sad. Sick.

The cold air bit at my cheeks and any flesh that was exposed—my ankles, my wrists. I unlocked Beck's bike, which she always kept right next to mine on the rack outside the dorm entrance. Everything was clattering—the bicycles, my teeth, my bones. It was so cold that the world seemed made of ice, everything brittle and wanting to break into pieces.

I kept looking around as I struggled with the lock. I kept expecting to see Margie the dorm mom come to the door, or Ainsley run out panicked and bleary-eyed. But it was dark and deserted.

As the lock fell away in my hand, I felt a shiver move through me. I lifted her bike off the rack and thought about Beck. Would she become one of those lost girls? A *48 Hours Mystery* or a *Dateline* story of the week? Where no one ever knew what really happened to her? Or would they find her broken body somewhere like Elizabeth? Or her bones a decade from now? I just wanted to hear her voice, for this all to be over.

Look, I can't keep going like this.

What are you talking about, Beck? Just leave me the fuck alone.

You know what I'm talking about. Don't you? Come on. Don't you? I had never seen her cry before.

*

As I rode toward the "haunted" cemetery, my thoughts turned to my mother and how I don't believe in ghosts. Because if anyone was able to haunt another human being, my mother would have haunted me. She never would have left me to live this life alone, even with the things I've done. I know that about her. She would have done anything, even in the afterlife, to protect me.

We are all very clear on what my mother would have wanted. I'm not even sure how, because she wasn't a person to ask for much. Sky, my lawyer, knows that she wanted me to help people, to make my own way. My aunt Bridgette knows that my mother would have wanted us to be close; she would have wanted Bridgette to love me as her own child. (And she's trying, she really is.) And I know my mother wanted me to find a way to be happy, to protect myself and stay safe. She would not have wanted me to be on my bike in the freezing cold, riding to an abandoned graveyard on the outskirts of a weird upstate New York village. I didn't need a medium to figure that out.

But my mother was dead, and everything about her—her soul, her essence, her personality, everything that made her who she was—went dark the day she died. She was not floating around in the ether, or living in heaven with God. She was dust in the wind, as are we all. At least I hope she's gone; I couldn't bear to think she was up there, watching. What would she think of me?

I whipped down the dark road from the school.

Somehow miraculously avoiding any icy spots that would have sent me careening. Up to this point, I had successfully managed not to think about my father reaching out to Dr. Cooper. But thoughts of him came unbidden as I flew through town. I hadn't talked to him in five years. After his last appeal was denied, Bridgette pressured me to find some closure with him. *Not for him, for you.*

But it was his hands that kept me away. I couldn't bear to look at his long, strong fingers, his wide, square palms. I didn't want to think of them on my mother, on me. I didn't want to think of what I'd seen those hands do. They were white and roped with thick blue veins that wound up his pale, dark-haired arms. Just the thought of them made me want to retch.

But to appease Bridgette, I took a call from him about a year after his conviction. He sounded so happy, so relieved to hear my voice. *I'm your father and I love you. Nothing, not even this, can change that. I just want you to understand that I'm sorry for all the ways I've failed you. I want you to know that you don't have to be alone.* And then he told me something else I didn't want to hear.

I don't think I said anything. I just muttered: *okay* and *yeah*, maybe *I know*. I just kept thinking about all the things he'd done to my mother. What did they expect from me? Did they want me to forgive? In real life, that doesn't happen. People don't forgive things like that. They don't find peace. It's pure bullshit. When something unspeakable happens, or when you do something unspeakable, it changes you. It takes you apart and reassembles you. You are a Frankenstein of circumstance, and the parts never fit back quite right and the life you live is a stolen one. You don't deserve to walk among the living, and you know it.

In the end, I think you'll be glad you spoke to him, said Bridgette uncertainly as I wept with my face in her lap. But that wasn't the end. It takes the state a good long time to get ready to press the button. It's a kind of institutional procrastination. Everyone keeps delaying and waiting. It's as if even the enforcers of the death penalty know how totally fucked up it is. They keep waiting for a loophole, a pardon, a stay of execution. They keep staring at the phone that never rings. But time was running out for my dad. Knowing this, I felt like someone had put a bag over my head and I was running out of air.

The cemetery loomed ahead and I slowed my speed, watching for the ghosts that I knew didn't exist. The clouds above had cleared and the night was dark blue, and the stars seemed so, so small and stingy with their light.

I pulled the little headlight off of Beck's bike and cast it ahead of me. Its beam fell on the overgrown cemetery with its skewed, weatherworn headstones. No, I was not afraid of the dead. It was the living that filled me with fear and anxiety. I leaned Beck's bike against the fence, and my footfalls were impossibly loud on the rocky path.

At then end of the trail, the beam of the headlight shone

dimly on the caretaker's shack. I had seen its roof from the road. But coming up on it like this, in the dark, it looked even sadder, more ramshackle than I had expected. It seemed like a pretty grim place to come to work every night, and a perfect place to off yourself.

The windows were smeared with some chalky-white substance, one of them broken in the corner. Did they leave it like this? So that it looked more haunted? According to the article I'd read, there hadn't been a caretaker on the premises since the suicide. Not surprising. I tried the knob and the door was locked. It was a newer lock, though. The old key I had didn't fit. I felt the wood groaning and bending beneath my feet. If I were heavier, I imagined I could step right through the wet and splintering slats.

I walked around the side to see if there was another door, and in the rear of the building there was. As the wind pushed the leaves and litter around on the ground, I slid the key in the lock and it turned with a satisfying click. The door pushed open with a haunted-house squeal.

Standing in the doorway, I heard rustling, tiny critter feet shuttling away from the noise and the small amount of light that washed in from outside. I shone the light, and looked into the single long room.

There was a desk with a tilted lamp. A corkboard dominated the far wall and was littered with frayed and wrinkled pieces of paper that had faded and grown old. Whatever announcements, and to-do lists, and schedules that had been tacked up there had long passed into oblivion. The white computer sat abandoned and way too big, like dinosaur bones. The eternal office chair had an air of expectancy, waiting patiently to bear someone's weight again.

I moved inside, feeling my heart start to pump a little bit. I'd have to be a robot not to be a little scared. I saw a frayed line of police tape, but no telltale stains, no shotgun blast in the wall. Just a room that was empty and had been empty and would, it seemed, be empty for the foreseeable future.

I looked around, shining my light in the dark corners and under the desk and into the storage closet. There was nothing here. Luke was probably at home having a good laugh. This, no doubt, was some joke. Or was I missing something?

I still hadn't figured out the biggest part of the puzzle: why Harvey Greenwald had ended his life, and what it had to do with me. It *had* to have something to do with me, didn't it? Luke was running some kind of weird agenda, right? Because otherwise, as a game, this pretty much sucked. Was it just going to be some lame haunted-house hop? He said it was going to be a history lesson. Is that all it was?

I was about to leave when my flashlight caught something. A bright white envelope tacked on the board among the yellowed and faded detritus. It had my name on it in the child's printed hand, which was now familiar to me. I walked over quickly and grabbed it down. Instead of ripping it open, I stuck it inside my jacket. I suddenly had a strong urge to get the hell out of there. But as I moved toward the door, I saw a large dark form pass in front of the side window. There was someone outside.

12

Dear Diary,

He's too small. That's the big problem of the moment. In his preschool class, he's by far the smallest child, though he's the oldest in his class. He weighs about twenty-five pounds and is about thirty-four inches tall, well under the normal range. And that in and of itself is not a big problem, though neither my husband nor I come from small people. It's just that, up until his last visit, he was progressing normally and suddenly, now, he isn't.

It might be hormonal. A hormone deficiency, says the doctor. They toss words and phrases around that land like blows to the kidneys. She started talking about human growth hormone and the pituitary gland, but how it was too early to be alarmed, and she prescribed a battery of tests. But I wasn't really listening. I was just thinking: Will nothing ever be easy for him? Will things always be hard?

His size is not the only problem. His teacher requested a conference last week. That, too, is a bit of a blur. He's not very social, she said. Meaning that he avoids the other children, and they avoid him. He has a hard time finding a "work buddy." He doesn't smile. And then, of course, the tantrums. How disruptive they are, how violent they have become. Have we thought about having him tested? There might be some (she paused to choose her words carefully) challenges. Twice she referred to him as having special needs.

He was a high-demand infant, my husband said as if this explained something. But the teacher just nodded uncertainly.

The truth is, if there is not some improvement, we can't handle him here, she continued. We care about him; you know that. But this is a small, private school and we're not equipped to deal with— Again, she stopped short and searched for a gentle word. But she never did come up with one.

I found myself thinking that she was so pretty and young, and I felt bad for her, even as I envied and resented her. How nice, just to be able to send someone else's problem home with them. It was a Montessori environment, small and intimate. The children worked together. There were three strong teachers and lots of order even within the free structure of the classroom. And while this is such a benefit to the children, when one child is causing continual disruptions, it hurts everyone. It drains our resources and leaves less of our attention for the other children. Surely, she said, you can understand that.

And I do. I wouldn't want my child's needs neglected because there was a problem child in his lovely, happy little classroom. There, I said it. A problem child. That's what he is, isn't he?

Silence is the fourth member of our family. He comes with us everywhere, enfolds us, shushes in our ears. And he is with us in the car on the way home. Neither of us knows what to say. Our marriage is strained to the breaking point. Every conversation devolves into arguments, and no topic is safe. There is so much pent-up anger, resentment, and sadness that any kind of heat brings it to a quick and roiling boil. Last night it was dinner. Whose turn was it to cook? Our rage at each other overflows the pot in a heartbeat. I am ashamed to say that there has been violence—a vase tossed (me), a hard push against the wall (him). And it's strange to say that there's a certain relief that comes in the fighting; it's the only way we connect now. Rage is the new sex. Bitterness stands in for passion.

Is it wrong to say that our child has destroyed our relationship? It probably is. But I've earned so many of the bad mommy badges, that one more can't make much difference. And it is all my fault; I know this. I have seen it over and over again, that look on the faces of health professionals, other parents, even my own sister. Sure, it masquerades as understanding, compassion, a desire to help. But really? It's judgment, plain as day.

Because everyone knows that a real woman, a good

mother, has a healthy and happy baby. And a bad mommy has a troubled child who cries and can't sleep through the night, who simultaneously rejects her and won't let her out of his sight. The child of a bad mommy doesn't get invited to playdates and Kindermusik and Mommy and Me yoga classes. She has a scent—it's fatigue and unhappiness—and all the other mommies can smell it and stay away. What if it's contagious? What if my child starts to rage instead of playing the tambourine? What if he throws a book that hits another child in the face and shows no reaction at all? What if he arches his back and screeches when I try to help him to do baby downward dog?

And they look at you, with that look, trying to figure out what exactly you are doing wrong and hoping that they're not doing it, too. And I want to tell them that I am just like them, doing all the same things and making the same mistakes. But silence holds his hand over my mouth. And I just walk away, don't go back to yoga, look for yet another pediatrician, try another activity. We don't need anyone, I think. We're better off alone. But of course that's not true.

"What's wrong with him?" my husband asks softly. Outside the day is bright and beautiful. We have the windows down and I can smell blossoming lilac. It was not the question I expected. Usually he rails against the teachers and the doctors, or launches accusations against me. You coddle him. You always give in when he cries. You let him into our bed. You don't discipline him.

"I don't know," I said. "I really don't."

And I don't. For all my self-blame, there's something inside me that knows he came to us this way. We didn't do this. I say as much, and I see a single tear travel down my husband's face. I have never seen him cry, not even at his father's funeral. My heart breaks for about the millionth time.

When we get home, the phone is ringing and I pick it up. It's Mrs. Peaches, the head of the school.

"I have a list," she says. "Of more appropriate places for your son. Should I e-mail it to you? Can I make some calls for you?"

"Oh," I said. "The teacher, she didn't say he couldn't come back. Just that if he didn't improve—"

"Don't misunderstand," she said quickly. "We're not punishing him. It's just that he needs an amount of attention that we can't give him."

"So," I said. "He can't come back?"

I could feel my husband looking at me, feel my stomach getting queasy with upset. I loved that school, everything about it, from the beautifully landscaped grounds to the bright, colorful classrooms to the stables.

"It might be best if he didn't," she said. Then, "I'm sorry. His teacher, I'm afraid, didn't make it clear how urgent we consider the situation. For the other children, especially."

I hung up in a fog, stumbled over to the couch. I think my husband murmured some words of comfort. We'll figure it out, he said. We'll be all right. But tomorrow I knew he'd go to work. And I'd be home alone with our son, figuring it out alone.

Usually, I would make some kind of slicing comment. But today I didn't have it in me. Maybe because I didn't, he sat down beside me. We were alone, my son and my mother at her place for the day while we dealt with the school. There, on the couch, for the first time in months, we made love. It was sad and slow, desperate. I was grateful to realize I still loved him, and I could see he still loved me.

What happens to a marriage? Before the baby, we were truly happy—with our lives, with each other. After he came, we just started to come apart. Would it have happened anyway? Maybe parenthood is a crucible; the intensity of its environment breaks you down to your most essential elements as a couple. Rather than bind, we destabilized. Maybe any other stressor would have done that to us. Maybe we were neither the people nor the couple we believed ourselves to be when times were good.

It was the birth control thing that really started to unstitch us. He felt so betrayed when he realized that I'd been taking the pill for the year he thought we were trying for another child. I had put on a charade for him, feigning disappointment each month, pretending to track my ovulation, taking prenatal vitamins. I'm ashamed of it now, the act I put on. Why did I do it? he wanted to know, utterly mystified. Why didn't I just tell him that I didn't want another child? Why didn't you know? I asked. Wasn't it obvious that I didn't? In motherhood, I am half the woman I was before. Couldn't he see that?

But that afternoon, both of us together on the couch, all of those arguments and the high emotion that caused them seemed distant and far away. We lay in the sunlit living room, giving ourselves a little vacation from our problems. Yes, I still loved him, the scent of him, the feel of his hands on me. Then we heard my mother at the door, our son's high-pitched voice. Is Mommy home? We quickly gathered up our clothes and bolted to the bedroom, naked and laughing.

"We're home!" my mother called.

"We're home!" he echoed. I heard him try the knob to our bedroom, which we had luckily remembered to lock.

"We'll be right out, sweetie," I said.

"Why is the door locked?" He tried it again, harder. I could hear him pushing his body against the door. Once, twice, three times.

"Just a minute," I said, pulling on my clothes. "Mommy's changing."

He gave a hard kick to the outside. "Fine," he said. I heard him storming off. My instinct was to rush after him, to comfort him. He wanted me and I wasn't there. I took a deep breath. Loving and caring for your child doesn't mean you owe all of yourself to him, every second, my shrink had said. She worried that I was overfocused on my son, that it was hurting both of us, fostering the unnatural dependence in him. She posited that all the trouble he was having in school might just be a ploy to stay home with me.

I looked over at my husband and saw that all the laughter had died from his eyes.

That night when I was tucking the baby into his bed, I saw him staring hard at the wall behind me.

"What is it?" I asked.

"There's a man behind you." I turned to look, but I knew there wasn't anyone there. There never was.

"Time for sleep," I said.

"He's a bad man," he said. His face was grim, but not alarmed. No. Never that.

This was not new. There were imaginary friends and pets, people lying at the bottom of our pool, lingering outside our windows. There were voices that told him to do things—like unlock and open the front door in the night, setting off the security alarm and rousing us from deepest sleep.

"What does he want?"

One of the psychologists to whom we'd taken him had advised us to go along, let the fantasy play itself out. Insisting that what he was seeing wasn't real, wasn't there, was a guaranteed red-faced, arched-back rage. Of course, said the doctor. How would you feel if someone told you that what you were certain you were seeing wasn't there? He had a point. But at the same time, weren't we just enabling these delusions?

"He wants you to know that he's sorry," my son said. "He didn't mean to kill those girls."

152

My whole body froze, all the moisture drained away from my mouth and my throat.

"But he said he'd probably have to do it again, if he could."

"Okay," I said. "Try to get some sleep."

It was critical not to overreact. Any show of high emotion filled him with a kind of manic energy. He'd never go to sleep. And those few hours that he slept in his own bed, before he came to stand in my doorway, were where my whole life was lived.

"Can you stay until he goes away?"

I lay down on the floor beside his bed, where I often lay until he fell asleep. The carpet was plush beneath me. Sometimes I read. Sometimes I tried to meditate. Tonight I just stared at the blue wall, my mind reeling and racing. How does he know? I wondered. Had he overheard a conversation between my mother and me?

After a while he turned over and fell asleep. I lay there, for I don't know how long, staring at the ceiling, trying not to shake apart.

13

I crouched behind the desk and started inching my way along the wall toward the exit at the front of the structure. There were some bulging boxes blocking my way, though, and I found myself in a junk maze—an old file cabinet, a dusty CPU, a stepladder, some rusted buckets of paint. I made myself very small and wished I had brought the Mace that Ainsley always wanted us to carry. It sat uselessly on the table by the door where we all kept our keys.

Someone was rustling in the leaves and litter outside, then creaking up the steps. Then silence. I couldn't control my breathing, which was coming deep and panicked, except to hold my breath.

Then there was a loud cracking sound, and a string of expletives issued in a deep male voice, one I recognized. I had a feeling those floorboards weren't going to hold. I made my way toward the door, and saw Langdon pulling his foot out from where he'd stepped through the porch. All the tension and fear drained from my body, leaving me weak with relief.

"Hey!" he called. "Lana, come out here. I know you're in there."

I pushed open the door, and he gave me an annoyed look.

"What in the world are you doing out here in the middle of the night?" he asked.

"What are *you* doing here?" I said. He looked funny, angry and embarrassed. I tried not to laugh.

"I was leaving the library and I saw you take your bike off campus," he said. "What are you *thinking*?"

I looked off to the road and saw his Volkswagen Touareg hybrid (the SUV for people who don't want to admit that they drive an SUV). I was puzzled how he could have seen me, gotten into his car, and followed before I had ridden out of sight. Maybe I wasn't as fast as I thought I was. Or maybe he hadn't been leaving the library. Whatever, I was glad to see him. This had been a much scarier errand than I thought it would be. I'm not always as tough as I think I am.

"You know," he said. He'd extracted his foot from the broken wood and was now sitting on one of the steps massaging his injured ankle. "There's a girl missing and you're out here in the freezing cold night on your bike. That is not the action of the intelligent person I know you to be."

"Are you okay?" I asked, sitting beside him.

"What are you doing here, of all places? And how the hell did you get in?"

He often smelled of cigarettes, but only faintly. A secret smoker like Rachel, hiding their deadly little habit, telling themselves lies about how much they smoke and why it's not so bad for them. I had always found this a little disappointing about him. I considered him so forthright, such a straight arrow. But then it's not actually as if he had ever lied about it. He's never claimed *not* to be a smoker. And it was really none of my business. I thought about the rumor Beck had reveled in sharing with me. That wasn't my business, either.

"Lana," he said. And now he sounded stern, like a father. "What are you doing here?"

I was ashamed to tell him why I was there. It was ridiculous really. But since I couldn't come up with an even remotely believable lie, I told him the truth about Luke's game. When I was done, he looked at me, awestruck.

"How could you let yourself get caught up in something like this with him?" he asked. He looked so surprised, so disappointed, that I flushed with shame. He was right. How could I? I thought of myself researching chess moves and looking up clues, running around in the night. It was embarrassing.

"It's harmless," I said lamely. "It's just a game."

"Is it?"

"What else?" I said. "He's eleven."

Langdon shook his shaggy head and rubbed his jaw vigorously, the stubble there rasping like sandpaper.

"He's an emotionally disturbed child and you're an adult in his life, his babysitter. You're enabling him."

I hadn't thought about it that way. To me, it seemed like Luke was calling the shots. It was his game, and I was doing his bidding. He was home asleep in bed, and I was running around in the night following clues. But, of course, Langdon was right. He was a kid. I was the adult, the supposed rational, reasonable one, the one who set the limits. I didn't have anything to say. I just sat there, feeling like an asshole.

"Let me see the poem," he said. I handed it to him and he took the wrinkled card and key in his hand. "Where did he get this key?"

I told him I didn't know. But Langdon didn't acknowledge me, just sat staring at the words in the beam of my flashlight. I was shivering from the cold.

"So what was the secret?"

I was tired of saying that I didn't know, so I just lifted my shoulders and shook my head. Langdon kept his eyes on me; it was a searching stare, a puzzle-solving gaze. He was trying to figure me out, to solve this odd situation in which we'd found ourselves.

"How are you going to find out?" He looked suddenly interested, curious.

"I'm not sure I am."

Obviously, it was the right thing to do to call off the game, just give up. I'd just admit to Luke that he was smarter than I was. That was his agenda, right? He just wanted to prove that he could get me to do what he wanted, create puzzles that I couldn't solve? Whatever burning competitiveness I was feeling was patently ridiculous. I needed to get over it.

I could tell that Langdon was curious, too, though. He was curious about Luke. After all, he was a geek like me. He was a man who studied, pondered, and treated the abnormal human psyche. And the psyche was, of course, the ultimate puzzle. Each individual person a brand-new mystery to solve—how did mental illness come to take root in this mind, how would it manifest itself, how could it be treated? *Could* it be treated or cured through therapy, medication, or alternative methods? Or must it merely be managed so that a person might be less of a danger to himself or others? Diagnosis and treatment, especially with children, were as slippery and elusive as eels. Young people were always changing, growing, and learning. So their illnesses were always evolving—sometimes worsening, sometimes disappearing altogether.

"Did you find the next clue?"

"No," I lied. I don't even know why I lied. But part of me felt like this was my game with Luke. It was up to me to continue it or not.

"There was nothing in there?" he said, nodding back toward the small building. He held out his hand for the light. "Let me take a look."

I handed him the light, and stood there shivering while

he banged around inside. He was clumsy; I heard him trip twice, knock against something once. I could feel that envelope burning against my chest in the pocket of my coat. I could hear Beck crying, *How can you be so cold?* I saw my father's hands gripping a shovel, digging and digging and digging. I saw Elizabeth looking at me, angry and disappointed, as I sometimes saw her in my dreams. Detective Ferrigno was right; we did argue that night. I was trying to comfort her, I think, and she lashed out at me. The memory was foggy and strange, if it was a memory at all. There was a perpetual merry-go-round of misery in my mind. I never have been able to figure out how to get off.

Finally, Langdon returned. "I didn't see anything."

"It doesn't matter," I said. "I'm going to tell him that I don't want to play. We'll go back to chess. Or maybe Scrabble. I'm better at that."

"That's best," he said. He stepped down from the porch and offered me his hand, gave me a little pull up. "The last thing we want to do is feed a damaged psyche. He's getting something out of this. And you don't know what it is. Chances are it's not healthy."

I didn't say that we were both getting something out of it. I wasn't certain it was healthy for either one of us.

"I suggest you resign your position, find something else." His slight smile told me he knew I wouldn't listen. He knew I had a problem with male authority. But maybe he also understood that I was so deeply hooked in to Luke and

Rachel already, I couldn't have walked away if I wanted to. Which I didn't, not really.

We started walking and came to where he'd parked his car beside the bike. He opened the hatch and lifted it inside.

"This is not your bike," he said, looking at it and then back at me.

I told him that it was Beck's and why I didn't have mine.

"So what's going on with that?"

"No one's heard from her," I said. There was a hard place of anger against Beck in my heart. "Her parents are here. The police have been talking to me and Ainsley, probably others, too."

"I thought there was a development tonight," he said. He shut the hatch and the sound of it echoed loud in the quiet night. "I heard she posted on Facebook?"

I shook my head. Beck didn't have a Facebook page, of course. As far as I knew. Maybe she had one now and hadn't told me. "I hadn't heard that."

"You don't seem worried," he said. Again, that stare, the scientist examining a sample.

"She's done this before," I said. I was trying for a non-chalance that I didn't feel. I *was* worried about Beck, really worried. But if I showed it, she won.

"Still," he said. "The police are taking this very seriously. A campus search is starting at first light tomorrow."

"Oh," I said. Why hadn't the detective told me about that? I always hated the little games they played.

I climbed into the passenger seat. And the car dipped as he got in beside me. "Don't hold all this in, okay? Don't cloak yourself in denial," he said.

He started the car and it came to life with lights and soft chimes, but otherwise it was nearly silent the way new cars are, almost as though there's no engine under the hood. "Make sure you're talking about everything with your therapist."

"I am," I said. "I saw her today."

"Okay," he said. "Good. This must be hard for you."

Langdon knew more about me than almost anyone. I had told him part of my secret during a mini-breakdown I'd had in my sophomore year. He almost never brought it up, knowing how painful it was for me to think about, let alone discuss.

"Elizabeth two years ago," he said, musing. "Your difficult history. You can talk to me, too, you know. We're friends, right?"

As we pulled away, I saw what I knew I couldn't have seen. My mind was playing tricks on me—not a new thing. I thought I saw a small, slim form slip into the trees to avoid the roving beam of the headlights as Langdon shifted the car into drive. I stared at the night for a long moment, but there was nothing.

"I know," I said. I tried for a smile. "Of course, I know that."

He gave me a quick, awkward pat on the shoulder, very

boyish, buddy-buddy. Totally chaste, no sexual charge at all. I've always been grateful for him. I think we draw people into our lives. It's as though we broadcast our deepest needs, and certain people hear the signal somewhere in their own subconscious and heed the call. For better or worse, we attract our teachers, our allies, and sometimes even our nightmares. Some of us have louder signals. Some of us have more sensitive receptors.

That night my sleep was hard won and restless. I dreamed of Beck's kiss and felt her hands on me, woke up thinking she was beside me. I drifted off to sleep again, only to be awakened once more. *Why are you doing this to me?* I heard a voice screaming. And it was my voice, and my mother's and Beck's—a chorus of misery and desperation. When I slept again, I went back to the night my mother died.

When's the last time you saw your mother? The cop had been a woman, and I remember thinking how mannish and rough she seemed. She had a pockmarked face and orange-red hair, cut as short and square as any of her male colleagues. She was large, not overweight, but broad, with big shoulders and a deep voice.

In the morning before I left for school, I said, just as my father had instructed me to say. The lie felt like cotton in my mouth, surely she could see the bulge. I wanted her to see. *Please*, I thought. *Please know that I'm lying. Please help me.*

My father sat in a chair by the gray wall, watching, always watching me. *Don't say any more than necessary. Answer their questions and offer nothing more.*

And was everything all right? Did she seem strange to you, upset about anything?

No, I said. *She was the same as she had always been.* What I didn't say was that my mother suffered from chronic depression, although she had some manic episodes. That morning, her mania was in full throttle and she was cheerfully clutter-clearing and scrubbing the whole house.

Leave my room alone, okay? I asked her. *Just don't touch my stuff.*

But she just kept singing and scrubbing and scrubbing the kitchen floor, which was spotless to begin with, and nothing was ever even remotely dirty or out of place.

Mom, I said. *Okay?*

A spoonful of sugar helps the medicine go down, she sang gaily, her blond hair a sweaty mess, her face flushed. I remember really hating her in that moment.

The cop had her eyes on me, and there was no softness, no humor or kindness there. They were just two black lasers, boring in, seeing everything. *Was she afraid of anyone? Had she mentioned anyone wanting to hurt her, or anyone following her?*

No, I said. *Nothing like that.*

164

She softened a little then, as if she remembered what she was dealing with here. *I'm sorry,* she said. *We have to ask questions, to do everything we can to find your mom. We'll find her, okay?*

Okay, I said. They wouldn't find her. I knew that.

My father was watching me so intently, I felt like he was trying to communicate with me telepathically. I put my head in my hand and started to sob.

But I woke up dry-eyed. I didn't cry anymore. There was an unpleasant tightness in my chest. Why did everyone in my life disappear?

14

It was the flashing lights that woke me up in the dim light of sunrise. The police had begun a search of the campus, looking for signs of Beck. The news of the online post was just a rumor, I'd learned when I got back last night. I already knew that Beck didn't have a Fakebook page, and never would.

But some of the other students on campus—you know *those* students, the ones who are always involved, jumping into the fray for Take Back the Night, or protesting against date rape, or a raise in tuition; those super-involved sorority sisters who are always raising money for Darfur, or running book drives for literacy, or baking for the hungry (let them eat cake!)—they had created a page for Beck (who had never spoken to any of them in all her years on campus): *Find Rebecca Miller!* There was a catalog of posts from the hundreds of friends Beck didn't even know she had.

People were bored. That was the problem with our culture.

Life, real life, is essentially dull. Even unhappiness is mundane, lacks texture, the hills and valleys of true drama. People love a mystery, a tragedy, a shooting, a disappearance, a gruesome murder. They love to think about dead pregnant women floating in pools, children down wells, a subway bombing, husbands strangling wives and hiding their bodies in the woods. It titillates, excites, makes them a little grateful for their own boring workaday world. Even those that feign compassion, who rain tears and bring teddy bears and bouquets of flowers, sit vigils, are secretly thrilled to be involved in something bigger and more interesting than themselves. And the media just chums the water, but don't get me started. Let's come up with a logo and jingle for disaster! Twenty-four-hour coverage, a *Dateline* special, a made-for-television movie, an instant book! Okay, I'm done.

After I took my shower, I noticed that my prescriptions were running low. Dr. Cooper is a psychologist but not a psychiatrist. She has a colleague, though, who prescribes for me. So before I headed to class, I called the office and told them I needed refills.

"Oh," said the assistant. I heard her clicking on her keyboard. "Miss Granger, I see here that you should have enough pills left for fifteen more days."

"No," I said. "Just five."

There was silence on the other line. "Let me talk to the doctor," she said. "And I'll call you back."

I tried to figure in my head when I'd gotten the last refill. But I was extremely tired, tired to my core. I was really careful about taking my exact dose of medications. I knew what happened when I went off and it wasn't pretty. I never messed with the dosage. Some people did, I knew. But not me. If pills were missing, it was because someone had taken them. And I bet I knew who. That would be a serious problem for me. Doctors and insurance companies were very, very strict with the kind of pills I was taking.

But I didn't have to worry about it with five days to go. I locked the rest of the pills in my desk and headed to class.

The white noise in my head was so loud that I could hardly focus on what Langdon was saying at the lectern. There were a lot of people missing from class. As I had left the suite that morning, Ainsley told me that people were turning out to volunteer for the search. But she wasn't and neither was I. We'd both been through it with Elizabeth, walking the grid in a cold drizzle. It had been like wading through a mire of fear and dread, hoping that someone would find a sign of her, praying that they wouldn't. It was too much to go through again.

The media circus had not yet begun. Outside our dorm there had been one local news van, and I'd heard there were a couple of reporters wandering around, asking questions. But Beck was no Elizabeth. She was not the all-American beauty, homecoming queen with straight As and a good relationship with her parents as Elizabeth had been. She was a tattooed, body-pierced, three-time runaway. Her picture, with spiky hair, lots of dark eyeliner, and exuding bad attitude, wasn't going to arouse the requisite amount of empathy and envy to be truly titillating. The missing or murdered beautiful girl brought up so much emotion. Like the pretty and pure Snow White with the poison apple at her candy lips, or Sleeping Beauty, pale and virginal in her glass vessel, it was innocence fallen into the hands of evil that really brought up the ratings. No one gave a shit about the ugly stepsisters or the wicked queen.

Not that Beck was ugly. In fact, beneath all that dark makeup and wild hair, she was one of the prettiest girls I'd ever known. Her skin was milk, her eyes almond-shaped and glittery green like the sea in summer. She was pretty in the truest sense and beautiful to her core, sensitive and kind (most of the time). But it was almost as if she didn't want anyone to know it. She was angry, rough around the edges, always looking to make a statement with her appearance and actions, quick to rise to an argument. She didn't always wash; her nails were bitten to the quick. No one likes a girl like that, a girl who doesn't mold herself to expectations, who doesn't work hard to please and attract. And so the national news teams weren't buzzing around, waiting for things to get interesting. Beck was right to hide her truest self inside. The world didn't deserve her.

My mother had been a truly beautiful woman. Beautiful and sad, long-suffering, her life ended by the man she loved and to whom she had devoted her life. She came from violence, too, but to all outward appearances, she'd escaped the horror of her past. Until she was condemned to repeat it. Naturally, the narrative of her story was irresistible to news-magazine shows, producers of made-for-TV movies, feature writers, and true-crime authors. There was little that the world didn't know about my poor mother, her tragic life, and her fucked-up family. The only thing they didn't know was the truth.

The other students were suddenly gathering their things, getting up, and leaving class. The movement jolted me from my reverie. I stayed seated in my place near the back and waited until Langdon and I were the only ones left.

"Did you even hear a word of that?" he asked when the room was empty. The air was cool, and the lights seemed dimmer than usual. He stooped and wiped the whiteboard clean. Actually, I looked down at my laptop and saw that I had taken pretty decent notes with the one-tenth of my brain I had been using to pay attention to the lesson. It was all about the difficulty in diagnosing troubled children, the implications of leveling a damaging diagnosis on a child who might grow out of his symptoms.

"I didn't think you'd be here," he said. "I thought you'd be doing the search."

I was still wondering why the detective never told me

about it. It seemed relevant that he'd keep that information from me. And if I thought about it too long, I started to feel anxious.

"I can't," I said. I bit back a swell of emotion. Better not to feel; I'd learned that the hard way. People were always telling you to express your feelings, work through them, explore them, release them. But that's an abyss, a dark spiral into the self. Better to just repress, ignore, push back, and try to make it through another day. "I can't go through that again."

I could still hear that scream, that surprised and horrified cry given by the girl who found Elizabeth. It rang through the afternoon like the calling of a crow. It was so raw, so primal; everyone around me froze in his tracks and looked toward the origin of the sound. It was an ugly moment. It was the moment we all knew.

Langdon packed up his leather messenger bag and then climbed up the aisle toward me. He chose a seat in the same row, but ever appropriate, he left a few spaces between us.

"That's understandable," he said. "I'm sorry."

"I'm fine," I lied. "Really."

"So, tell me if you don't want to deal with this," he said. "But I've been doing a little research."

"Oh?"

His legs were so long that they knocked against the seat in front of him. He ran his hands up and down the thighs of his velvety, brown corduroy pants. His nails were neatly trimmed, pink and square. He had clean hands that had only ever done good things—graded papers, made scrambled eggs. I wanted to reach out and grab one, to feel it soft but strong in mine. But I tucked my hands under my thighs. He leaned over and turned my laptop before I could stop him, examined my notes.

"Not bad," he said. "Lucky you're a genius."

I waited for him to go on. But he turned the laptop back and just kept rubbing his legs. He kept his eyes on the seat in front of him.

"So," I said. "What kind of research?"

"About Harvey Greenwald."

I'd almost forgotten about him. There were so many dark thoughts competing for my attention, he hadn't come up in the shuffle yet that morning. That abandoned building in the graveyard seemed like weeks ago. I thought I'd told Langdon that I was going to stop playing the game, and that he'd agreed it was for the best. Why was he looking for answers? And why was he telling me about it? But there's not a geek alive who can resist a mystery.

"So you found out his secret?"

"I did," he said. "You want to hear it?"

He must have read something on my face. "I'm sorry," he said. "It wasn't my business. I guess curiosity just got the better of me."

Someone laughed long and loud in the hallway outside the classroom and we both turned to look but saw no one.

I turned back to him. "Tell me."

"Harvey Greenwald was a cross-dresser," he said. "He kept a shed out in back of his house with a wardrobe of women's clothes."

Somewhere inside me, a door started squeaking open. It was the doorway to my dark places, the one I kept bolted. I felt my breath grow thick in my throat. How securely could it have been closed, if a child could undo the lock with a poem?

I could almost envision Harvey Greenwald's shed, a rickety wooden structure in the back of an ill-tended yard. It was filled with cheap enormous shoes, and tacky polyester dresses, maybe some hats. It would smell of mold and booze and cigarettes. It would be lit by a bulb hanging on a wire.

There was a stone stuck in my throat; I issued a little cough to clear it. But it was lodged tight.

"He'd go out there and dress up," said Langdon. "His wife thought he was watching television. He had an old set out there and he turned it on to whatever game was playing."

"So that was his secret?"

"The allegations against him turned out to be false," said Langdon. "Two neighborhood kids discovered him one night. Apparently he chased them, threatened them—in full drag. The kids ran straight to their parents. They claimed he exposed himself, then later admitted it wasn't true."

I kept my eyes on Langdon. His face was grim and serious. He took the pain of others very seriously.

"Greenwald had a history of clinical depression," he said, when I said nothing. "Exposure of his secret pain was more than he could handle, I imagine."

"That's awful," I said. It *was* awful. How many people carried around a secret pain like that, one that tortured them, eventually laid waste to their lives?

"It is," said Langdon. He turned to look at me. Then, gently: "Does it mean anything to you?"

I shook my head slowly. "No," I lied. "Nothing at all."

"So if it doesn't mean anything to you," said Langdon. "Then it must mean something to Luke. What is he trying to tell you about himself? Because it has to be one of those two things."

"Why?" I asked stubbornly, even though I suspected as much myself. "What if he's just a kid trying to entertain himself?"

"Well, I've been thinking about this," he said. "If Luke is a callous-unemotional child, with narcissistic personality traits, then a game like this is because he's obsessed with you. Or because he has something he wants to reveal about himself."

"So you think he's trying to tell me he's a cross-dresser?" I almost laughed.

"I have no idea," said Langdon. "But he might be having some gender confusion. It's not uncommon, especially with troubled children."

"How did you discover Greenwald's secret?" I asked. I hadn't found anything about it during my Internet search.

"Online," he said. He shifted his eyes from me. Was he being purposely vague?

"I didn't see anything about it," I said. I have to admit to a prickle of competitive annoyance. Why had he found what I hadn't been able to?

He gave a little half shrug. "It was there," he said. "A smaller piece that ran after his death."

I looked at the clock on the wall and moved to gather up my things. I had to go; I didn't want to be late getting to Luke again. And he and I had lots to talk about, didn't we? I had to take a cab, so I could ride my bike home later. I said as much.

"I'll take you," said Langdon when I told him I needed to go. "My car's right outside the building."

"I thought you wanted me to quit."

"Well," he said, "since you're obviously not going to, I'll give you a ride."

For some reason, I hesitated. I had the weird feeling that it would upset Luke. But I quashed that. It was a silly thought and the fact that I was having it meant that I was already too involved with him. Like his mother, who obviously spent her whole life walking on eggshells around him, giving him so much power that she needed to lock him away when he raged.

As we pulled out of the parking lot, there was a thick fog hanging in the air. The day was weirdly warm and damp. And the campus was suddenly glutted with police cars, a few more news vans, a bunch of cars probably belonging to volunteers. But we didn't see any people moving about. Doubtless they had all headed into the haunted woods.

Oh God, I thought. *What will they find?*

She disappeared one night so long ago
They never found a trace.
The years went by and still no sign
Just the memory of her face.

Then one night, her son returned
His mind ruined by secrets and lies.
He started digging beneath the earth
Where the truth so often hides.

In the dead of night, he took his shovel.
He dug deep into the ground.
The deeper he got, the more he knew
What he'd lost would not be found.

Horrible, really. Utter nonsense. The kid was a terrible poet, and I was starting to hate him for it. I kept turning it over in my mind. His latest clue was more vague than the last one, not much to search on. My one stab at it: "Missing woman, son looking for answers, The Hollows, NY" brought up a slew of Web listings that didn't seem to hold anything on first glance.

I really wanted to tell Langdon about the next clue. But I had lied to him last night, and that part of me that was a little annoyed that he had figured out Luke's clue when I hadn't wouldn't allow it. This game was a challenge issued by Luke, so any help I took from Langdon was cheating. And the fact that I'd had to cheat already meant that Luke was winning. And the stakes seemed suddenly very high, his hints and clues brushing against my secret places. I didn't think Luke was trying to tell me anything about himself. Not at all.

The heat was blasting from the vents in Langdon's car and slowly the chill gave over to warmth. I felt better the farther we were from campus. A place that had once seemed like a retreat from the ugly world, it was becoming tainted, another place of chaos. When my aunt and uncle were trying to talk me out of coming to school in such a remote place, Bridgette said something that stayed with me: *You can't hide from who you are. Not forever.* I thought I had proven her wrong; I had hidden quite well from the person I used to be. When I think of my childhood, that kid seems like another person living another life, like a distant cousin, twice removed. My memories are like movies on a screen. It was the second part of her warning that I hadn't considered. When you're eighteen, four years seems like an eternity. But it's a heartbeat. And that's how long it had taken for the past to come back.

I still hadn't even dealt with the issue of my father. I'd ignored a call and a voice mail this morning from Bridgette, too. We'd just had our weekly catch-up chat, so if she was calling in the middle of the week, there was something she needed to discuss. Was it about my father? Had he reached out to her? Or had she heard about Beck?

"Are you okay?" asked Langdon.

I realized that I was frowning, and rubbing the back of my neck. "No," I said. "You know, not really."

"Okay," he said. "Understandable."

We pulled up in front of the house. There was still a half hour before Luke would get home. It was a half day at school today for some reason, which was why I had to go right after class. We'd have the whole afternoon together.

"Be careful," Langdon said, after I'd thanked him for the ride. "Don't let him know he got to you."

"What makes you think he got to me?"

He lifted his eyebrows, gave me a little half smile he seemed to have perfected—professorial and yet smart-alecky all at once.

"Uh, you were out in the middle of the night, wandering around a graveyard shack where a guy killed himself—all because of a poem he wrote. I'd say he got to you."

I thought about offering a protest, reminding him again that it was just a game I was playing with a kid in my care. But I didn't bother.

He beeped his horn when he saw that I'd opened the door, and I felt a little wistful as he drove his gray Touareg off into the gray afternoon.

*

Inside, I immediately set up my laptop and hooked into the wireless router. Rachel had given me the code so that I could go online. First, I tried to track down that article about Greenwald that Langdon said he found. But even after scrolling through pages of links, there was nothing. I knew he wouldn't lie. I must have been doing something wrong. Or maybe he used a more powerful search engine; he would have access to LexisNexis at the library.

I checked my e-mail and saw a note from my aunt:

Call me, honey. We need to talk about something. And I heard about that missing girl at your school. I want to check in with you, okay?

She was a good person, my aunt. I thought that my mother would be so appreciative of how hard she'd worked at her relationship with me. And I thought she'd be a little angry with me for how hard I worked against her. I was a terrible and ungrateful child. But, of course, that wouldn't be news to anyone.

There was an e-mail from Ainsley, too.

I'm going home. I can't be here right now. My teachers said that I could take my classes online, so that's what I'm going to do until things are settled. Sorry to leave you here alone. I just can't go through this again. Tell Beck I'm sorry when she comes home. If she's hurt or worse, I'll hate myself. But if she's fucking with us, I'll never speak to her again. I totally mean it.

I was surprised by a powerful wave of sadness and fear. I didn't want to be in that room without either of them. And I had no home to escape to; I certainly wouldn't go to hide in my aunt's perfectly lovely guest room. It wasn't home and it never would be. I had always envied Ainsley her goodness, and her nice parents.

P.S., she wrote. I hate to tell you this. But some people are talking shit about you on Facebook. You might want to check it out. I'm sorry. I really am. I know I'm a sucky friend for abandoning you like this.

I didn't blame her. If I had a real home, and loving parents who would nurture and protect me, I'd leave, too. But I was used to being on my own. (It would really hurt Bridgette's feelings to hear me say that.)

Next stop: Fakebook, Beck's misery page. Oh, the outpouring of sadness and love. *We are praying for you, Rebecca! Please come home safe*, wrote a girl I'd never even seen before. *You hot, girl*, wrote another moron. *What I wouldn't do to see you again* :(, wrote a girl whom I knew Beck had once experimented with sexually but whom she now hated passionately.

What was it about a situation like this that brought out

181

all the drama queens and glommers-on? How could people live with it, injecting themselves into an event that had nothing whatsoever to do with them? They were nightmare chasers, sucking up other people's tragedy, anesthetizing their own boredom for a few days or weeks.

I scrolled through about a hundred posts that varied little from one another. Until I came to one that must have been what Ainsley was talking about.

What does Lana Granger know about Beck? What were they fighting about the night Beck went missing? And wasn't she fighting with Elizabeth the night she went missing, too? And, naturally, people jumped at the chance to dish.

That girl's a freak. She looks like a boy. (Nice.)

I hear they were lovers. (No.)

Don't argue with Lana Granger or you go missing or dead! (Moron.)

Aren't her parents dead? (Shit.)

She's got problems, and she's fugly. (Really? Fugly?)

You guys don't know what you're talking about. They're best friends and have been forever. Shut your stupid mouths!!!! (Ainsley, of course.)

Didn't her father kill her mother? (That one made my blood chill. Who knew that? The poster's profile image was blank, and his page had no information at all. His name: Lester Nobody.)

Whaaaaat??? Is that true? That's fucked up.

Google that shit, yo.

I let my head fall into my hands. I thought of the newspaper article I'd found in Beck's drawer. It was all coming out. After a second I felt myself shutting down inside, the fear, despair, and panic disappearing down the big drain I had in my center. I closed the lid of my laptop and all that idiot chatter was gone, and the waves of emotion I'd been feeling since last night, gone, too. *When you've been exposed to massive psychological trauma*, Dr. Cooper explained, *your mind learns how to do this. It's survival. But those feelings don't really go away. You can't repress them forever. They will demand that you deal with them, one way or another.*

After a quick glance outside for any sign of Luke, I found myself drifting up the stairs. There were still ten minutes before he was due home and I wondered if it was enough time for me to get a leg up on the whole scavenger hunt thing.

Instead of heading to Luke's room, I wandered into Rachel's. It was a peaceful, pretty space. The watery-gray afternoon light washed in. She had folded the throw blanket over the right foot of the bed. The radio had been left on and some kind of ambient, New Age music was playing. The room smelled like her perfume as I walked in and stood at the foot of her bed, then to the bedside table where her books and reading glasses sat in a tidy pile. At the low armless chair and ottoman by the window, I took a quick peek outside. The street was empty.

I ran my hand along her dresser. It was spotless, the surface shining and free from dust. Like everything in the house, it was perfect—a study in style and cleanliness.

"I am obsessively clean," Rachel had admitted to me. "I clean to relieve stress."

I felt so comfortable with her that I almost said, *My mom was like that, too.* But I had managed not to mention my parents at all. And she, maybe sensing my cues, had never asked.

"She scrubs and scrubs even though nothing's ever dirty," said Luke. We'd been eating dinner together when she made her admission. "It's like she's trying to wash something away. Something no one else can see."

Rachel didn't say anything, just pushed some chicken around her plate.

But Luke kept looking at her, pinning her with his gaze. "So what is it, Mom? What are you trying to get rid of?"

She swallowed her food. And I thought how reversed were the roles between them. He seemed like the parent, leaning forward, looking for eye contact. She was the bullied child, shrinking into herself.

"Just dirt, darling," she said, not looking up from her plate. "Just dirt."

It was then that I realized she was afraid of him. Who could be afraid of their own child?

*

On a simple silver tray, there was a simple silver locket. I found this odd. She wasn't a locket type of person. It wasn't her. I saw Rachel as practical, unsentimental. Then again, she was opening a bookstore in the electronic age. Maybe she was prone to fits of nostalgia. It was a nice piece, platinum, from Tiffany & Co. I opened it carefully with my fingernail, but not before catching sight of myself in the mirror.

What are you doing? I asked the pale person in the mirror. *She's fugly. She looks like a boy.* You'd think at this point in my life, I'd have been immune to schoolyard taunts. My whole life, I'd been enduring bullies and their nasty, slicing words. I've never understood why some people seem to delight in cruelty, in making people feel bad about who they are. I ran my hand through my hair—which looked like pitch in the dim light, short and messy. Not styled messy, but like actually messy since I hadn't bothered to draw a brush through it today. I didn't spend a lot of time in mirrors. In fact, I actively avoided them. I wasn't one to primp and preen. I was more of a wash-and-go kind of person.

If I looked at myself, I had to think about who I was, how I was moving through the world. And that's the last thing I wanted. Still, I picked up Rachel's brush and ran it through my hair. I looked, really looked, at my face. I was too much like my father. Why couldn't I have been more like her? I thought.

185

I was aware in this moment that my actions constituted a terrible breach of privacy, something I would have railed against. I, who keep so many secrets, was poking around in my employer's bedroom. I put the brush down quickly.

Inside the locket was, predictably, a picture of Luke. In the opposing frame, there was a chiseled-looking blond man in his thirties. Was it Luke's father? They looked nothing alike.

Luke's father, like my parents, had been conspicuously absent and unmentioned. And I, naturally, had never asked about him. There was no mention of divorce, ugly or otherwise, or warnings about his showing up at the house. Luke never talked about him—no discussions about weekends with his father, no phone calls or cards that I saw. I knew it was a sore spot, since our first back-and-forth. Maybe he had died. You wouldn't keep a locket on your dresser with a picture of someone you'd divorced. Would you? But wouldn't Rachel have mentioned it if Luke's father had died? I usually didn't like to pry. But maybe it was time, since Luke was clearly prying into my past.

There was a slim, low-profile desk in a little alcove behind the master closet. Rachel's silver laptop sat open. I pressed the touch pad and the screen came to life with a blooming, purple lotus flower. But the box itself was password protected.

I sat in the white leather desk chair and slid open the top center drawer. Inside, there was a book, bound in dove-gray cloth. Embossed in silver across the middle was the word *Journal*. As I ran my finger along the cover, I heard a car door slam outside. I shut the drawer quickly, leaving the journal unopened, and headed downstairs.

15

Dear Diary,

It's a silly thing to write, isn't it? Dear Diary. It's such an innocent, hopeful salutation. As if logging your feelings in a book, narrating your life, has any meaning, does any good at all. But, for me, this is the only place I can be really honest. Everywhere else I'm wearing a smiling mask, putting on a show of myself and my life. You are the only one who knows the totality of my feelings, the depth of my spirit, however dark and bottomless.

It's only in parenthood that we realize how truly powerless we are in this life. I imagine this is true for all parents. You cannot cushion every fall, soften every blow of disappointment. You can't alleviate the sting of rejection or failure, mend every hurt. When your child suffers, there's an ache that doesn't go away until the tears are dry, and the smile returns.

I imagine that's what it feels like for the parent of a normal child. I am powerless, too. I am powerless to protect others from my son.

There was the boy he bit so hard, so deep, that the tiny arc of teeth marks bled and turned purple before my eyes. His mother and I had been sharing a cup of coffee at my dining room table. I'd actually been enjoying myself. We'd met at preschool. And either she hadn't heard the rumors about my son or chose to ignore them, but she said her boy had asked for a playdate. I was almost giddy with relief. Someone wants to play with my kid! We were sharing a laugh, just like normal parents, over how funny children could be sometimes when a shriek of pain and dismay rang out from the room where the boys were playing.

I won't forget the look on her face, or how hard she tried to be polite as she cleaned the wound, with my fluttering frantically around for Band-Aids, Neosporin, and my son looking on with an expression that could only be classified as malicious curiosity.

"I'm so sorry. Really, I'm so sorry," I said as she shuttled her weeping child toward the door, gathering up his backpack that looked like a cute little monster, his hat and scarf. To my son: "Can you say you're sorry? You know we don't bite our friends."

"I'm sorry," he said. He clearly didn't mean it. "Anyway, he's not my friend."

"It's all right," she said. "Really, these things happen. We'd better go."

It would have been better if she'd raged and been angry. But on her face there was only concern for her son, and for me. I could see that she felt sorry for me. I watched silently as they drove away in their red Honda.

"I didn't like him," he said. "He was stupid."

"Is that why you bit him?"

"I bit him because he asked me to bite him. He wanted me to bite him."

I stood there at the door with him. He was lying and I knew he was lying. And he knew that I knew he was lying. It was a metacommunication that passed between us. He slipped his little hand in mine.

"We don't need any friends, Mommy."

"I'm glad you feel that way. Because we don't have any."

My sister and nieces came to visit a few weeks ago. She and I have had our differences over the years, though admittedly it's largely my fault. I have always been the prickly one, the one prone to temper and the one who holds grudges. And unhappiness hasn't made me easier to get along with, I'm sure. But I was truly flooded with joy when she and the girls got off the plane. I waved and ran to them; my sister dropped her bags to take me into her arms while the girls (just two and four) clambered around our legs. So wrapped up in my son and all the drama surrounding his life, I had badly neglected my family.

The girls were cherubs, chubby and golden-curled, Gerber faces and sapphire eyes. They were so normal. They giggled, they cried, they played, they fought. They reached for their mother and clung, or ran off laughing. They were toddlers in all their wild beauty. They weren't silent and watchful. Their tantrums weren't rages. They were disorganized and messy; how I envied my sister.

We had a lovely first evening. My mother was there, of course. We ordered pizzas, opened a bottle of chardonnay. Even my son seemed happy, charming and social, being so helpful, attentive to the girls. My mother and I exchanged looks: What's he up to? But eventually we relaxed.

I think it was when he realized how enamored I was of my younger niece. What a bright light she was, so funny and silly. She had such a warm, sweet way about her. She wasn't talking much, and my sister was worried about it. I even envied her that, the small worry that her younger was less vocal than she should be at two. She's fine, I told her. She's perfect.

I was feeding her pasta shells in butter with a spoon.

"Self!" she said with a defiant little frown. I handed her the spoon.

"No!" she said. "You!"

"Silly," I answered.

And it was a game we played for a while. The game of the normal two-year-old, the internal struggle between wanting to do things for herself and wanting them done for her. I was, weirdly, in heaven, basking in the glow of normalcy. And so I didn't notice at first. But then it was like the sun moved behind the clouds, and I felt a chill come over me.

He was dressed for bed, as I'd asked him to do, standing

in the darkened kitchen. My sister had taken her older for a bath. I was supposed to bring the baby when she was done eating.

"Grandma helped me with my pajamas," he said. He sounded like a jilted lover.

"You're a big boy," I said. He was six going on seven, big enough to do things for himself. The teacher at his new school and his psychiatrist had both indicated, albeit subtly, that I was doing too much for him. "You shouldn't need help with your pajamas."

"There was an old woman in my room," he said. "She told me you didn't love me anymore."

"That's silly, darling," I said. I fought to keep my voice light. Too often I was sharp and angry with him lately, stretched as I was to my limit with his visions, fantasies, and lies. "Go to bed. I'll be there in a minute to read your story, after your cousin is done eating."

He was quiet. Then, "Is Dad coming home tonight?"

"No," I said. "He'll be home on Saturday."

I realized that my whole body was tense. And the baby started to fuss, as though she sensed the shift in energy.

"All done?" I said.

"All done," she confirmed. "Bath."

"That's right," I said. I gave her a kiss on the forehead and tousled her hair. She had piles and piles of hair. "Oh, I love those golden curls."

I brought her to my sister, and left them in the bathroom.

I heard the music of their voices as I walked down the dim hall. High and low, singsong, then stern, then laughing. They brought laughter with them; something that we had far too little of in our house.

I lay beside him on his bed, and started reading. He touched my shoulder lightly and I turned to look at him.

"She's not your baby," he said to me. "You'll never have another baby."

I was so immune to him that his words didn't even hurt me.

"I know," I said. "I never wanted anyone but you."

I had hoped that would appease him. I should have known better.

In the early, dark morning the sound of my sister screaming tore me from sleep. The run I made across the house felt like the longest distance I've ever crossed in my life. I was already praying before I even knew what was happening.

I burst into my sister's room and the scene revealed itself to me in bursts. She was holding the baby, cradling her as the child wailed. The child's hair was shorn, cut ragged, with patches bald to the skull. On the ground around my sister's feet were those golden curls I'd so admired, confetti from a party. And glinting in the lamplight a long, silver pair of kitchen shears.

16

I managed to get myself back to the kitchen and behind my laptop before Luke let himself into the house, bringing the cold air with him. He looked flushed and expectant, dropped his bag by the large standing vase by the door, and walked toward me. I pretended to be engrossed in my schoolwork.

"Were you upstairs?" he asked, standing in the kitchen doorway.

"Hmm?" I said, pretending not to have heard. Then, looking at him with a welcoming smile, "Upstairs? No," I said.

"I thought I saw a shadow," he said.

"Trick of the light, maybe," I said. "Would you like a snack?"

"Yes, please," he said. He shed his jacket, hung it neatly in the hall closet. He was a tidy little boy when he wanted to be, precise and orderly. He came to sit across from me, and I closed the lid on my laptop.

"How was your day?" I asked.

"Horrible," he said mildly. "Just like every day there."

I went over to the refrigerator, took out a bowl of green apples, a block of white cheddar cheese, and some of the hard black bread that I knew he liked.

"I'm sorry," I said. "I know it's not always easy there."

We'd talked about how unruly the classes were, how challenging were lunch and recess. He and some of the better-behaved, more intelligent children were removed in the afternoons for lessons. But that only made them targets for some of the more aggressive children. Even among misfits, Luke was a misfit.

"So," he said. "Did you figure out the clue?"

"I did," I said. I told him how I'd searched and found The Hollows Historical Society site, and actually went to the building. "Very clever," I said. I tried to be as patronizing as possible.

He tried to hide it by looking down at the table, but I saw him frown, saw his disappointment at my answer. I brought him over his plate, along with a glass of milk and a checkered cloth napkin.

"Did you discover his secret?" he asked. He took a bite of apple. There was a twinkle of mischief in his eye. I thought about what Langdon said. *Was* he trying to tell me something about himself?

"Yes," I said. He frowned again.

"You did?" he asked. He was getting agitated. And I would be lying if I said I didn't enjoy it. "How?"

"How does anyone find out anything these days? Online," I said. He could smell the lie, and we locked eyes.

"So you know he was a *pervert*?"

I didn't say anything, just took a bite of the apple I had sliced for myself. Let the patient talk, Therapy 101. They will tell you what is wrong, and they may also already know how to fix it. A good therapist just opens the line of communication, and lets the patient lead the session.

"That he molested children," said Luke. "That he touched little boys. Exposed himself." He was looking to shock me, unsettle me. But he didn't know how hard that actually was. Nearly impossible, I'd say. I knew how ugly was the world, how we harm one another.

"I know he was accused of that," I said. "Yes."

Did he not know about the cross-dressing? Was that not the secret? I wasn't going to toss it out there.

"Why else would he kill himself?" said Luke. "If he wasn't guilty."

It was comforting to realize that he had a child's way of looking at the world, all black and white, no understanding of the nuances of depression and despair, all the varied layers and textures of unhappiness. How it can bury you until your world is so dark that death actually looks like an escape hatch.

"People who kill themselves generally suffer from severe clinical depression," I said. "Their reasons for choosing suicide are not always rational. It's often a chemical imbalance that leads them to the choice."

Luke put a slice of cheddar on top of an apple slice and chewed thoughtfully. He was like a little machine, ingesting nourishment, processing information. He looked like he wanted to say something but didn't.

"But what's the point?" I asked him. "I mean, what were you trying to get across with that poem? Why that man? Why that place?"

He blinked at me, examining my expression, my body language. We were in a very subtle standoff, each of us trying to figure out how much the other knew, what the other wanted, and who was winning.

"The *point* is to find the next clue," he said with mock innocence. "Did you find it?"

"I did."

"And?" *Chew, chew, chew.* He washed down what was clearly too much food with a big swallow of milk, then made a show of letting out a belch. I ignored his little display.

"I haven't started thinking about it yet," I said. "I have class."

"And a missing friend."

"Right."

The refrigerator dumped some ice cubes into the bucket, and again, the sound made both of us jump, then laugh a little. It was becoming a joke between us.

"I'm curious," I said. "How did you get to that house to plant the next clue? And *where* did you get that key?"

"Wouldn't you like to know," he said. It was somewhat

less obnoxious than it sounds. Luke had a great deal of superficial charm; his beauty and the wattage of his smile were disarming. I had to remember not to put down my guard.

"You're not going to tell me?" I said.

"When we get to the end, I'll tell you everything." He gave me a sweet, warm glance, and patted my hand as though he were the caregiver and I his terribly slow charge.

"What if I don't want to play anymore?" I said, somewhat more petulantly than I had intended.

"But you do," he said. He released another belch. "You really do."

I think it was clear then who had the upper hand. He had hooked me into his game, and I had no choice but to play. I found myself thinking about that dirt on his tires, his knowledge of Beck, the clues that grazed the edge of my secrets. What did he know about me? Or was it all in my imagination? Was he, after all, just a lonely kid playing a game with the closest thing he had to a friend? Carl Jung believed in a dark side, a self we pressed down and tried to hide. He held that whatever we dislike, whatever unsettles or disturbs in others only does so because we are repressing similar qualities. That theory made a kind of sense here.

He brought his plate and glass over to the sink and washed them, placing them neatly in the rack as was his habit.

When he turned back to me, he cocked his head to one side. "How did you get here? We still have your bike."

I thought about lying, telling him that I'd taken a cab. But I decided that it was a silly thing to do, giving him more power than he deserved. "I got a ride," I said.

"From?" he asked a bit peevishly. There was a sudden change to him, an odd stiffness to his frame that I hadn't seen before, a stillness to his face.

"From a professor," I said.

"What's his name?"

"What do you care?" I asked. I didn't like his tone or the way he was looking at me. I found myself thinking about last night, the small form I thought I'd seen disappearing into the trees. It couldn't have been him. Rachel would never have allowed him out that late. Could he have snuck out? Was he following me? The thought was more worrisome than I can say.

"You won't tell me?" he said.

"Why is it an issue, Luke? I got a ride from my professor, who also happens to be my adviser and friend. It's none of your business who he is."

I didn't want to say Langdon's name in front of him. I didn't even know why.

"Is he your boyfriend, too?" he asked nastily. "Do you *fuck* him?"

"Luke!" I said. I felt like he'd slapped me.

"My mother would have come to get you," he said. His body had literally gone rigid, his arms sticking out. I rose to my feet. I did not want to remain seated. The air was electric with his coming rage, a steep drop in the psychic barometric pressure.

"Who is it?" he said, his voice rising. "What's his name?"

The ridiculousness of this situation struck me, and I realized that Langdon was right. I had empowered him by playing this game with him. He thought we were friends, that we were equals. He'd developed some attachment or fantasy about me, and he was acting out of that place.

"Take a deep breath," I said, keeping my voice low. "Calm down."

He came at me quickly, until he was right in my face. I held my ground, but kept my eyes down. I knew where he was, shot through with impotent rage. I'd been there myself as a child. I remember how it's a hurricane inside, a terrible roar that drowns out all reasonable thought, everything around you. All you are is anger and sadness, and it's a loop that feeds on itself. You go deeper and deeper, with nothing to draw you back to reality. Remember, I have problems, too.

"Who is he?" His face was right in mine. I could smell the cheddar on his breath.

"We can't talk about this until you calm down," I said.

"Did you tell him about our game?" he asked. But this time it was a shriek; he backed me against the wall with it. *"Did you?"*

"We can't talk about this until you calm down," I said again.

He released a kind of anguished cry that was more despair than anything else, and I heard all the notes of my own childhood in it. I wasn't afraid of him. He couldn't hurt me, not in a fair fight. Instead of coming at me, he stormed up the stairs screaming, pounding on the walls as he went, slamming doors down the hall—his mother's room, the bathroom, the empty guest room. Then from the sound of it, he was trashing his room upstairs. I followed slowly, creeping up one step at a time.

"You weren't supposed to tell anyone," he was wailing. "It's our game."

There was a succession of heavy thuds, then a loud crack. The television hitting the floor maybe? I stood outside the door. I could see that the locks were loose in their settings, and that the doorknob was a bit wobbly. What happened here at night after I went home?

Then, from inside, more shouting, *"Who is he? Who is he? Who is he?"*

I sat at the top of the landing and waited for him to burn himself out. But he didn't, not for more than an hour. And that's how Rachel found us when she came home, Luke screaming in his room, me sitting on the top step, my head resting against the wall.

She made me a cup of tea while Luke, obviously aware that we were downstairs talking, had taken to pounding on the floor of his room. The glasses in the cabinets were rattling. What a fucking brat he was. I mean, seriously.

"I'm surprised this didn't happen sooner," she said. "It's funny. I was just looking at my calendar and thinking that you'd been with us a month. That's the longest anyone has ever lasted with him, by like three weeks."

"It's partially my fault," I said.

"No," she answered firmly. She raised a palm at me. "Don't say that. Luke is responsible for his own behavior. It took me years to accept that."

I told her about the game we'd been playing, about the clues he left, his scary poems. She didn't seem surprised, just nodded and made affirming noises as I told her everything.

"He's so good at reeling people in," she said. She gave a little laugh and a shake of her head.

"Stop talking about me!" he screamed from upstairs. More pounding ensued.

She put down my mug and sat across from me. "He knows exactly what to say and do to hook people into his games. They tell me he manipulates the children at school, that he promises them treats if they misbehave at a certain time. A Snickers bar for a meltdown at twelve thirty-four or something like that."

That was not the picture he painted of himself at school. I thought he was being bullied, pushed around because he was smart and small. I could relate to that, someone being rejected because there was something strange and different about him. I guess he knew that somehow.

"Why?" I asked. "Why does he do that?"

"Because he can," she said. "That's the only reason. He gets so bored; he needs constant stimulation. He can't handle the monotony of normal day-to-day school life. So he creates chaos just to entertain himself. That's really the only reason, hard as it is to accept."

Of course, I knew that. I had enough education and experience at Fieldcrest to know that she was right in her assessment of him.

"Did he tell you I abuse him?" she asked. I didn't respond. "Well, he wouldn't say it outright. Just flinch when you get near him, or show you some injury and then be like a textbook abused child saying he fell or something."

"The bruise on his shoulder," I said.

"Self-inflicted," she said. "He did it here by repeatedly banging himself against the wall. Then he went to school and put on his little show. I was called in, naturally. Parents of troubled children can sometimes resort to violence. Not me, though. The doctors there are smart. It didn't take them long to figure out what he was doing."

"I'm sorry," I said. "That's awful."

She raised her cup to her lips but then she didn't drink, just put it down on the table.

"I watched a documentary once about these crazy people who keep wild animals as pets," she said. "They buy these baby chimps or lion cubs, even bears. And at first, it's all cuddles and milk from a bottle. Then, surprise, surprise, a year later there's a deadly, wild beast living in the backyard."

She paused a second, finally took a sip of her tea. Then she ran her fingers under her lashes, wiping away tears that had welled there.

"These animals, caged and miserable, will kill the minute they get the chance. But, you know, you can see that these crazy pet owners love their creatures, really *love* them. They're lonely people, rejected, and this lion or baboon or whatever fills some void they have inside. They just don't realize that the creature doesn't—can't—love them back."

She looked at me to see if I was following her. I was.

"And I found myself thinking that I knew just how they felt. The only difference was that I thought I had a kitten, and he grew into a tiger."

Upstairs, Luke started pounding on the floor again. He must have been jumping, or the house was just really shoddily constructed, because our cups shivered on the table with each rattling blow.

"It runs in my family," she said, looking up at the ceiling. "My father battled crippling depression, as well as chronic anxiety. And my brother was a lot like Luke, until he killed himself when he was sixteen." I thought about the man in the locket and wondered if it was her brother.

She seemed so tired, heavy with fatigue. And who could blame her?

"I used to pray for a normal life," she said. "I couldn't wait to get out of my house. I wouldn't have planned a child, not with my genes, not with the place I was in when I got pregnant. But that's life. Things don't always go as planned."

She looked at me suddenly, as though she was snapping out of a trance. "I haven't told anyone that. Not in years. I'm sorry. It's a horrible thing to say."

"No," I said. Another loud boom resonated from upstairs. "I understand."

"I know you do," she said kindly. She put her hand on mine for a moment, and then took it away. How did she know that? I didn't know what she meant, and I didn't ask.

"I have to go," I told her. "I'm sorry to leave you like this. But I have a crisis at home."

She nodded. "I suppose you won't be coming back," she said.

"Oh, no," I answered. "I'll be back."

She beamed me a wide grateful smile, and I realized that somewhere along the line we'd become friends.

17

After I left the Kahns', I returned to my empty dorm room. It was dark and cold, and I wasn't there a minute before I wanted to leave again. Dr. Cooper had left a message on my cell phone, and after I made myself some macaroni and cheese, I called her back.

"I was just checking in on you," she said. "I dropped a bit of a bomb on you last session."

"I was going to call you," I said.

"Do you need to come in?" she asked.

"I do," I said. "I think I really do."

"It's dark and really cold," she said. "I don't want you to ride your bike."

She was always on me for riding my bike without a helmet at the best of times. I didn't exactly relish another nighttime ride myself.

"I'll take a cab."

"Actually, I know my husband is on campus right now. He helped with the search today. It's a little unorthodox, but if you're comfortable with it, he'll happily give you a lift and I'll drive you home after our session."

Jones Cooper, the man who investigated Elizabeth's disappearance and Harvey Greenwald's suicide. Strange how he kept turning up.

"He's a cop, right?" I asked.

"He's retired now, working as a private investigator. He was just helping out today, volunteering. He doesn't have anything to do with Beck's case."

My distrust of the police had been long established in our sessions. I felt an immediate sense of discomfort when they were around. They annoyed me because they thought they knew everything, and really they knew nothing. With all their special forensics equipment, cutting-edge technology, body-language reading, handwriting analysis, whatever other little tricks they pulled out of the collective hat, they still got it all wrong. It was human nature to see only what you want to see, and nothing would change that, no matter what tools people had at their disposal. The truth is only what you think it is.

"Is that okay with you?"

"Sure," I said with a lightness I didn't feel. "That's great. If he just rings downstairs at the Evangeline dorm, I'll come right out."

I thanked her and ended the call.

Was it weird that I had just been reading about Jones Cooper in the article about Harvey Greenwald? Or that he had worked Elizabeth's case, and I had the feeling he never liked me? Oddly, the fact that he was married to Dr. Cooper had never bothered me before. It was something that I knew, but just filed away as irrelevant.

Dr. Cooper never spoke about her husband. And she was such a stickler about boundaries and privacy that I never worried that she might talk to him about me. But they *were* married. How likely was it that she would be able to keep the secret of my past from him? Especially back when he'd been working Elizabeth's disappearance, which involved me in a peripheral way. And now he was volunteering on the search for Beck. Was this some kind of trick the police were playing? Maybe they were hoping I'd say something to him that they could use. But that would mean my therapist was colluding with the police. Or maybe I was just being paranoid. Paranoia—the voice in your head that tells you everyone has a secret agenda that he's running against you. The confusing thing is that sometimes it's true.

If you don't say anything, they can't hurt you. It was my father's voice in my head. *Don't give them anything, no matter how small, that they can use to manipulate and work their way into your cracks.* They could try to trick me all they liked. But it wasn't going to work, because I had learned from the best.

I opened my laptop and entered Cooper's name into the search engine, and started scrolling through the long list of articles in which his name appeared. By the time they rang me from downstairs, I knew a lot about former lead detective Jones Cooper.

I had also found something else: the location of Luke's next clue.

Then one night, her son returned
His mind ruined by secrets and lies.
He started digging beneath the earth
Where the truth so often hides.

There was a slew of articles about Cooper's first case as a private investigator, a cold case. A woman named Marla Holt had gone missing back in the eighties, and she was never found. There was always some suspicion surrounding the husband, but ultimately, because she had been having an affair, the police concluded that she'd run off on her family.

Last year, after the husband died, her son returned to The Hollows hoping to find out exactly what had happened to his mother. He discovered her body buried deep in The Hollows Wood next to an abandoned barn. And in finding her, he discovered the real truth of her death.

As I read the articles, my whole body started to shiver. Though it wasn't quite the same set of circumstances, the similarities between that story and my own cut a deep valley of dread through me. The details, like the details of Harvey Greenwald's suicide, just grazed the boundaries of my truth. Did he know me? Did Luke know who I was? The panic of the discovered liar was a drum beating in the back of my head. I wanted to race out the door, and go straight to that abandoned barn in The Hollows Wood. I needed to find out what he knew about me; it was a desperate and terrified drive. But I looked out my window and saw Cooper's SUV idling in front of my building.

Like his pal Detective Chuck Ferrigno, the lead on Beck's disappearance, Jones Cooper seemed like a nice guy. He was big and beefy, ruddy-faced and clean. He was the kind of guy who could wear a barn jacket and still look tough. He got out of the car to open the door for me. He waited until I climbed inside, then closed it carefully after me. His handshake had been warm and firm, but not too firm, the way some men use it to show how strong they are.

"Didn't your mother ever tell you not to take a ride with strange men?" he joked as he got into the driver's seat. He had a scent, not cologne but something soapy, and crisp.

"Well, since Dr. Cooper seems to think you're all right," I said, "I figured you were a safe bet."

"She *is* an excellent judge of character," he said.

He started the engine and the big SUV rumbled to life. He pulled slowly onto the drive that led out of the school.

We passed by the crowd of volunteers still gathered in the parking lot. The gym was lit up brightly and milling with people. I knew it was where the police and Beck's parents were running the command center. There were more news vans than there had been this morning. The story was heating up. Beck hadn't used her phone or any of her credit cards since the day she went missing. I knew this from my last check on the Facebook page. I hadn't heard from the police or from Beck's parents. It seemed like I was being purposely kept out of the inner circle. But again, maybe that was just paranoia talking. Not everything is about me.

"Must be a hard time for you," Cooper said.

I nodded, still staring out the window. I found I couldn't use my voice, didn't trust it not to betray me. I drew and released a deep breath.

"She's my friend," I said. "I hope she's just pulling another one of her stunts. I really do."

"Me, too," he said. "Three-time runaway, right?"

I nodded.

"But never like this?" he said. "Causing so much worry?"

"No," I admitted. "Usually she was in touch with someone after a day or so."

As we pulled past the gym, I saw flashlight beams bouncing in the woods. They were still out there looking.

"Do you remember me?" he asked after a minute.

"Yes," I said. "You worked Elizabeth's case. You were there when they found her."

He'd had a lot of questions for me back then. Someone said that they overheard Elizabeth and me arguing.

Someone had heard me say: *You can't tell anyone, Liz. It's not true.* I didn't have any memory of that event, just the floaty, foggy images that came back in my dreams. But there was no evidence of any foul play in Elizabeth's death. So eventually, they dropped it.

"That's right," he said.

He'd been involved in a number of missing-persons cases over the course of his career, according to the Web. Though, of course, it was a small town with a small police department. So naturally, as the lead detective, he worked most of the big cases.

"Did you find anything today?" I asked. "I wanted to be out there. But—I just couldn't go through it again."

"I understand," he said. "No one should have to go through a thing like that twice."

Three times, I thought, but naturally didn't say.

"We didn't find anything," he said. "Not a trace. The Hollows Wood knows how to keep a secret."

I looked over at him to see if he was making some kind of an insinuation, but he didn't look at me, just kept his eyes on the road. He seemed lost in his own thoughts. He was right. It did keep secrets.

By the time I'd gotten to the lookout point that night, Beck had trailed so far behind me that I figured she had turned around. I felt the unloading sensation I always felt there, as if I could drop all the bullshit of my life, put it down like a backpack filled with stone. I was glad she was gone. Part of me kept waiting for her to come through the trees, but she didn't. And after a while I relaxed. There was a patch of icy, crunchy grass, and even though it was cold, I lay down on it, flat on my back, looking up at the stars. I could hear the breath of the wind and nothing else, not a hooting owl or critters moving over the leaves on the ground. I was bundled up tight in my wool coat, hat, hood, scarf, and gloves. So only the skin on my face was bitten by the cold.

How I craved solitude. All my life, even before the worst thing happened, even as a child, I just wanted to be alone. Out in the world, I had to hold it all in, all my dark thoughts, my anxieties, my twisted thoughts and fears. All the things that made me a misery to my mother, that caused me trouble in school, with other children. All the things that were quieted now with medication, I had to hold it all in as best I could. But alone, I could just let the tension unfurl. No eyes on me, no judgment, no whispers. They mark you, you know, when you're different. Children can smell a freak and seek to ostracize him, eject the diseased member from the group—and rightly so. I'd be rid of myself if I could.

You might wonder why I wasn't afraid to be alone in the haunted woods in the night. What went on inside my head was infinitely scarier. *I* was the monster hiding in the woods. I wasn't afraid of anything out there.

Finally, after I lay there awhile and calmed myself down, I heard Beck moving through the trees.

"Goddammit," she said breathlessly as she moved into the clearing. "You really like to make people work for it, don't you?"

I was aggravated and relieved all at the same time, a familiar response to Beck's arrival anywhere.

"I didn't ask you to follow me, did I?" I said. I didn't like the sound of my voice, sharp, deep, and angry.

"I'm sorry," she said. "I didn't mean what I said."

She sat herself heavily down beside me.

"I know you're not fucking Langdon," she went on. I still didn't say anything. Her nearness was making me uncomfortable. She didn't seem to notice, as usual, or care. She lay down beside me so that our faces were side by side, both of us looking up at the night sky. She reached out for my hand and I didn't pull it away. She turned to look at me, but I kept my gaze up at the sky. It was safe and her eyes were not.

"Sometimes anger is the only emotion I can tease out of you," she said softly. Her breath came out in white puffs.

I was quiet a minute. "How do you know I'm not?"

"How do I know you're not what?" she asked.

"Fucking Langdon."

"Are you?" she said, jaw dropped. I enjoyed seeing her look surprised; it was so rare that she didn't know everything. She was one of those people who got angry and confused when they were proved wrong, as if she couldn't believe that her instincts might be fallible in some way. "You're not!" she said.

"No," I said. "I'm not. He's not my type."

That face, that pretty, pretty face, was so close. The memory of her kiss came rushing back at me, and my body reacted in all those horrible, wonderful ways that it did whenever she was near me.

"What's your type?" she breathed.

It was a short drive. And Jones Cooper was not the kind of guy to rush to fill a silence. Most cops know the value of keeping their mouths shut, understand that nervous people rush to fill in the quiet spaces where their anxious thoughts and guilty feelings tend to expand and become unbearable.

I thought about prying for more information about the case, but I figured it was risky. With that nonsense on Facebook, and the uncomfortable conversation I'd had with Detective Ferrigno, I figured it wouldn't be too long before I was talking to the police again. I didn't want Jones Cooper to have anything to add, like: *She kept asking about the search, wouldn't let it go. Even after I told her that we hadn't found anything.* I probably needed to call Sky. I was probably going to need a lawyer. Innocent people always think that they don't need lawyers. But I knew that innocent people need them most of all.

"Thanks for the ride," I said. We were pulling up the

gravel drive of the Coopers' lovely house. There was a warmly lit porch with a painted red swing, still a wreath on the door. In the spring, the walk to the front door and the edging along the porch were always alive with colorful perennials, cheerful and welcoming. A huge bare oak tree dominated the yard; I'd seen Cooper out there often, raking leaves. He seemed to take some satisfaction in it, had a meditative air about him as he worked. Otherwise, it was probably a job most people would hire out to a neighborhood kid. Did neighborhood kids still do jobs? Or were they too busy broadcasting themselves and their silly little lives on Facebook and playing Angry Birds?

"You have a lovely home," I said. I had opened the car door myself, but he had come around just the same.

He looked back at it. "It's a lot of work," he said. "I guess I don't always spend enough time appreciating it."

"Thanks again," I said. I know I felt his eyes on me. He had cop's eyes, searching, seeing, knowing. And I felt the heat of his gaze on my shoulders as I walked into the door of Dr. Cooper's office, which adjoined the house. I noticed, not for the first time, a plaque on the other side of the door. It read: jones cooper investigations. And there was a separate bell for what I imagined was another office space.

"Anytime," he called out. I turned back toward him, and he wore a slight, musing smile that I didn't much like. He was one of those, the ones that see.

217

18

Dear Diary,

I keep thinking that I'll have something nice to write here someday. But so far, that's not the case, as you know. I'm sorry.

My husband has grown ever more distant and cold. And when he's not an automaton in our life, our battles have become increasingly bitter, almost always escalating toward violence. He travels often now, seems to be gone more than he is here. And my son and I have grown used to living life without him. He's a guest, a visitor, and not always a welcome one. I think there's someone else. I wish I cared.

When you're young and in love, you only think of the future as a bright light that you will enter together. You never imagine that the day-to-day of work and home life and children is a spinning wheel that dulls down rather than sharpens your love. I can't even remember what I thought was so wonderful about him. I think it might have simply been that I thought he was nothing like my father.

I hate to say it, but it's better when my husband is not here. It's just easier, because when he's here I have to choose between them. There is a terrible tug-of-war between father and son, and I am the rope.

You've got it wrong, my husband said when I expressed this idea to him. You should never have given him so much power. I am your husband. He is our child. He doesn't get to hold one end of the rope. That's not how it should work.

I know he's right. When he's home, he holds up a mirror that shows how unhealthy my relationship is to my son. And I don't like to see it. Because it's not like I chose this; it's not as if I wanted things to be this way. It's just that there's a terrible chemistry between my son and me. His personality extracts all sorts of things from my personality that I didn't even know were there. Dysfunction isn't a choice, it's a disease. In parenthood, we only do what we know how to do. What I know how to do: cater to, coddle, acquiesce, comfort, and condone. Turns out what my husband knows how to do is run. He has dropped his end of the rope. And all I feel is relief— because I can never please both of them and you can't stop being a mother.

This is not what I've come to tell you, dear diary. And even as I sit here in this dim room, shame keeps me from writing. How can I tell what my son has done? I don't even know where to begin.

A couple of weeks ago, after he went to bed, my mother and I shared a glass of wine on the back porch. It was one of those fall evenings when the heat of Indian summer has left the air, but before the chill of winter has settled in. The humidity has disappeared for the season, taking with it the mosquitoes and gnats. And the air feels like someone just lightly touching your skin. The sun had set but the sky was still glowing. I was actually feeling good. I was enjoying working part-time at a local bookstore. My son hadn't been in trouble in his new school (of course, it was his fifth in five years and the year had just begun).

Maybe it was because she'd had more than her usual one glass of wine with dinner, or maybe it was because she'd been with him every afternoon that week while I worked.

"Darling," she said. "I have some things I need to get off my chest."

You have to know my mother, how easy she is, how unfailingly kind, how warm and funny. In my life, I have never heard her utter anything but the most patient and loving words. Even when my father was arrested, tried, and convicted of murdering five teenage girls while he was working as an office-equipment salesman—even when he was executed—she never said a bad word about him to my sister or me.

We had to move to another town, change our last name to my mother's maiden name. And, thankfully, since this was long before the age of the Internet, we were able to live a seminormal life in his wake. She never uttered a word, except to say that he was a man in terrible pain, who'd done horrible, unforgivable things. But that he'd always been a loving husband and father who had provided for us. And, of course, she'd never had any idea what he really was inside.

That was a true thing that we could cling to, she'd said. And it would serve us all if we could pretend that it was another man, a stranger, who'd killed those children. Because in a sense it was. I don't know about my sister, but that is indeed what I did. I pretended all my life that my father was not the man he was. And it worked for me.

It did not work for my sister. I secretly pitied her for how she suffered through years of therapy. I was angry with her for confronting my mother with her difficult and indignant questions: How could you not have known? And how could you counsel us to live in denial? How could you take us on a cruise the week he was executed? Did you think we could all run from the horror of our reality?

My mother just said she was sorry, but she did what she knew how to do. She was trying to protect us the only way she could. How could she have done more? There was no blueprint, no helpful book written on how to help your children move on from the murder conviction and execution of their father. Remember, she begged us, that she, too, was in terrible pain. And of course my sister and mother worked it out. I stayed away from the conversation, because I was really fine with denial, with holding it all in, pretending it never happened. That was so much easier. I wondered why my sister didn't see that.

But that's my mother, unseeing, uncomplaining, utterly accepting of the people in her life. She didn't like to talk about unpleasant things. So, I felt my whole body stiffen as we sat on the porch.

"I've been doing some research," she said. She cleared her throat. "Your sister has been helping me."

"Oh?"

"There's a place, a school that specializes in children like my grandson."

"Children like him?"

"Disturbed children," she said, looking straight at me. "Troubled children, dear. He is that. Of course you know he is."

A little gasp caught in my throat and my eyes filled. She reached out a hand and laid it on top of my arm.

"It's not your fault," she said. "But you need to do something. You know that your sister will never come here again with her children. Your husband has all but left you. And I have to say, I'm at my limit with his rages, and those visions—which, by the way, I don't believe are quite sincere—and all his lies. He's isolating you."

I sank my head into my hand, not knowing what to say.

"There's a school," she said again. "They're making some headway with children like him. There's therapy, discipline, a different way of teaching. The children live there eight months out of the year, so it's not forever. It's like boarding school."

A cold dread settled over me. What was she saying?

"I can't send my child away, Mother," I said softly. There was a crow sitting on the railing of our deck. He was big and jet black, looking straight at me. I tried to shoo him away, but he wouldn't go. I couldn't look at my mother, heard her take a swallow of wine and put her glass down on the table between us.

"He's getting older," she said. "And bigger. He'll be eight next month. How much longer will you be able to control him?"

My mother was a woman of allusions, of subtleties. She was the kind of mother that led you to making the right choices and then allowed you to take all the credit. This kind of direct confrontation was not her style. How desperate she must have been, how worried.

"What happened?" I asked her. "What did he do?"

She released a sigh, took another swallow of wine. "He tripped me," she said easily. "I fell down the stairs."

I looked at her. "What? When? Mom, are you hurt?"

I had noticed her limping and asked her about it on Tuesday. She'd said her sciatica was acting up, which I knew meant she was getting overtired. And I felt guilty for going back to work part-time. My son was resentful about it; my mother was getting too old to care for children every day. But I selfishly didn't ask her if it was all too much for her. I liked having a job, getting out of the house, talking to people. I felt like a real person for the first time in years. I was giddy with it.

"On Monday," she said. "He claimed it was an accident. But it wasn't."

"How do you know it wasn't?" I asked before I could stop myself. I so wanted her to be wrong about this.

She shook her head and offered me a sad, tight smile. She was still a pretty woman, petite and always put together, with her makeup done.

"I saw him, too late, stick his foot out," she said.

She was patient, not angry that I didn't want to believe her. There was a little quaver to her voice and the sound of it shattered me inside. "But really it was the look on his face that told the tale. He didn't run down after me. He just stood there. Honey, he smiled."

I grabbed her hand. "Oh, Mom, no. Please no."

"You must know what he is," she whispered. "You must."

I could hear my sister shrieking, *You knew what he was, Mom! You must have known. He slept in your bed.*

"The medication," I started, but didn't finish. His most recent diagnosis was bipolar disorder, which no one believed. But the medication seemed to be helping somewhat. He was calmer, sleeping through the night.

"There's no medication for that child," she said. "He is what he is, just like his grandfather. It's bad wiring, dear. I didn't know it when I saw it the first time, in my own husband. But I can't pretend not to see it now—the blankness, that black hole inside him."

"No," I said. It wasn't true. There was some goodness in

him, some of me, some of his father. I didn't believe he was irredeemable. A mother knows these things. And I told her as much.

"Then send him someplace where they can help him, where they can teach him to live right, if nothing else. You can't do it here. You're enabling him. I'm sorry, sweetie. But it's true. You just move him from school to school, hoping his reputation doesn't follow, that he doesn't hurt anyone else. But he always does."

I cried and cried. She stroked my hair and told me that she loved me, but that she couldn't be alone with him every afternoon anymore. I'd have to quit my job, or work only when he was in school. And anyway, it was about her time to return to Florida.

We stayed up talking for I don't know how long. In the end I agreed to look at the school, to consider it. I would call my husband in the morning and ask him to come home. Our situation, I would tell him, had reached a crisis and decisions had to be made. He would help me; I knew he would. In spite of everything, I knew he still loved me.

When I went upstairs to check on my son, his door was open. I knew that I had closed it because I always did. The light in his bathroom was on. Had he heard us? Had he been listening in, as we had often caught him trying to do? But he was sound asleep. Curled in his comforter, still very small for his age, and underdeveloped in every way but intellectually, he looked like the angel child I'd never had. I tried to imagine him pushing children from jungle gyms, biting classmates, hurting the class guinea pig, tripping his grandmother. All the things he'd done to others, which I knew were true but had never witnessed. And he looked so small, his cheeks flushed with sleep. How could he be what he was?

The next day, the call came from the school to pick up my son early. The principal was waiting for me the hallway near the main entrance. He was a young man, blond, pasty, wearing chic, slim black trousers and a crisp white button-down. I had liked him on sight when we first met; but all his warmth and joviality had disappeared.

My son was sitting on a couch in the office waiting, looking proper and innocent in his navy-blue-and-white uniform, with its little red crest embroidered on the chest of his polo shirt.

I sat beside him while the principal took a seat behind the desk.

"Would you like to tell your mother why we're here?" he asked. "Or shall I?"

My son shrugged, looked casually at his fingernails. "It was an accident," he said lightly.

"He gave a classmate a peanut butter sandwich today," said the principal. "This student has a severe nut allergy. And he was rushed to the hospital."

Mr. Cruz, that was his name. They are all running together, these school officials with their stern faces and devastating words. I had packed the lunch this morning—macaroni and cheese, baby carrots, an apple, some steamed broccoli in a thermos.

227

There was a strict no-nuts policy at this and most schools. Every mother with a school-age child knows that.

"I didn't pack him a peanut butter sandwich," I said.

"But he had one nonetheless," said Mr. Cruz. "He told the student that it was hypoallergenic."

"Why would he do that?" I said. I looked at my son, who was still looking at his nails. "Why would you do that?"

No answer.

"There was a kerfuffle on the playground a couple of days ago," said the principal. "The other student pushed your son. A teacher intervened."

"Why wasn't I made aware of this?"

"You were sent an e-mail," said the principal, straightening up his shoulders. "It was a fairly minor incident. But whenever there's a physical conflict, we inform the parents."

I never received an e-mail. But it suddenly occurred to me that I hadn't been home in the afternoons. He could have easily gone to my computer and deleted any message from the school. He was staring at me now.

"Is he all right?" I asked. "The child."

"He will be," said Mr. Cruz. "There have been other incidents, as you know."

"I'm sorry," I said. "I don't know what you mean."

"Do we have the right e-mail address for you?" he asked, looking at his computer screen.

"What other incidents?"

Mr. Cruz regaled me with my son's activities over his first

three weeks of school. He pulled the fire alarm on the first day. He was caught doing so by the security camera. He relentlessly taunted a little girl for being adopted, causing her to have an epileptic seizure brought on by stress (according to the girl's mother). He wrote profanity on the chalkboard during math class when he'd been asked to solve a problem on the board. Now this.

"Do you deny any of this?" I asked my son.

"No," he said. "But I did think I smelled smoke. That girl called me a shrimp, because I was the smallest kid in class. I was just giving her a taste of her own medicine. And the problem the teacher gave me was too easy. I had some extra time."

Here I saw what my mother had been talking about: the smile—the slight, cruel little turn at the corners of his mouth. I hadn't seen it before. My heart filled with dread at the sight of it. The principal asked him to wait outside, which he did, exiting in the most sullen way possible with a dark backward glance and a slam of the door. It was theater, though. He didn't care. He wanted to be thrown out; he wanted to be home with me.

"The sandwich was a clear retaliation for the events of the day before," said Mr. Cruz. "The other student is quite large, somewhat of a bully, and suffers from learning challenges. He did overpower your son, who has been taking some guff for his small size."

I felt myself nodding. The room was growing hot, and the principal's voice distant.

"So I see why he was angry. But the premeditation is what disturbs me, as it should you. He sought revenge in both cases and exacted it. That's not normal. The other things— the fire alarm, the profanity on the board, okay. We deal with that here. But this—it's disturbing. The other boy could have been killed. And he knew it."

"Yes," I said. "I agree that it's very upsetting. What do we do? We brought him here because you specialize in difficult children."

"We are not equipped to handle a behavior problem like your son. You'll need to find a facility more suited to his needs."

I couldn't believe how many different ways there were to express this sentiment, which I had heard a total of five times now. I don't remember the rest of the visit, or the car ride from the school to our house. I quit my job that afternoon, and I called my husband and asked him to come home. But it was too late.

Knowing what I knew, I shouldn't have left them to go to the store. I should have known that he heard my mother and me talking that night, that he knew I had already called the school upstate.

I should have had Mr. Cruz's words ringing in my ears: But the premeditation is what disturbs me, as it should you. He sought revenge in both cases and exacted it.

What happened is unclear. My mother's memory of the events is fuzzy. And my son claims—passionately and tearfully—that he had no idea what precipitated my mother's fall in the bathroom, where her head knocked against the marble tub and she lay unconscious until I returned home from the store. My son was upstairs playing video games, and it was another fifteen minutes of my putting groceries away with no sound from behind the bathroom door in my master bathroom (which she never used) before I got concerned. I finally pushed my way inside the unlocked door and found her lying there, still and pale.

She regained consciousness in the hospital, but has a severe concussion and her doctor wanted her to stay overnight for observation.

"What happened, Mom?" I asked her when we were alone. She'd told the doctor that a rug slipped out from beneath her and she'd crashed backward.

"A very common fall," he'd said. "You're very fortunate it wasn't worse, and that you weren't alone."

She swore to me that she didn't know. She thought the rug might have slipped, and in fact it did look as though it had been bunched up on the floor.

"But why did you use that bathroom, and not the guest bathroom?" I asked.

"The door to the other bathroom was locked," she said. "I thought he was inside, using the toilet, too embarrassed to answer when his grandma knocked on the door."

*

It could have been an accident. There is no evidence to suggest that my son had anything to do with it. I inspected the rug, and there was nothing except a little extra water on the floor. The shower often sprayed out onto the tile if it wasn't turned in the right direction. And perhaps I missed it this morning, didn't wipe down the floor well enough. Maybe it was my fault.

In my heart, I don't believe he would have willfully hurt his grandmother. I know he has problems, serious ones. But I know he loves her. In a lot of ways, he's like a scientist. He does things just to see what the outcome will be. It's not malice but a lack of empathy, an inability to envision consequences to others. You probably think that I am deeply in denial, diary. Maybe you're right. But I have to cling to it, my faith that my son does have a heart. It might be slower than other hearts, but it does beat.

My mother is sleeping now, and my husband is home with our son. He seemed relieved to be called home, to be needed. And he knows that we need to talk, to make some decisions about our life and about our boy. We have to help him, if we can. And we have to help ourselves, as well as everyone else who may cross his path.

19

Dr. Cooper was waiting for me in her doorway, looking motherly and concerned. She had a mass of copper curls and a pretty, freckled face that always seemed to hold precisely the right expression. In her aura, I felt myself relax.

"How are you doing?" she asked as soon as I was inside.

I shrugged. "Not too great."

"Okay," she said. "Come in."

Everything came tumbling out of me—everything to do with the police, with Luke, the scavenger hunt, Langdon. I told her about the Fakebook page and all the accusations there. She listened nodding, not reacting.

"Maybe your friend Ainsley has the right idea," said the doctor. "Have you thought about going home?"

"I don't have a home," I said with more venom than I would have intended. I would have liked nothing better than to go home, someplace where I was safe and loved and accepted. But that place didn't exist.

She pulled her mouth into a sympathetic line, bowed her head a little.

"To your aunt's house," she said. "You know your aunt would welcome you. She wants to be there for you."

"And, while I'm down there, drop in on my father? On death row?"

"You're angry," she said. "I get it."

"It doesn't really seem fair, does it?" I asked. "I mean, is it *me*? Doesn't this seem like quite the shit pileup?"

"It does," she agreed. "But we've talked about fairness before here. Life is not fair. Horrible things happen to people, sometimes in disproportionate amounts. And I'm sorry that all of this is converging on you."

You get what you get, and you don't get upset; that was one of my mom's favorite lines. But I always got upset. I'm sure I was as big a pain in the ass as Luke when I was a kid. Though I hope I wasn't as mean to my mother as he was to Rachel. I don't think I was.

"Someone who's ill equipped to deal with it, who has dealt with too much already," I said. I hated to be whiny, but I was really feeling sorry for myself.

"You *are* equipped to handle this," she said. "And I'll help you, no matter the outcome."

I hugged one of her big soft pillows to my center and curled myself up deep in the corner of her couch.

"Maybe we can table the discussion of your father for now," she said. "He has reached out to you. It's up to you whether you want to communicate with him or not. Maybe now is not the time to make the decision."

"What does he want?" I asked. "Did he tell you what he wants?"

She released a breath. "You want to address this tonight, with everything else going on?"

I nodded.

"He wants to know how you are. He wants to know if you are healthy and living well. He wants to know if you have managed to put the ugliness of your past behind you, what your plans are after graduation. And he wants to have a conversation with you. He said that there are things he needs to tell you that he doesn't want to share with me."

I stared at a painting she had on her wall. It was a soothing oil painting, swirls of gold and pink and white. I was always searching it for shapes. That night I saw a chrysalis with a butterfly folded deep inside.

"It's to his credit that he sought to reach you through me, rather than finding a way to reach you directly," she said. "It shows a true and honest concern for you, whatever his crimes."

"What else?" I could feel it, that other thing hovering in her consciousness.

"His private investigator, Paul Rodriguez, claims to have new evidence," she said. "Your father wonders if Mr. Rodriquez has reached out to you."

I didn't answer, just kept looking at the painting—now an angel, her wings curled protectively around her.

"I'll remind you that you don't have to talk to him or to the investigator."

"He's not innocent," I said.

Now I saw a tornado, twisting and turning, decimating the village beneath it, spitting up debris.

"I watched him bury her body," I said. This was not news to Dr. Cooper. "I sat there as he dug the hole in the ground and rolled her body, which was wrapped in our Oriental dining room rug, into the grave he'd dug. I lied for him, because I was afraid that he'd bury me right beside her."

She watched me carefully. "I understand," she said. "We've talked about this. You didn't actually see him kill her."

"No," I answered. "But who else? Who else?"

Who else?

My mother had a lover allegedly, according to the defense. Not a fling, or a one-night stand, not a brief encounter that never should have happened and that she lived to regret. She, allegedly, had a long, enduring love affair and friendship with a man other than my father. If it was true, I never knew about it, of course. That's not a thing one shares with her child, I imagine—not that I know anything about affairs or about parenting.

This affair was the reason, the police concluded, for my father's homicidal rage. The rage that caused him to murder her, dispose of her body, and then declare her missing. When I think about it, that she loved someone and he loved her, it gives me an odd sense of relief. I'm glad to know that somewhere in her life she was happy. Because she wasn't happy with us.

When I think back upon that afternoon, what I walked in on when I came home from school that day, my whole body freezes. Sometimes it's like a puzzle, shiny bright pieces scattered on the floor of my memory. Odd things, like a strange pair of shoes by the door, the tinkling of music coming from my mother's room. My palms slick and red with blood. The siren of my own screaming. My father standing in the kitchen weeping. I wasn't supposed to be home; art club had been canceled because our teacher was sick. I often wonder, though I try not to, how things would have been different if I had not come in when I did.

There were dates in her old calendar, including that afternoon, assignations marked only with the initial *S.* That's what led them to conclude that my mother was having an affair. But this man, this lover, this suspect for a time, he was never found. They'd been careful, very careful—almost as if they knew something horrible would happen. Or maybe he—the other man—was the only one who knew it. And he was able to disappear without a trace.

It was this man who my father claimed had killed his

wife. My father had found her murdered, he finally admitted. Then he hid her body, because he knew that he would be accused. Because he, too, was having an affair.

He has always claimed his innocence, that his only crime was acting in panic and hiding her murdered body. I've seen him interviewed; he's very convincing. And there is a whole camp of people who believe him, have been lobbying for his release for years. Maybe he believes it, too. Maybe, over the years, he has convinced himself that it's true. The psyche is a powerful thing, it can bend and obscure reality, turn it into exactly what we desire or expect. How much of the world is just a figment of our imagination, and the imaginations of those around us?

That's the kind of question that would have kept Beck and me up all night. How I wished she were there to talk to. She'd know what to say, how to comfort me, how to make the whole thing seem ludicrous. We'd fire up a joint and smoke it all away. She did like her mind-altering substances, our Beck, and I was certain she'd been the one taking my pills. Who else? Not the prim and proper Ainsley, who had run home to Mommy and Daddy.

"How about I write to him?" said Dr. Cooper. The room was feeling overwarm and I was so tired. "I'll tell him that you're struggling with some things right now and you're not up to a conversation with him or his investigator. That *when* you are—*if* you are, at some point—we'll get in touch."

238

That sounded good. It was an optimistic blow-off, a hopeful fuck-you. *I'll get in touch* is probably not the sentence someone on death row wants to hear. But then again, we're all on death row, aren't we? Most of us just don't know it. On the day she died, did my mother know it was her last day on earth, did Elizabeth—no pardon, no appeal, no stay of execution?

"Okay," I said. "That sounds like the right thing to do for now."

She handed me two prescriptions. "Dr. Black sent these by messenger. He said be careful with these once you get them filled, lock them up. He won't be able to bend the rules more than once. The street value of these drugs is apparently quite high, so the protocols are strict."

We talked a while longer. She advised me to stay off Facebook, and, yes, of course call my family attorney and let him know what was happening, get his advice before talking to the police again. She suggested again that I take a little hiatus to Florida, or that I ask my aunt and uncle to come up for support. But how could I? They did so much for me already and I did nothing but cause them trouble, ruin all their holidays and vacations just by being alive.

I was feeling better when there was a hard knock at the door that startled us both.

"Dr. Cooper," came a voice through the door. She was already up and moving forward. I wanted to call her back.

"It's Detective Ferrigno with The Hollows PD. Do you have Lana Granger in your office?"

"You are interrupting a session with a patient," she said. She opened the door and blocked the entrance with her body.

"I'm sorry, Maggie," said the detective. I could see his dark, bulky form outside. Then I was aware of the flashing lights through the window. "We need to bring Lana Granger in for questioning."

"This young person is in a fragile emotional state," said Dr. Cooper, still barring the door.

"I understand," he said. "But we still need to speak to Miss Granger." Did he lean on my name oddly? Did they know?

"Lana," said Dr. Cooper. Her face was pale with concern. "Write down the name and number of your attorney. I will call him and meet you at the police station. Do not say anything until someone is there to represent you."

"Okay," I said. She handed me a pad and pen and I did as she'd asked.

I saw the detective cast an annoyed look in her direction as she allowed him entry into her office. Then I gathered up my things and let him lead me outside to his squad car. I assumed that he was trying to rattle me by making such a big show of bringing me in. But he didn't know me very well.

*

They left me in a cool gray room for a while, where I sat patiently waiting. I kept my body still and my eyes focused on the table in front of me. If I had been smart, I'd have shed a few tears, looked frightened. I knew they were watching me; I could see the red light on the camera mounted in the far right corner of the room. They wanted you to fit a particular mold, and when you didn't, they were suspicious. That was one of the things that had sunk my father, that first aroused suspicion. He didn't seem worried enough when she was missing, grief-stricken enough when she was found. He didn't howl and collapse, didn't put on the show everyone expected to see. But we are a family of stoics; we aren't hardwired to display our feelings. Inside, my father was shattered. For two nights I listened to him sobbing in his empty bed while I lay alone in mine.

He and I never had much of a relationship. He traveled much of the time, and what I knew about him even as a child was that when he was around, my mother cried a lot. There was fighting, yelling carrying through the Sheetrock walls. He was dark-haired like me. He sat at the head of the table when he was home, and we ate dinner while he awkwardly tried to facilitate conversations. *So, tell me about school. What are your teachers like? How's the violin coming along?* We endured him.

When he was away, we often ate dinner in front of the television, picking out our favorite movies and sitting cross-legged on the floor in front of little standing trays. We painted in the afternoons, or went for long walks on the beach. Then I'd do my homework while my mother cooked our dinner. My early life with her—when we were alone—was quiet. I wasn't a normal kid. I had a few friends. Okay, I didn't have any friends, until I was much older. I had doctor's appointments and took medication. I was often overwhelmed by events at school. There were always problems, and I frequently needed to come home. I try not to think about it. I wasn't a nice little kid, and I always just wanted to be with my mother. How hard it must have been for her.

But I have trouble painting a picture of her now. Sometimes I can't remember her face, or the sound of her voice. Because I was a child, I knew her only as she related to me. That's why she has slipped away, I think. Because I am no longer a child, and she has been gone for so long.

What would she say to me now? *Take a deep breath*, she used to say when I spun out of control. *Just be yourself*, she'd advise when I was nervous about people or a new school (there were many schools). *Just do your best*. It was all she had. But unfortunately that was not the best advice for a kid like me.

The door opened and Detective Ferrigno walked in. He was a man who always looked tired, who always seemed to be carrying a burden. He sat heavily in the chair across from me and started to rub his eyes. He leaned his elbows on the table and then held me in his gaze. He smelled like hamburgers and onions.

"You and I need to talk about a few things," he said.

"I would prefer to wait until my attorney is present," I said.

"You're not under arrest," he said. He gave me a comforting shake of his head. "I just need your help."

I offered him an uncertain smile. "And I want to help. But I need to speak to my attorney first."

"Why?" he asked. His concern, his mystification, was not quite sincere. "Are you hiding something from me?"

I focused on details to calm myself. There was an analog clock on the wall that seemed to have stopped at ten past twelve. The gray paint was peeling in places, and there was a crack in the ceiling.

"Of course not." I put my hand on the faux-wood table. It was bolted to the ground, as was my chair.

"Then we don't need to go *there*, do we? You know, attorneys and all that."

I was done talking to him, communicated this by looking away from him and not answering. There was a rhythmic sound, blood pumping in my ears. I knew I didn't seem scared to him, but I was. What *was* this all about? What did they want from me?

"Okay," he said. "How about I talk and you just listen? Maybe you'll feel like chiming in?"

The fluorescent lights above us buzzed unpleasantly in

the thick silence of the room. He was waiting, watching me. I gave him an indifferent glance, then looked at the mottled laminate floor—easy for cleaning blood, vomit, what have you.

I think about you all the time, she said. Beck's voice was soft and her skin was so white it glowed in the moonlight. She was shivering. I wanted to reach out to touch her, but instead I wrapped my arms around myself.

Do you think about me? she whispered. *Do you ever think about that night?*

No, I lied. *I don't.*

She rolled over on her side, pressed up against my shoulder. Then she put her head in her hands and started to cry.

How can you be so cold? she asked, and the note of despair in her voice cut me to the bone. She was a girl who needed to love and be loved. She was all heat and noise; her energy burned and roared. Her anger was a hurricane, and her love was more terrifying than that. I felt like a glass vial beside her, empty and brittle, quivering in her thrall. Oh, I wanted to hold her, I did. I wanted to tell her that I loved her and that I thought about her all the time when we were apart. But I was too fragile and she gave off too much heat. I was about to shatter.

After a while she looked up at me. Her eyes were wet

and red, her cheeks flushed. She was so beautiful she glowed.

You don't have to hide, she said. She reached for my face and I didn't draw it away. *I know who you are.*

You don't, I said. My voice was hoarse and low.

But I do. She moved in closer, and I couldn't pull away from her. I tried to push her away, but it was a weak effort and she saw it for what it was, kept pressing in. Finally, I let her curl her arm around my neck and draw herself nearer, nearer until she was straddling me. She ran her fingers through my hair and now it was my turn to shake.

Shhh, she said. *It's okay. Let me love you.* And she said my name. My real name. I was shaken to the core by the sound of it on her tongue. She did know me. She knew all of me. *OhGodohGod, she knew everything*. I had never been more terrified.

And then she put her mouth to mine, and I wrapped my arms around her. Her kiss was so hot and wet, so sweet, and I let myself drown in it.

"This is what we know," Detective Ferrigno said. He started ticking his thumb and fingertips together. "We know that you and Rebecca had a fight big enough to draw attention to yourselves in the library and that you stormed out."

He waited, maybe looking for a reaction. Then he went on.

"We know that a few minutes later she followed you. Another student saw you walk the trail that led into the woods."

Again he paused, but I kept my gaze leveled at the wall.

"It was late and dark, and you claimed not to have been feeling well, and still you headed off onto one of the running trails."

Still, I wasn't going to say anything. He was too experienced to be agitated with my silence. So he just kept going.

"Rebecca went after you. She called to you, and you didn't acknowledge her. She, too, was witnessed heading onto that same trail."

He waited a moment, presumably to allow me to make a comment. But I had nothing to say.

"Two hours later, you emerged from the woods alone. No one ever saw Rebecca come out."

I picked a piece of lint off my sleeve, an action that seemed to annoy him. It was a cavalier act of body language. It said, I don't care about you or what's happening here. Now I saw a flash of temper on his face.

"You have lied to me a couple of times now," he said. "And that doesn't look very good."

I cleared my throat, but still I said nothing. He had all the information, right? What did I have to contribute? Nothing.

"My question is, what transpired between the two of

you in those woods. What was going on in there for two hours?"

I folded my arms across the table and laid my head down. He cocked his to the side, then he leaned back in his chair. I watched it tilt precariously and thought how embarrassed he'd be if he fell. Outside, I heard the sound of voices, one of them raised.

"You know what I don't like? What's bothering me?" He was talking to me but looking toward the door. He knew time was running out; soon my lawyer would be here and he'd have to leave. I blinked my eyes to show him I was listening.

"Two girls go missing from the same small university in two years. And both of them are connected to you."

I thought about Luke's snide remark. It's a statistical anomaly, he'd said. True. When you add my mother into the equation, things start to look really strange, don't they? I'm a misery magnet. Anyone connected to me had better watch out.

"The investigator on that case thought that you were hiding something. Elizabeth's boyfriend claimed, still claims, that they never fought that night. Someone saw *you* arguing with her that night, though."

That sent a little jolt through me.

"No," I said, before I could stop myself. "She was upset. I was trying to comfort her, to calm her down."

"Ah," he said. "She speaks. What was she upset about?"

"I don't know," I said. "She was really drunk. And so was I. I went to get her a glass of water, to try to help her sober up a little. But when I got back to where we were, she was gone."

"Hmm," he said.

"Her death was ruled an accident," I said.

"There was no evidence of any foul play," he conceded. "But the investigator on the case? He was never quite satisfied with the ruling."

Jones Cooper had done his investigating back then, that was for sure. I had been over and over the fuzzy details of my last encounter with Elizabeth. I did remember now saying that I'd gone to get her a glass of water. *It's okay*, I told her. *Just stay here. I'll get you a glass of water. You need to sober up.* The drunk leading the drunk.

But I didn't remember if I ever actually gave her the water. I shouldn't have left her. I should have dragged her with me. She had been shaking, tears of blue mascara on her face. Why did I leave her? I told Jones Cooper all of this a hundred times. I sensed he never believed me. He sensed that I was hiding something, and he was right. But it had nothing to do with Elizabeth. I told Detective Ferrigno all of it again.

"What does any of this have to do with Beck?" I said. My voice broke, betraying the depth of my emotion. And he looked surprised by it, drew himself back a little with a frown. In general, I knew myself to have a disconcertingly flat affect. It couldn't be helped. It had to do with my meds, without which, I assure you, I could be quite the opposite.

There was a loud knock on the door then, and Sky Lawrence walked in, bringing with him the scent of expensive cologne and an aura of authority. He was stooped and ancient, with a shiny bald head and a suit that looked too big, as though he'd taken something that had suddenly shrunk him in his clothes. He was not aging well. He'd always seemed old, but I didn't remember him ever looking like a golem. Still, he drew all the energy in the room to him when he entered.

There was some banter between him and the detective, something about leveling charges or releasing me. And after a few minutes, I was exiting the room with Sky. We walked down a long hallway together until we entered a waiting room where I saw two people I didn't expect to see: Langdon and my aunt Bridgette.

My aunt rose to greet me, took me gingerly in her arms. I knew she expected me to pull away, but I found myself clinging to her and her to me. Maybe Beck had melted something in me that night, something that had frozen solid. But the thaw was more pain than pleasure.

They took me back to my dorm, which immediately revealed itself as a bad idea. There were so many people milling about that it looked like a county fair. A gaggle of reporters hovered around the front entrance, being kept at bay by some of the university security guards. I wanted to hide my head and run as we exited the vehicle, take cover from the storm of questions and judgments. But I forced myself to walk at a normal pace from the car to the dorm, flanked by Langdon, my aunt, and Sky. Apparently, the news was out that I had been brought in for questioning.

Are you a person of interest in the case? What were you two fighting about? Where is Beck? Were you lovers? It was a hailstorm of idiotic and sensational questions, but I kept my face blank and didn't speak—or breathe—until we were inside. The lobby lounge area went silent as I entered, which was almost worse than the shouting outside. I felt everyone's eyes on me as we moved toward the elevator. We all rode it in silence, my aunt holding tight to my arm, up to my floor. I could smell her perfume; it was warm and flowery, a bed of poppies where I wanted to lay my head down and sleep forever.

But when we entered the dorm room, we found Frank and Lynne waiting for us. They sat at our small bistro table, drinking tea, looking shrunken and fatigued.

"Mr. and Mrs. Miller, this might not be the best time," said Langdon on seeing them.

"And when would be a better time?" asked Lynne. Her voice was shrill and quaking. "Our daughter is missing and Lana was the last person to see her. They went into the woods together and only Lana walked out. She knows something about Rebecca. What is it, Lana? Where is she?"

"I don't know where she is," I answered.

"They found her scarf during the search today," said Frank. He ran a shaking hand through his hair. "That pink chiffon scarf she always wore. There was blood on it."

My aunt moved in to comfort her, led her over to the couch with an arm around her shoulder.

"We know she cares about you," said Frank. He was leaning over the table toward me, one arm extended out in a kind of reaching gesture. "If you know something, now really is the time to tell us. We're coming unglued here."

"Lana isn't going to be answering any questions tonight," said Sky. He looked so odd in this context. He didn't belong in this part of my life, and he seemed like one of those Colorforms figures from when I was a kid. He was flat and plastic, affixed to a scene that wasn't real in the first place.

"Where's your room?" he asked, and I nodded toward the closed door. I was surprised that the police hadn't searched it. That couldn't be far off, I thought as Sky led me along.

"She's done this before, Mr. Miller," I heard Langdon say gently to Frank.

"Not like this," Frank answered. He shook his head

vigorously, as if he was trying to shake something off. "This is different."

Lynne was crying now, really sobbing, and the sound made me uncomfortable in the extreme. As Sky closed the door behind me, I lay down on my bed. I could hear the noise outside my window, the voices outside my door. I wished everyone would just go away.

"Is there anything I need to know?" he asked. He sat at my desk and took a pair of glasses from his pocket. "Of course, I'm not a criminal attorney. If it comes to that, I know someone."

I liked his casual, practical nature, as if nothing would surprise him and as if there were a contingency plan for any outcome of this situation.

"No," I said. "There's nothing you need to know."

He looked at me through his round, gold-framed spectacles. "There is the matter of some missing time. Two hours, right?"

"I was in the woods," I said. "I go there a lot, to be alone."

"Were you alone?"

"I need to sleep," I said. "I've never been so tired."

He regarded me a while longer, then stood with effort, picked up his briefcase.

"Get some rest," he said. "But be prepared to talk in the morning."

I pulled up the covers and curled myself up. I wondered

where my aunt would sleep, how long Langdon would stay, what tomorrow would hold. I thought about Luke and the raging tantrum I'd left him in, his next clue. But most of all I thought about Beck, kept hearing over and over the last words she said to me: *Why are you doing this to me?*

It was about 2 a.m. when my phone woke me. I dug it out of my bag and answered it without looking at the caller ID.

"Beck," I said. I was still half asleep, dreaming about her.

"No," he said. His voice was mocking. "Still can't find your friend?"

"Luke," I said. What a little asshole. "Do you know what time it is?"

"What kind of a question is that?" he asked. "Of course I do."

"What do you want?" I asked. I fell back against my pillow. Sleep had abandoned me completely; I was wide-awake now.

"Are you alone?"

"What do you want?" I asked again.

"I wondered how you were doing with our game."

I got out of bed and walked to the window. The crowds outside had dissipated, and the room beyond my door was quiet. I heard the distant drumbeat of panic that I'd heard when I first discovered the next clue. I had so much else to worry about that it had quieted for a time. But now the rhythm was picking up again, a steady jungle beat.

"Do you know where the next clue is?" he asked. His voice sounded deeper, older than I knew it to be. Perhaps because he was talking softly. I thought about hanging up and calling his mother. But I stayed on the line. The truth was, I liked talking to him. At least he was interesting, something else to focus on besides my own misery.

"Maybe," I said.

These clues, all to do with the tragic secrets and lies of tortured souls … well, let's just say they spoke to something deep inside me. What did this boy know about me? And how? And why was he teasing me with it?

"If you know where it is, I suggest you go find the next clue," he said. "There isn't much time." He sounded like a comic-book villain, which I guess was his only frame of reference.

"Tomorrow," I said.

"How can you be so cold?"

It was a whisper, but he might as well have screamed it. Those words, Beck's words, shot through me. I thought of the dirt on his bike tires, the form slipping into the shadows. He was there that night. He saw.

When he started laughing, I hung up. When he called back, I turned off my phone.

*

I got dressed swiftly and walked into the living area. What did he mean, time was running out? What had he seen that night? Who had he told? Did he know where Beck was?

I thought I was alone in the suite, then I saw my aunt's suitcase and discovered her sleeping in Ainsley's bed. I wanted to wake her, thank her for coming, and then ask her politely to go back to Florida. Things were about to get ugly, and she'd been through enough.

But I knew that it wouldn't fly, and if I woke her up, she'd try to pull me into conversation. I just couldn't talk anymore. The worst part about my aunt is that she knows me. That's the problem with family. You can put on a mask and a costume for the rest of the world, but you can't hide from the people who changed your diapers.

I pulled on my coat and slipped from the room, moved down the dim hallway, and took the fire stairs down to the laundry level in the basement. It was empty, but well lit. I followed the gray hallway, the scent of fabric softener heavy in the air, and wound up at the back door that let out near the bike racks.

As I rode through the night, my legs pumping, my heart racing with exertion, I thought about what Rachel had told me. Luke manipulated the other students in his class, teased certain behaviors out of them. *Because he can*, she said. *Because he's bored and needs constant stimulation.* He'd hooked me. When I pulled on the line, he reeled me in. We pick our own predators.

It wasn't long before I saw headlights come up behind me. I pulled over into the shoulder and turned, expecting to see Detective Ferrigno or a squad car. How was I going to explain this? Instead, it was Langdon's Volkswagen. He pulled up ahead of me and climbed out of the car.

"What in the world are you doing now?" he asked. His voice bounced off the street, echoing strangely. His palms were open as he approached me. "Have you completely lost your shit? I mean, are you not in enough trouble?"

"Are you following me?"

"I was sleeping in my car outside your dorm," he said. He looked embarrassed suddenly, ran a hand through his mass of hair, gazed down at the road between us. "I was worried about you. I had a feeling you were going to do something crazy."

"I figured out the next clue," I said. It sounded lame, even to me.

He closed his eyes and shook his head. "Are we talking about that stupid scavenger hunt? We're not. Are we?"

I dropped the bike and walked over to him, handed him the second poem. If he remembered that I'd lied to him about finding it, he didn't bring it up. He stood squinting at it.

"I can't read this," he said finally, handing it back. "Not in this light."

I read it to him, and when I was done he was watching me with an expression that I couldn't decipher.

"This is really getting fucking creepy," he said. "Get in the car."

I went to the car, and he retrieved my bike, hefting it into the trunk. I thought he was going to take me home. But instead, he kept driving ahead, heading toward The Hollows Wood.

20

Dear Diary,

It has been a while since I last visited with you. And a lot has happened since then. I think it's funny how life is like that, forever dashing your expectations. You just start to accept the conditions of your world when everything around you changes again.

I am in love. There, I said it. It's true, and it's a magical feeling. I had forgotten what a head trip is a good love affair. And after years of just one shitty thing following the next, it feels like heaven. I go to sleep thinking about him. I wake up thinking about him. I am a teenager, giddy and nervous, waiting for the phone to ring. And it's delicious.

Today, I met him at a swank hotel in town. After I dropped my son off at his new school, I hurried home and showered. I changed into a new dress I bought for the occasion, a simple black sheath. For the first time in years, I had bought underwear that wasn't designed solely for comfort—a lacy push-up bra and matching bikini panties. And guess what?

I've still got it. I am not just the beleaguered mother of a troubled child. I had my hair done a week ago, punching up the gold highlights that had turned mousy and flat, opting for a shoulder-length straight bob. And when I look in the mirror, I see her. The girl I used to be—bright and happy and full of hope. I am not her. But I remember her.

The valet took my car, and I stood on the steps of the hotel and looked out into the harbor. I could hear the halyards clanging on the boats and smell the salt in the air. Florida. We have moved to Florida, a new school, a new life. I think, I dare to hope, that we have done the right thing.

I stood in the doorway of the grand dining room. The high mirrored ceilings and enormous chandeliers reflected the light streaming in from the floor-to-ceiling windows. And the tinkling of silverware and the hum of conversation were a kind of music that carried me away. I drifted over to the table where he waited for me. He rose and took me into his arms. We didn't linger long over lunch.

And the good news, the best news of all, is that this man who's setting me on fire—well, we're already married. Yes, that's right, diary. I am having a red-hot, sizzling, secret fling with my own husband.

After my mother's accident, she decided that it was time for her to go back to Florida. Who could blame her?

And, maybe in a way, it was a blessing. I couldn't lean on her anymore. I had to call my husband that night and ask him to come home for good. I told him that I needed him and

that I couldn't manage alone, and that he was right. I'd made
so many mistakes relating to our child, and I needed him to
help me rebuild our family.

And, you know what? He did it. He made changes in his
job—less travel, more time working from home. We sat down
with our son and we told him that things were going to
change. That he had one opportunity to change his behavior
in this new place, in a new school, or we would have no
choice but to send him to the place my mother had
suggested.

There was a school in Florida, not very near my mother
and sister, about two hours south. We decided to move there,
enroll him in their new program for troubled children, and
build a new life, start over. We would be closer to my family,
but not so close as to burden them with our problems.

It's an understatement to say that our son wasn't happy.
But I think that he saw us, for the first time, as a united front
and he realized that he had very little choice. No more divide
and conquer.

The move was not easy; none of us really relished the idea
of living down south. But the school was highly regarded, and
they'd been having success with cases like ours. Through
education, medication, and therapy, children like our son
were being managed and helped. There were even therapy
and education session for us. My husband and I saw it as a
last chance to have a seminormal life with our child.

He would board four nights a week at the school and

return home to us Friday through Sunday night. This served to remove him from any dysfunctional relationships that might be contributing to his illness (whatever that was—we've had as many diagnoses as there are out there, from bipolar, to ADHD, to schizophrenia, to borderline personality, to malignant narcissism). This was the hardest part, because he and I had never been apart.

I don't have to tell you how all of this went. The rages, the tears. He locked himself in a bathroom for eight hours. He tore the curtains off the wall in his room. He tried to set the clothes in his closet on fire. But the difference was, this time, I didn't seek to comfort and coddle. I didn't give in to his demands. I held back and let my husband handle our son. And, guess what? He did a much better job than I ever had.

Our son seemed to calm under my husband's firm guidance. If our boy was fire, my husband was cold water. With my husband, tantrums and breakdowns didn't escalate the way they did with me. I would lie on the bed in my room and listen to the high-pitched sound of my son's voice, the low, easy rumble of my husband's, and then silence or even— imagine—laughter.

The night before he left for school was the hardest. I lay beside my son on his bed while he begged me not to send him away.

"I'll be good, Mom," he said. "Don't send me to that place."

And everything inside me hurt, but I held my ground.

"It will be fine," I said. Even though I wasn't sure I believed this. "And it's not forever. We'll all learn how to do better together. And then you'll come home. Anyway, it's just four nights away."

He sobbed. And after he finally fell asleep, so did I. In the morning, my husband took him. My son didn't even look at me. He wouldn't even say good-bye. I told myself that this was the first step toward normal.

And something happened while he was away that week. I expanded. I stretched out and became myself again. I didn't spend my whole day dreading the call from his school, or bracing myself for breakdowns over homework or what was for dinner. I didn't worry about his nightmares, or his visions, or his lies, or who he might hurt. For the first time he was in a place where they were actually equipped to handle all of it. And toward the middle of the week, over pizza and a bottle of wine, I fell in love with my husband again.

We're hiding it from our son, this love affair we're having, this newfound happiness. The weekends are still hard, and Sunday the worst of all. He hates the new school, of course, but we're already seeing changes. And we're learning that it is okay for him to be unhappy and to deal with it. He'll need to change his behavior to be happier, and that's something we haven't taught him. Because when he's been unhappy, I've tried to change the world to make him happier. I never asked him to be accountable for his own happiness. And for someone like my son, who has emotional challenges, this failure on my part has had some terrible consequences. Another child might have just been whiny, or spoiled or entitled. Our boy is filled with rage when things don't go his way.

We feel that it would set him back if he knew how really happy we were while he was away at school. I know; that's another bad mother badge for me. But you don't understand; you can't. Normal children demand all of you, night and day. They want and deserve to have you all to themselves, some of the time at least. But troubled children want all of you and then more and more. They want things inside of you that you didn't even know were there. They mine the depths of you, pillage every resource and then still it's not enough. I have been filling myself up again—spending time with my husband, working out, reading, seeing films. I've applied for a job at the local bookstore café, just something to reconnect me to the world, to my love of literature. When our boy comes home on the weekends, I'm a better mother, a better person. I am fresh to the fight on Friday afternoon.

Since the first time I've started visiting with you, diary, I feel strong. I am in love again. I am hopeful for my son and for our family. I am almost afraid to say it. But I really believe, in my deepest heart, that everything is going to be all right.

21

Once I pushed a little boy off the jungle gym at school. I won't forget the look on his face as he fell. The wide surprise in his eyes, the O of his mouth as he felt himself tilt off the metal surface and gravity took him down hard. He landed on his arm funny and it broke, twisted at an unnatural angle beneath him. There was a snap, an ugly sound that caused me to cringe inside. And then a loud wail of pain and fear. A swarm of adults flew from their playground posts. I stood above him, looking down. Much was made of my "flat affect" in that moment, my total lack of remorse.

It was one of several times I was removed quickly from a school and installed in another. People looked at me strangely. The teacher, who had been so warm, was suddenly stiff and cool.

"He fell," I remember lying.

"No," said the teacher, who had been on the playground. "I saw you push him. Why did you do it?"

"He made fun of me," I managed.

But I was young, unable to articulate my feelings. The fact was that this boy had been quietly and surreptitiously torturing me since the first day of school. I was small for my age. I had a very high IQ, was separated out for gifted programs. And this overdeveloped mouth-breather, for whatever reason, had it in for me. He pulled my hair, stole my pencil box, hid my show-and-tell. I dreaded him, dreamed about him, lay awake at night worrying about what he'd do the next day. I didn't tell anyone about him. Because I was such a chronic liar, no one ever really believed the things I said. As a child, I had what I can only describe as daydreams. I saw people who weren't there, imagined conversations with them. I thought they were ghosts sometimes. I heard voices in my head that told me to do strange things, like wash my hands fifteen times, or avoid a certain food all day, otherwise my mother would die. It was part dream, part imagination, part lie. It's impossible to explain. Anyway, that's why no one ever believed me anymore.

My fear and rage toward this boy was a throbbing, swelling thing that lived inside me. That afternoon, he'd eaten my sandwich. So I was hungry, as well as miserable. When he came up behind me on the jungle gym and whispered in my ear that I was too small for third grade, that I should stay with the babies in preschool, the thing, the white-hot rage that was always simmering, expanded and exploded from me. I jumped up and spun around and used all my strength to knock him back.

The truth was, I didn't think he'd fall. I was pushing him *away*, not too concerned with where he'd *go*. It was true that I did not feel remorse that day, though I do now. What I felt more than anything was relief. He'd stay away from me now. They always do, you know, when you really hurt them. The bullies always stay away then; they're cowards at heart.

And curiosity was the other big thing I felt. I was deep in wondering about that snap, and the broken bone, and how would they fix it, and how bad would it hurt. And what would the body do inside to knit that broken thing back together. And I couldn't stop thinking about that; I was totally focused inside on those questions, coming up with theories and wondering who I could ask or what I could read that would give me all the information I wanted. So that's why I seemed flat, though somewhere deep inside, I *was* upset. It was just buried deep under layers and layers of manic thoughts and strange voices.

Dr. Cooper and I have talked this through. I understand who I was then better now that I'm older. There was a little bit of OCD, a little bit of my being too intellectually smart while emotionally underdeveloped. There was my hormonal imbalance, which has corrected itself mostly since puberty. There are other theories, too, about what might be wrong with me. But that's the thing about mental illness; there's no such thing as a cookie-cutter diagnosis. We're all crazy in our own special way. Some of us just have it worse than others.

Langdon and I were trekking through the cold, haunted woods. He was grumbling and complaining, tripping every few feet.

"I'm not really the outdoor type," he said.

"No kidding."

Prior to our activities over the last few days, I don't recall ever seeing Langdon out of doors. He was a man who seemed designed to dwell only in a library or classroom, possibly in a bookstore café, sipping some type of warm, herbal beverage from a travel mug. Not that I was throwing any stones; my feet were growing numb and that heavy fatigue that had settled over me felt like a weight on my back.

We came to the clearing and I saw the decrepit old barn sagging in the moonlight. It looked like it was built from cards, might crumble onto itself with a good wind. A shiver of dread moved through me. I froze at the edge of the trees and found I couldn't go farther.

"He brought her out to a place like this and buried her body."

Langdon stood beside me. He seemed to intuit that I was talking about my life, not about the life that had ended here.

"I watched him do it," I went on.

I could see my father digging and digging while I sat shaking and crying. I kept watching the rug, willing it to move. Maybe she was still alive. But no, her skull was shattered.

The shape of it; I'll never forget that or all the blood. "I watched him bury her."

He dropped an arm around me. "I'm sorry," he said. "I can't imagine what you've been through."

"Luke knows about me," I said. "He must. A body buried in the woods? But how did he find out?"

It was a half admission. I didn't tell him about the call, or how Luke was taunting me, what he had said. If I told him that, I'd have to tell him everything, and I couldn't. I couldn't tell him what happened between Beck and me, and how Luke seemed to have some knowledge of that. There were so many layers to my lies, so many moving parts to my problems. I was becoming tangled in the fishing line of my deceptions.

"So that's what this is about," he said. "That's why you're so hooked into this game."

I folded my arms around myself, gave a single nod of my head. It was obvious, wasn't it? Only an instinct for self-preservation would have me this desperate to follow his clues.

"Who else knows about your past?"

"You," I said. "Beck." But of course neither of them knew everything. "Dr. Cooper."

There was no connection between the three of them, no place for them to intersect and exchange information about me. Not that either Beck or Dr. Cooper would share anything about me with some strange kid even if the opportunity arose. I said as much. Neither of us made a move toward the clearing or the barn. It was spooky, even for me, who prided myself on not fearing anything.

"And what about the first clue?" asked Langdon. "I thought you said it didn't have any meaning to you."

"My father tried to kill himself in prison," I said. "But, unfortunately, he didn't succeed."

I felt Langdon's eyes on me. It was kind of a callous thing to say, and I could feel him analyzing my words, my demeanor, like any good shrink would. But there you have it. I wished my father were dead. He deserved to be dead. Not her; my mother should have been alive and none of this shit should have been happening. I couldn't wait until they pumped his body full of poison. He'd turned my life into a horror movie, and now he wanted closure. Fuck him.

"So you think Luke knows that?"

"Apparently."

"There was nothing else about that clue that resonated with you?"

I could feel him pressing at me. He didn't buy that it was just about the suicide. And that's because it wasn't.

"No," I said. "Nothing."

Again, the silence of his analysis. I turned to look at him and his face was paler than usual in the moonlight. I heard an owl calling, and something rustling in the leaves caused us both to start. A black cat hurried from the brush and crossed our path. Perfect. As if my luck wasn't bad enough.

"You've forgotten the other possibility," said Langdon. "That this is about Luke and not about you at all."

But I didn't think it was, not after the telephone conversation we'd just had. The moon moved from behind the clouds and the clearing was washed in a silvery-blue light. I moved toward the barn, and after a moment Langdon followed. He reached out for my arm.

"Maybe this is a bad idea," he said. "We should just go."

I shook him off and kept walking. Aunt Bridgette and Dr. Cooper were always going on about how hiding from who I was and what had happened to me was just a temporary fix. *At some point, you're going to have to face it*, said my aunt. *You're going to have to own it. Until then, it owns you.*

My aunt, my mother, and my grandmother had all moved and changed their names after my grandfather was convicted of the crimes he had committed. My aunt said that she used to lie awake at night, imagining what would happen if anyone discovered that she was the daughter of a murderer. Now she has a blog where she bares it all. It's embarrassing and painful to read, but she's received some positive attention for it. And she's established a foundation to help the families of convicted murders. I think that's why she's so hell-bent on "helping" me. *You should write about your experiences, put them on paper. There's power in claiming and narrating your life.* But I don't want to see those words on the page. My story is more complicated than Bridgette's. And I can't just cast my mother and myself as victims and

271

my father as the villain. It's so much more complicated than that. We are all complicit in our own disasters, aren't we?

But there was something inexplicable about Luke, about his trail of bread crumbs leading me into the forest—the pull was inexorable. Maybe it was time. Everything was rising up, and it was time to face it or be swallowed by it.

There was a hole in the ground, cordoned off by wooden posts and a frayed piece of crime-scene tape: Marla Holt's grave. A door-size piece of wood had been laid over the opening, but it had clearly been moved aside a number of times. From where I stood at the edge, I could see beer cans and cigarette butts accumulating at the bottom. People had no respect for anything, it seemed. A woman had died here, been murdered and buried. And yet some people still apparently considered it a cool place to party.

I kept walking toward the barn.

"Seriously," Langdon called. He was lingering at the edge of the grave. "That doesn't look safe. Don't go in there."

But I kept moving and he didn't come after me. He seemed frightened now. I always knew he was kind of a wimp; I didn't hold it against him. I assumed he'd come in after me if he needed to, but there was no reason to act the hero until it was necessary. He was nothing if not completely rational.

I stood in the doorway and heard a whistling where the light wind outside was finding its way in through the cracks and gaps in the rotting wood. There was graffiti on the wall, the usual unimaginative scrawls: **Tami luvs Justin TLUV4EVA** and **Justin Bieber Rules** (really?) and **Go Fuck Yourself Trevor**. Liquor bottles, cigar and cigarette butts carpeted the dirt floor, a filthy, careless confetti. There was a little pit where someone had stupidly built a fire. I saw used rubbers, and a composition notebook covered in something red and gooey, magazines faded and swollen with moisture. The whole place was a testament to how badly people sucked, how stupid and boring they were, how totally base. Places of neglect always made me hate the world, how no one takes care of anything, or worries about the consequences of their actions. Beck would have understood that. I could have told her that and she would have nodded her head, and said, *Fucking losers*. But she had abandoned me, just like everyone else.

I walked a careful circle around the space and looked for something shiny and new in the sea of rotted debris, a straight line in a chaos of furled and uneven edges. The moon was bright, so I could see fairly well and I didn't see anything. But part of me knew that Luke wouldn't have put anything in here. He wouldn't have liked it in the barn; the disorder of it would have unsettled him. And I knew that because it unsettled me.

He wouldn't have lingered looking for a good place to

hide his clue, someplace obvious but not too obvious. I knew then where he'd left it. In the grave, of course. Because that was the worst place to hide it—the place that would most upset me.

When I returned to the grave, I saw that Langdon had moved aside the wooden cover and climbed inside. I found that very surprising. It takes some sangfroid to climb into an abandoned grave filled with who knows what kind of garbage. He was lifting himself out as I approached, and then stood panting from the effort, dusting off his pants.

"Why did you do that?" I asked him. Suddenly I had the strong sense that someone was watching us. I scanned the open field, the trees around us. Maybe the police were fol-lowing me. It would make sense, since they seemed to think that I had something to do with Beck's disappearance. Now they seemed to think I had something to do with Elizabeth, too. But I didn't see anything in the dark shadows.

"I saw something," he said. He was bent over, still out of breath. He was one of those thin people who were out of shape in spite of outward appearances. He was sedentary, a creature of intellect. His brain was so big, he hardly needed his body at all. At least that was my impression of Langdon. I remembered what Beck had said that night. *I heard he has a boyfriend in the city.* Was it true? I didn't know; we didn't have that kind of relationship. Usually there was a careful, respectful distance between us. This was as close as we'd ever been.

"What did you find?"

He had an envelope in his hand. I saw my name scrawled on the surface, but it had already been opened.

"You opened it?" I said as he handed it to me.

He shrugged. "Sorry," he said. "Curiosity killed the cat and all that. I thought better of reading it, though."

I snatched it from him. I kept hearing Luke raging about how I shouldn't have told anyone and how it was our game.

"Why are you here?" I asked him.

He glanced toward the trees, around the clearing, as if sensing, as I had, that we were being watched.

"I don't know," he said. He offered a weak smile. "I'm your adviser. I'm advising you."

He looked a little embarrassed, with a half smile and a hike of his shoulders. He put his hands in his pockets, keeping his thumbs out. He started rocking a little up on his toes. The result was that he looked boyish and unsure of himself. I unfolded the envelope and took out the sheet of paper. It was the stationery I'd seen in Rachel's drawer, from the box she kept next to her journal—white linen with a silver-embossed edging.

"You didn't read it?"

He shook his head, but I wasn't sure if I believed him. My hands were shaking, from the cold, from fear. The stress I was under was like a vise, slowly tightening every second. Dr. Cooper had left a note for me at the police station.

She'd apparently waited until my aunt arrived. They wouldn't let her in to see me, my aunt had said. I was supposed to call her when I got home. *Don't hesitate to call me. Don't let the pressure get too intense. And don't forget your meds.*

The smart thing to do would have been to hand the letter to Langdon, go back to my dorm room, and let my aunt take me back to Florida—if the police would let me go. The truth was, I really couldn't handle this. And Luke's game seemed, in that moment, like it might be the thing to push me right over the edge.

I didn't want to read it. I wanted to tear it up and throw it away. But, of course, by the light of the moon, I did read it. Curiosity didn't kill only the cat.

You shouldn't have let her touch you.
You shouldn't have let her see.
You should have known all along that
You belong to me.

Where did she go when you left her?
Why did she run away?
Why is it that no one you love ever seems to stay?

She knows all your secrets.
She knows all your lies.
Guess what?
So do I.

Inside the envelope was the tiny gold star on a chain, the one I'd given to Beck, its clasp ripped away. Everything inside me went still. And I knew two things. I was in deeper trouble than I had imagined. And Luke Kahn had not written that note.

22

"There's money," I said. "Lots of money. And I'll get it all when he dies."

"How much?"

"I'm not sure," I told her. "More than two million, I think. A lot of it went toward his defense and appeals. But there was a lot to begin with. Old money, generations of wealth which he inherited later in his life."

"And it's yours?"

"After he dies," I said. "Or some of it when I turn thirty. Whatever comes first."

Beck liked the idea of money, the way people who have never had money like the idea of it. They think it's a kind of magic, a panacea, the cure for all of life's woes. They imagine dream vacations and hired help, clothes and cars, yachts and jewelry. Only people who have money know the truth about it. It makes life easier, sure. But it doesn't fix any of the important things that break and are lost. It doesn't bring back the dead, or turn back the clock. It might look nice on the outside, but it doesn't change anything on the inside. No matter where you go, or how you get there, like my aunt is so fond of saying, there you are.

"And the money is still his, even though he's in jail?" asked Beck.

"Yes," I said. "His lawyer manages it for him. But it's not like they can just seize your assets because you went to jail. My mother's family never filed a civil claim. No one ever saw the point in that."

"The point is to get his money," she said.

"They already have money," I said.

The conversation annoyed me. Beck had her share of angst, but as far as any real grief was concerned, she was completely innocent.

I found myself thinking about this for some reason as I stood holding the paper in my hand. I didn't take the necklace out of the envelope, let it sit in the crease at the bottom.

"What does it say?" Langdon asked.

I folded up that paper and put it in the envelope. There was a siren going off in my head, loud and long, more like an air-raid horn.

"It's private," I said. He must have read it. How could he have opened the envelope and not read the contents? It just didn't seem possible.

"Really?" he said. "You're not going to tell me?"

I started moving toward the car, and I heard him follow.

"Fine," he said. "You're right. This is none of my business. I just hope you know what you're doing."

I had no idea what I was doing. I was flying blind. I just knew that Luke hadn't written that note. I don't know how I knew, something about the words and the rhythm, the maturity of it, the possessiveness. Luke was possessive, but in a childish, tantrum-throwing way. He would wrest what he wanted from you, snatch and grab. He didn't have the self-control yet to tease and manipulate it out of you. Did he? He was still slamming doors and stomping up steps. He was still a kid.

But if not him, then who? To whom did I belong? Who knew all my secrets and lies? And did that person know what happened between me and Beck? Did they know where she was now? The game was no longer a game. It was a matter of life and death.

That night in the woods, my whole body came alive for Beck in a way I'd never experienced. I'd been wrapped up tight in an armadillo shell for as long as I had been aware of myself sexually. I was terrified of the touch of other people, of the reactions deep inside over which I had no control. Puberty came late, long after it was suspected to have passed me over altogether. It rocketed through me, setting my hormones ablaze. Desire was a sudden blast that sucked all the air from the world. And still I wrapped myself up tight.

I wasn't sure who I was, or what I wanted. So I chose to want nothing at all.

But Beck—she was my polar opposite. She wanted everything all the time. She'd been with boys and girls, and loved them both the same. *Love is love*, she said. *We can all get each other off, one way or another.* She was easy with her body, free with her touches. She would get naked anywhere with anyone. Sexuality radiated out from her like a beacon, and I couldn't help but be drawn to her and repelled by her at the same time.

"Don't be afraid of your own pleasure," she whispered.

Her breath had been hot and wanton. She started tugging at my clothes, her mouth on my neck. The ground was cold beneath me, hard and uncomfortable. But she gave off so much heat, opening her coat and the shirt beneath. Her body looked like milk in the moonlight, glowing a translucent blue, and I couldn't stop my hands from touching her. Skin contact ... babies need it from their mothers, flesh on flesh. We all need it, all the time. But the virginal, the chaste, the sexually repressed—we hide our skin in long pants and shirtsleeves. We hide it, protect it, even as it burns to be touched. I could have died right there as Beck got to work on peeling back my layers.

"Don't," I breathed. "Please."

But we both knew it was far too late for that. I was shuddering as she undid my belt buckle, the button on my jeans, unzipped my fly. I was a useless lover; I didn't even know how to pleasure her. But she moaned at my tentative touch, pushed her tongue deep into my mouth.

She moved her hand slowly down my belly, and I reached up a hand to stop her. I grabbed her wrist hard.

But she just shook her head and smiled. "I know," she said. "I already know."

And I let her. I let her touch me. I let her know me. And it was so. Goddamn. Good.

A short while later, she would rip that star from her neck and toss it to the ground. *How can you be so cold? I hate you. I fucking hate you.* That was Beck, a tempest, powerful and unpredictable, thunder and lightning—so unlike me in every way.

Langdon pulled up in front of my dorm, and he looked grim and disappointed in me.

"I'm here for you," he said. "You know that. Whatever you need."

"I know," I said. I wanted to show him what was in the envelope. I wanted his help. But I couldn't. I didn't want to pull him into my mess. If the last few days had proved anything, it was that I was better off alone. I got out of the car and watched him drive away. *Why is it that no one you love ever seems to stay?* Because I push them all away. No mystery there.

*

My aunt was waiting for me when I walked in the door. She'd turned on the gas fireplace and was sitting huddled under a blanket nursing a cup of tea.

"It's freezing here," she said. "How do you stand it?"

"You get used to it," I said. I liked the cold. It allowed me to bury my body beneath layers of clothes. *Why don't you get yourself a spiked collar?* Beck had spat at me once. *Just to be sure everyone knows to stay away.*

I sat beside her. Have I mentioned that I love my aunt? I think I've only said unkind things about her, made fun of her a little. But she looks just enough like my mother that I feel a desperate closeness to her. And she looks just enough like my mother that she causes me to be deeply, deeply sad and lonely. Because she is not my mother, and she never will be. But that's the only wrong she's ever done me. She has been unfailingly kind and present for me, and I have never once thanked her for it.

She was pretty in the firelight, her golden hair catching the light as it fell around her face in soft waves. She had some lines around her eyes and mouth, a middle-aged pull to her skin. But she had good genes and money, looked forty-something when she was fifty-something.

"Where were you?" she asked. She pulled the blanket tighter around herself.

"Walking," I said. Lies came so easily to me.

"Is that safe?" she asked. She was one of those people that asked a question to which the answer was obvious, hoping to elicit the correct response, making you think in the process. It was annoying.

"I don't know," I said. "Probably not."

"You've always done that," she said. "Walked off on your own to think. But you're not alone, okay. I'm here for you, whether you want me or not."

I nodded, looked at the licking flames of the fire. Everybody kept saying that. Why couldn't I bring myself to take anybody up on it? "Thank you," I said.

"Listen," she said. She sat up and put her teacup down. "Sky thinks we need a criminal attorney. He says the police believe you had something to do with Beck's disappearance, and they're reopening the case of Elizabeth Barnett."

I needed to tell her, I needed to tell someone about this last clue, about the necklace. But if I did that, I would have to tell everything. And I just couldn't do that.

"I think you need to come clean, sweetheart," she said. "You need to go to the police and tell them who you are. They're going to find out. They're going to discover that you've changed your identity. And when they do, it's not going to look good. They may already know everything."

I wondered at her calm, at how there was not even a note of fear or accusation in her voice.

When I didn't answer: "You need to tell them everything."

"Do you think I had something to do with Beck disappearing?" I asked.

She kept her eyes on me, her gaze level and cool. Then she reached out her hand and I took it. "I changed your diapers," she said. "You've had problems in your life, bad ones. There was a time when we didn't know what would become of you. But I know you. I *love* you." She closed her eyes, as if swept away by feeling.

It wasn't an answer. I think she was trying to say that she loved me no matter what I had done. Someone had changed my grandfather's diapers, and my father's. And they were monsters. Did she think I was a monster, too? Was I?

"So, no," she said. "I don't believe you would hurt anyone. I don't."

Was she naive? Or was she just in denial? Or did she know me better than I knew myself? There was murder in my blood, in both strands of my DNA. I had done everything in my power to escape it, but no matter where you go, there you are.

I lay down on the couch beside her and put my head in her lap. She ran a hand over my forehead, over my short spiky hair.

"Sky has been in touch with one of his colleagues," said my aunt. "She'll be here tomorrow."

"I have to work," I said.

"Honey," she said. "It's not business as usual, you know."

I noticed how she studiously avoided using the name that was not really mine. She had always been awkward with it, but she knew I couldn't tolerate the name my mother had given me.

As soon as Rachel knew what was happening to me, would she really want me babysitting for her child? But I had to talk to Luke; unless I was told not to come, I was going.

I fell asleep thinking about that poem and who had written it, about Beck's necklace and the last words she said to me. I heard her screaming my name, my real name, as I ran away, as far away as I could get.

23

The crowds outside the dorm had turned into a throbbing, bloodthirsty mob by morning. Word that I had been taken in for questioning had spread farther and wider, and the media coverage was heating up. There were news vans and a large crowd of onlookers. I watched them from behind the curtain in my room, trying to pick out individual faces. People were drinking coffee, chatting, some had actually brought chairs. It looked more like a tailgate party than anything else. Were people this bored? Did they have so little to do?

The dorm mother had come early and suggested to my aunt and me that we leave.

"I'm sorry, Lana," she said. She *did* look sorry, sympathetic and concerned. "But the other parents are making a fuss. People are understandably unsettled by all of this. Of course, *I* know that you had nothing to do with this. You're a sweet soul, always have been."

When Sky arrived, he agreed that we should leave as soon as possible.

"This is not good for anyone," he said. He took a pressed, bright white handkerchief from his pocket and wiped at his freckled, bald head. What kind of man still carried a pressed handkerchief? Obviously, someone too delicate for a situation like this. He handled money, which was quiet and never caused this kind of trouble. I was worried about him.

His assistant had managed, through the magic of the Internet, to rent us a small house just outside the center of town. The plan was to sneak me out when things quieted down. But the crowd only grew.

When I was a kid, I used to wish that there were underground tunnels. You could just climb inside from some kind of basement access where a tunnel buggy would be waiting to take you wherever you needed to go. I wished for that now. I wished I could just walk into a tunnel and disappear forever. I remember reading that about The Hollows. There were miles and miles of underground tunnels from the iron mines that used to be the major industry here.

The police were going to have to make an arrest soon, I knew. Lynne and Frank had been on television last night, pleading for Beck's safe return. I saw the footage that morning, and both of them looked ghostly, disheveled, dark circles under their eyes. I had two distraught messages from Ainsley on my cell phone, but I couldn't stand to hear her voice, so worried and far away. I deleted them and hadn't called back.

290

There was a soft knock on the door, and Sky pushed in without waiting for me to answer.

"I think we can get out back," he said. "My assistant is bringing the car around. We can lay you down in the back-seat and get out of here."

"How does that look?" I said. "I'd rather just walk through the fire, you know. Hold my head up and let them see me."

"But then they'll follow us," he said. He was calm and practical. "We want to get you and your aunt some privacy until this matter is settled. Get packed."

I took my medication and packed a small overnight bag. And when I left my room, I looked it over as though I'd never see it again. How could things ever go back to being what they were before the night in the woods? They couldn't. No matter what happened, the stigma of this would follow me. By tonight, I knew, everything I had successfully hidden for the last seven years was going to come out. It couldn't help but be discovered; it was too raw, too sensational, it would sell too many newspapers, magazines, and TV ads. Because that's what it's all about now. We are a junk culture of voyeurs, planted in front of our televisions watching the worst and most wretched people make disasters out of their lives.

I walked out of the room and heard Sky and my aunt talking in the kitchen. I tugged on my peacoat and shoul-dered my bag. I took a black wool cap from one of the hooks by the door; it was Beck's. I pulled it over the mess of my hair, donned my sunglasses. There wasn't a mirror in the front room, but the last time I'd dressed like this, Beck said that I'd taken my androgyny to a whole new level. The feminists say that gender is a social construct, something that doesn't exist in the physical, but only in the imagination of our society. I am inclined to agree.

Their voices were low, and I couldn't hear what they were saying. On the table by the door was the Mace that Ainsley had bought for me, and for the first time since she'd given it to me, I remembered to shove it into my pocket. The door to the hallway was open, and the next thing I knew, I was walking out into the empty hallway.

It was always quiet in the morning, everyone in class or sleeping in. But it seemed unnaturally so that morning. There was a hush, a drawn-in breath. People had cleared out of the building. That's what most sane people did when there was a murder suspect on the premises.

Soon I was on the fire stairs, creeping down fast and quiet. Then I was pushing out into the cold, bright morning. I could hear the crowd in the front of the building. Something was going on, because the volume went up— someone was leaving or arriving.

There was no one in sight out back. I walked, unseen, from the back door and headed straight into the woods.

I came up behind the Kahns' house. I rang the bell at the back door and waited, though I knew no one would be home. Rachel would be at the shop, and Luke in school. The air seemed to be growing more frigid, but maybe it was just because I had been out so long, walking and walking. It would have taken me twenty minutes to get here on my bike. It had taken me nearly two hours on foot through the woods, a route I chose in order to stay out of sight. After a few minutes, I tried the key I had. It did fit in the back door. I wouldn't have to go around front, where I had a greater chance of being seen. I stepped with relief into the warm kitchen. I locked the dead bolt and pocketed the key.

I dropped my bag by the table and I took out my cell phone. There were about a million messages, a list of alternating calls from Sky and Bridgette. I shoved the phone into my pocket and headed upstairs to Luke's bedroom. On my way up, I peeked out the side window by the door. I half expected to see a crowd gathering outside, but it was clear. It was just the quiet street, trees bending in the window, windows dark, in a neighborhood where most people worked all day.

Why was I here? What was I looking for? It was clear to me that Luke had not written that note. But he was obviously involved somehow with whoever had. So I was hoping to find something in his room that would tell me who it was. Somebody had seen Beck and me together that night. Who was it?

I hadn't forgotten Rachel's journal, but that wasn't why I'd come. So I passed her room and went straight to Luke's.

The locks on his door were even looser in their mounts, one of them dangling by a single screw. The door was ajar and I pushed it open. The room was tidier than it had been; it looked as if he and his mom had finished unpacking. The video-game system was no longer on the floor among a pile of games. It sat on an orderly-looking console, the game cases organized on one of the shelves. The bed was neatly made.

His computer stood on the desk under the window. I sat in his chair and touched the mouse. He didn't have an e-mail account set up on his computer, and I remembered Rachel saying that she hadn't allowed him to have one or to do any social networking. It was too hard to control, too many ways he could reach people, or the wrong types of people could reach him. She also said that she limited his Web access. But I had a feeling he might be smart enough to get around that.

I opened the Internet browser, went straight to his history. But I was disappointed. After a few minutes of scrolling through, I saw nothing but visits to online booksellers and video-game purveyors, gaming chat sites. He'd visited Wikipedia and some nature sites, probably for a report he'd been writing about bats. I kept thinking about Lester Nobody, the person who had posted on Facebook. Was it Luke? He had not, as far as I could see, visited any social networks, or any of the various Web-mail providers. But I kept clicking, back and back through his digital history.

Way down, around the time that he'd given me the first clue, I found a visit he had made to the Web site for The Hollows Historical Society. He'd clicked on the "Haunted Hollows" link, and visited the pages about the caretaker suicide and the Marla Holt grave site. It impressed me suddenly how sick the whole haunted tour was—profiting as it did from the misery and tragedy of others. But maybe it was a way to drain horrible events of their power, to make them earthly, manageable. Maybe it created a kind of distance from the real terrors of life and the world, made them seem like make-believe, almost funny. Or maybe people were just totally depraved and fucked up. I would have voted for the latter.

Next I checked the search-engine history. Again, at first glance it was pretty benign: questions about getting to the next level on his video game, general inquiries about bats in New York State, cool and scary scavenger hunts, killer chess moves (little bastard; I'd done the same thing). You could tell a lot about a person from his search-engine history. Don't we all enter our questions into a little box on our computer screens? We expect all the answers to be there now, at our fingertips. Whatever ails us, worries us, interests us, makes us wonder. It's all just a few keystrokes away, the whole universal net of knowledge accessible in a heartbeat. Our stream of consciousness is recorded now in digital form. Wading through Luke's, I almost—almost—breathed a sigh of relief. He was just a kid after all. He found some spooky stuff online and he was trying to scare me. Any connection to the things that I was hiding was coincidence. I almost thought that. I almost had myself a good laugh.

Then, down near the bottom of the list, I saw my mother's name. The sight of it cut a valley through me. He'd entered it weeks ago. In fact—I did some quick figuring in my head—he'd entered the name into his computer a week before I answered Rachel's ad. I sat, staring at the screen, struggling to piece together how that might be and what it might mean. I ticked back over the last few weeks, months, to think how he and I might be connected. But there was nothing, just a dark churning in my mind. He does know me, I thought. He knows who I am. And with this thought, I felt equal parts terror and relief. The weight of lies is a terrible burden. It's always a relief to lay it down, no matter how horrible the consequences.

There was a noise downstairs and I froze. I waited, feeling my heart thump in my chest. Then I heard it again and relaxed. It was the stupid icemaker, dropping cubes in the tray. I turned back to the screen and again began to follow the trail of his research. There was a mass of information about my mother and her murder—feature articles, entries on the crime Web sites, links to documentary footage, newsstory clips.

Naturally, there was also a wealth of information about my father. There was the group lobbying for his freedom, led by a private investigator and a journalist who had recently published a book. They believed that my father, due to the sensational nature of the case, didn't get a fair trial. Because he himself had been an acclaimed journalist before the murder, the media feeding frenzy was significantly ramped up and the pressure on the police to make an arrest was high. There was another man, my mother's alleged lover, who was never found. The police, they claimed, arrested the most likely suspect even with a dearth of physical evidence, largely because of "the eyewitness testimony of a distraught and mentally disturbed child." That would be me.

The group had another member—my father's fiancée. She was a lawyer who'd worked on his case and subsequently fallen in love with him. As you might imagine, I worked very hard not to think about any of this, ever. I never watched television. I had hidden myself away in a little school under another name, and Bridgette and Sky had worked tirelessly to keep me cloistered and protected. But here it all was, scrolling out before me on an eleven-year-old's computer screen.

I saw pictures of a much younger me, looking as grim-faced and pale as a corpse, blank really. That's what the media kept saying about me: that I was blank, unemotional, odd. I was always sandwiched between my aunt and my grandmother (who died the year after my father was convicted. It took all the life out of her, really. You could see her draining, shrinking, growing gray).

In the pictures, though it was more than six years ago, I didn't look that different than I do now. I had the same short haircut, the same stooped, too-thin frame. I had always considered myself exceedingly ugly—and the taunts of my classmates had served to confirm my low opinion of myself. I was more comfortable with my looks now. I no longer imagined that people were gawking at my small body, my pallor. Because I'd figured out how to make these things work for me. And I'd figured out that no one cared, not really. No one gave a shit about anything but himself. People were addled by their own chatter, their own personal litany of fears and insecurities, self-loathing, and selfish desires. Hardly anyone could hear over that. I was invisible if I wanted to be. And that's what I would have been if not for Beck. She was the first person to notice me, the real me. She was the first person who ever really wanted me, who wanted to love me.

I pushed myself away from the computer. I couldn't look at it anymore. I was about to leave, get my stuff and run as far away from this house as I could get when I noticed the light on in Luke's walk-in closet. It beckoned me in.

I stood among Luke's legion of blue jeans, chinos and cords, and primary-colored shirts, organized by shade and sleeve length. I snooped through a few of his drawers—underwear, socks, folded T-shirts in soft, scented stacks. Something, a draft, a sound, caused me to look up. And that's when I saw the attic access door. I reached to pull on the dangling string, and the door came down easily. And a ladder unfolded smoothly with it. I looked up into the dark maw of the attic, and didn't hesitate a second before I climbed up.

24

Do you believe in fate, diary? Do you believe that our whole lives are laid out before us, a path from which we cannot veer, with a predetermined end from which we cannot escape? I never believed in that. I always believed that you created your life. I always thought that all your power lay in your choices. I don't believe that anymore.

The choices we made to bring us to Florida, to enroll our son in this new school, to be a family, a real family for maybe the first time? These were the right choices. They were positive and proactive. And it was, for a time, good for everyone, most especially our boy. But were these choices really? Or were they reactions? Reactions to something that life had thrown at us, something we didn't choose and didn't want. Is there a difference between reaction and choice? I don't know the answer.

The good news is that our years down here have made all the difference for my child. Thanks to the teachers and counselors at his school, the success of a cocktail of medications he has been taking, his behavior has normalized. And the onset of puberty, albeit a much delayed onset, seems to have mostly corrected the hormonal imbalance he'd been suffering from. He'll always be small. He'll have little hair growth, and no discernible Adam's apple. And, even I have to admit, there's something decidedly feminine about him. But he's calmer. Of course, he's calm almost to the point of being flat. That's the medication, though. He has loving moments, sweet moments. Moments when he seems just like any other kid. And for us, that's a miracle.

People sometimes mistake him for a girl, but this doesn't seem to bother him.

"I don't feel like a boy or a girl," he told me recently. And I didn't know what to say. "I don't know who to love."

"Romantic love is overrated," I told him. "Love yourself first."

He nodded, seemed to understand. But maybe he didn't. I only meant to say that I didn't care about his sexual orientation, that he was free to be whoever he was. I just wanted him to find a way to be happy, in spite of his challenges.

And for the first time ever, I have hope that he might do that. He has attended the school for four years now. And his doctors believe that he is well enough, strong enough, to come home and go to a normal high school. And I agree. I am ready for him to return to us full-time. I only wish he was coming home to happier parents.

My husband and I have agreed to stay together for the sake of our son. I know: what a cliché. But there we are. Because our child's mental health is so fragile, and I don't believe he can handle another blow to his psyche, we have agreed to live our separate lives together. We won't argue or fight in front of him. We have promised each other not to do that, and I hope we can be true to our word. I am not always great at biting back my feelings, or keeping from goading him when I'm angry. And my husband's temper, his rage—it's a force to be reckoned with. Is it any wonder our child has so many problems?

Whatever renaissance we briefly experienced in our love has waned again. I still have those dates in my calendar, those secret assignations where I pretended that he was my lover. It seems silly now. Any married couple knows that passion might be the pilot light of a successful relationship but it is not nearly enough to sustain you through the years. When hardships befall us, we don't come together. We break apart.

He lost his job a while ago, or rather, his job disappeared from underneath him, leaving him in a professional free fall.

It was the blow to his ego, the loss of pride, the loss of the one thing he knew he could do better than anyone else. That's what did him in. Because even when he was failing at home—disturbed child, marriage in tatters—he'd always had the work that he loved. The assignments that took him all over the world, the prizes and accolades, the television appearances—they nourished him. Without it all, he was starving.

Naturally, he blamed me. Because it's always my fault. I had asked him to spend more time at home, so he took fewer and fewer assignments. We moved from New York, the hub of the universe, to Florida—its armpit according to my husband. Later, he took a position as an editor at his paper's local field office. It felt to him like being put out to pasture. He was doing less and less of what he loved. At first, he said it was a gift, his opportunity to write the book he'd always wanted to write. But he didn't do that.

Initially, our renewed passion distracted him from his career issues. But that proved short-lived. That was always the problem; without the big stuff—the passion, excitement, success—the little stuff was never enough to sustain us. The fighting started up again, the blaming, the accusing. It often got physical. I am ashamed to admit that there was a small, dark place inside me that enjoyed those battles. It was almost as if we craved and needed the drama. It was a welcome distraction from the day-to-day of a job he hated, the bills, the laundry, the house. Sometimes it seems as if, as a couple, we aren't equipped to handle a normal existence. It's almost a relief to connect in anger when we can't connect any other way.

Now even our son has normalized to the extent that he will. Tomorrow, he's starting at a well-regarded private high school near home. And my husband has sworn that he intends to hunker down into his novel—which is what all journalists do when they've been downsized. But I'm not sure that the quiet work of sitting and writing will agree with him— without the bustle of travel, the pressure of deadlines, the thrill of the interview. He's just begun and already he is noticeably more cranky, sulky, frustrated.

And me? What about me? you ask. I suppose I'm all right. I volunteer at a group home for abandoned adolescent girls. Drawing on my distant and none-too-impressive fashion background, I teach them how to dress for success. I teach them about the message they send with their bodies, the clothes they choose, the signals that inadequate hygiene telegraphs to other people. I show them what's appropriate for school, for job interviews, even for dates.

It might seem silly and frivolous. Does it? But I can see the girls' self-esteem improving as they start to take pride in their appearance, maybe for the first time. I pay attention to each of them, helping them with hairstyles, light makeup, bringing clothes from my own closet, buying some things for each of them. I teach them to choose clothes that are appropriate, pretty, but not suggestive. And it's funny how paying attention to these small things seems to make a big difference in how they feel. And I think I'm helping. And in helping them, I'm helping myself.

Sometimes my son comes with me. And the girls treat him like a pet, doting on him and telling him how cute he is.

He still does have that delicate, doll-like beauty he always had. I have discovered about him that he feels comfortable surrounded by the company of women and girls. Something about him relaxes and grows easy; he smiles with them, even laughs. He fits in with a group of girls struggling to find themselves, to find their way. He lets them dress him, put makeup on him like a doll. And maybe it's weird. But he seems so happy that I let it be. He wipes the makeup off in the car, before we get home to his father.

So that is our life right now. And even though I wouldn't say that we are happy and there are so many things I'd like to change, I don't see how things could be any different than they are. We have reacted to our circumstances, and those reactions have formed our life.

I think this will be my last entry, diary. I hope you won't be offended, but I am not sure I need you anymore. It's time to move on from navel-gazing and moaning about the hardships in my life. Journaling about my feelings is starting to feel like a waste of time. There are no answers here with you. And I think it's time to start the business of accepting my life as it is, and just living every day the best way that I can.

I have come to believe that all those New Age ideas to which my sister clings, and which sound so nice on paper—all of that stuff about choosing your own destiny and making your life and asking the universe for what you want—that maybe all of it is just bullshit. There's no divine and mystical force, no karma, no what-you-give-you-get-back kind of balance. No, I no longer believe that we create our lives. I think that maybe life creates us.

25

I climbed the ladder and it creaked beneath me. A heavy, musty smell wafted down on a breath of cold air as I emerged into a large, nearly empty space. A milky light washed in from a round window on the far side of the attic, and the effect was to give a misty-gray, nearly ghostly quality to the air.

It would have been spooky if not for the litter of candy wrappers on the floor. Kid contraband. The type of sweets—Snickers, Milky Way, Mars bar, gummy worms, Swedish Fish—that Rachel would never allow Luke. *Sugar turns him into a monster. We both know it and he craves it just the same.*

I followed the trail of crinkled colorful paper to a pile of boxes stacked like a fort at the back end of the room. I wondered briefly how either of them, Rachel and Luke, had managed to get the boxes up here. Both of them were slight and not especially strong. Then I realized that the boxes were empty. Luke must have smuggled them up at some point to construct himself a little hiding spot.

As I passed the row of boxes, I saw that he'd brought up his beanbag chair, an iPad, three giant bags of candy. There was a stack of magazines and books, a couple of photo albums. I sank into the beanbag and started sifting through the pile. There were library books about the history of The Hollows, some psychology texts. There was an old *Vanity Fair* magazine that held one of the more in-depth articles about my mother's murder. Where had he gotten it? It was three years old.

I imagined him up here, eating candy and reading library books. And I almost felt sorry for him. Was he lonely like I had been? Did he come up here to hide from the stressors in his life, as I did when I disappeared to my spot in the woods? I could envision him, reading, eating candy, feeling that special kind of freedom you have when no one knows where you are. He probably came here while his mother thought he was locked away, and maybe it made him feel like he wasn't a prisoner after all.

I picked up a slim book from the stack. It was heavy, in spite of being a paperback: *Mines and Tunnels of Upstate New York*. It was a photography book and trail guide to various sites around the areas where hikers, spelunkers, and cavers could go beneath the earth and explore the natural caves, crevices, and tunnels, as well as those blasted by the iron miners that helped settle some of the area, including The Hollows.

In fact, the largest section of the book was about The

Hollows and some of the neighboring areas. I felt a catch in my throat as I started flipping through the chapters and came to a dog-eared page. It talked about a site about a mile into The Hollows Wood, not far from where Beck and I had been that night. There was a brief passage about the woods, and how it was known by area residents as the Black Forest because of the resemblance of its flora and fauna to the forest in Germany by the same name. *It is the haunted forest of fairy tales and nightmares*, declared the author, *so creepy and quiet that one could almost believe it was home to the witch's cabin and the Big Bad Wolf, and populated by the restless spirits of the forest. Something about the area confounds cell signals. So make sure you take your old-school compass with you and that you let someone know where you're going.*

The wind was picking up, and I rose to look outside again. I was alone, and no one knew where I was. Suddenly that didn't seem like such a good thing. We need other people, we really do. As much as I'd always liked to think that I was better off on my own, I wondered if it was true. There were people who wanted to help me, who cared about me in spite of everything. I thought about Bridgette, who was probably having a cow. In that moment, feeling my isolation in a way I never had before, I thought about calling her. But I didn't want to hear the fear and disappointment in her voice. I didn't want to deal with her expectations of me. Maybe that's why we choose to isolate ourselves, those of us who do. Because in so many ways, it's just easier.

I went back to Luke's depressing little hideout and picked up the book again. It meant something. Why had he marked off that page? Was it the next clue in the scavenger hunt? The last poem hadn't ended with anything that led me to another place. It was angry, as if he'd lost his focus. It wasn't like the other clues, which was why I suspected someone else had written it. But what if I was wrong? What was I supposed to take away from it? Had he known I'd be lost, that I'd come here for answers and find his aerie? No, that was giving him too much credit. I was certain that he would be furious at me for being here.

I'd come to see who he might have been communicating with, and quickly discovered that he really didn't have his own e-mail account, just as Rachel had told me. Maybe he had access to another computer somewhere. But where? At school? At the library? I sank back into the beanbag and closed my eyes. I felt just like I did when I was playing chess with him, five moves behind, certain he had a master plan for my destruction, though I had no idea what it was. And, there was some kind of clock ticking, apparently. But only he knew when time ran out.

I got up from where I lay beside Beck and awkwardly started pulling myself together.

"Where are you going?" she asked.

"I'm freezing," I said. "It's thirty degrees."

I was shivering but not from the cold. I was afraid, angry. Passion and desire had abandoned me, and I felt myself shutting down. Even though I could still smell her on me— her skin, her hair, her perfume. Even though I knew I loved her and maybe had for a while, I wanted to be as far from her as I could be. She knew too much. She'd seen too much. What had I been thinking? I remember the simmer of a terrible rage, the rage of the liar discovered.

"Are you mad at me?" she said. "You can't be."

She'd pulled her pants up, sat down, and curled herself into a ball, her arms locked around her legs. Her eyes were big, looking up at me. She had dropped her usual mask of indifference. I saw her in all her sadness and vulnerability; she was my mirror. She was as lost, alone, and in need of love as I was. I almost sank down to her and wrapped her up in my arms. But I didn't. I was that selfish, that cruel. That's the problem with damaged, broken people. We're unpredictable. We'll draw you close, then shove you away. It's nothing personal. Emotions are painful, frightening. It's so much better to be dull and blank. There's less risk. Don't open yourself wide; they can't hurt you if you don't.

"I want to go," I said. I fastened up my coat. When I looked at her again, she was crying.

"You felt it," she said. "I know you did. You love me."

She stood and brushed herself off. The look on her face—it was a grimace of disappointment and disbelief.

"Give me a break," I said. "It was *sex*."

That's when she yelled at me, when her voice rang out into the night, angry and sad. *How can you be so cold?*

The anger inside me, the twisted thing that wanted to hurt and strike out, that wanted to say cruel things and wreak destruction … it was so powerful. I hadn't felt it in so long, I had to marshal all my resources to control it. It frightened me, the things I wanted to do to her, the things I wanted to say. I imagined striking her hard in the face. I saw myself digging her grave. I heard myself calling her unspeakable names, things that if I said I could never take back. I was shaking with it. She saw it; she saw it in my face and she recoiled from me. Her eyes were a mirror where I saw myself. I was a monster. I ran from her, from myself, and from everything we were together.

I left her there—in the dark, cold night … I left my best friend crying. She was sobbing actually, from pain that I had caused her. And now she was gone. I thought she had run off, that she was punishing me, as I heartily deserved to be punished. I thought she'd turn up all sassy and victorious to see the pain she'd caused. Because Beck liked that. She liked people to hurt for her. That was how she knew they cared. But now I had to wonder. Who else had been out there that night? And what had he done to Beck?

I was sunk deep into the beanbag, flipping through that old book that maybe no one but Luke had ever read.

The silence seemed to expand. And then I heard a door open and close downstairs.

I froze, listening to slow, heavy footsteps resonating through the wood floor of the attic. Not Rachel, not Luke—the footfalls were too heavy, too deliberate. Rachel was soft and light on her feet, tapping out quick staccato beats. Luke was all banging—tossing his bag and coat down, storming into the kitchen.

Whoever was in the house was moving carefully down the hall. I heard the copper gong that hung in the hallway give off a hum. I thought of my bag on the floor, in plain sight. There was a terrible pause, a moment of silence. I forced myself to breathe deep. Then I heard him (it had to be a man) move back down the hallway toward the staircase. I'd left Luke's closet door, the attic access, wide open. If someone were looking for me, it would be very easy to figure out where I'd gone.

There was another agonizingly long pause, in which I thought maybe whoever it was would leave. Maybe the front door was open for some reason, perhaps it had swung ajar and a neighbor came to investigate. Or perhaps it was the handyman Rachel had mentioned. The man who was hanging her paintings, erecting bookshelves, hauling away junk left by the former residents. It could have reasonably been any of those things.

But then I heard someone on the stairs. I put the book into my pants and started crawling quietly along the dusty floor. Maybe the handyman had a quick errand to do in the house, or had to drop something off. I just had to stay quiet, undetected.

From my vantage point on the floor, I saw the other exit from the attic. There was an identical hatch with an attached ladder that opened down the hallway from Luke's room across from Rachel's. I moved over toward it slowly, my mind ticking through options.

I'd have to wait. If I heard someone come up from Luke's access, I'd exit quickly and run. If I got caught, I had the Mace in my pocket. But then there was only a silence that stretched on so long I began to convince myself that I was alone after all. I thought of my medication in my bag, how I hadn't been good about taking it at precisely the same time every day. How I'd already passed the time for my dose this morning. My mind played tricks on me when I went off my medication, something I hadn't been foolish enough to do in years. Maybe that was what was happening now, a crack in my chemical armor, demons leaking from my subconscious to my conscious mind. Funny how, in certain circumstances, the worst-case scenario becomes the best.

Oh, how the seconds snake and crawl when you're afraid. But how attuned are your senses, how your blood pumps to fuel your muscles for flight, how your focus tightens. The brain releases its flood of chemicals to increase your chances of survival. There's a certain power in the prey response, a rush that nothing but fear will deliver. Then there was a soft sound that lifted up through the open hatch to Luke's room.

I realized in that moment that Luke could get out of his room anytime he wanted, even when Rachel locked him in. I knew from snooping around that she took pills at night; so her sleep must be sound and impenetrable. All the banging he did, all the pounding at those cheap locks, pulling them out of their mounts. It was just theater; how it must drive Rachel crazy. Not that it was the best choice to lock your kid in his room. Maybe she deserved the anger he felt toward her. But what did I know?

My parents, so distressed by my behavior, sent me to board part-time at a school for troubled children. The school was forward thinking for its time, blending education with talk and medical therapy. It was a safe place, and I got well there.

I don't have any horror stories of abuse to recount—but the staff locked us in our rooms at night. We each had our own space to sleep in, and it was actually a relief to know that no one else could get in. It was a school for crazy kids, after all. I had been staying there four nights a week, spending weekends at home. At first I was distraught, nearly doubled over with despair at missing my mother. I know that, but there's no real visceral memory of pain. It's honestly kind of a blur. There was class, then therapy—group and individual. There was the new cocktail of medications

I took, and what they gave me to sleep at night. Initially I was overwhelmed and foggy. But eventually, it all normalized and it became my life. There was a certain measure of relief in being away from my parents. It was quiet—no more fighting.

The kids there were all handpicked because Dr. Chang believed that we would benefit from his program. We were all gifted. His critics accused him of "creaming," skimming the least disturbed kids, the most intelligent, those who were most likely to respond to medication and therapy, in order to obtain the best results for his program.

Whatever. It worked. The raging creature that lived inside me quieted. The voices, the nightmares, the sick daydreams and bizarre ideas, ceased. Or at least they were buried, deep, deep below soft fuzzy layers of consciousness, a hard pea beneath a stack of mattresses.

On the weekends, I was so happy to see my parents, my mom especially, that I worked hard not to stress her out. And she did the same for me. We would go for walks and talk. She would read to me as she had always done, lie on the floor of my room while I fell asleep. The things that used to frighten us both were gone, and we got to know each other for maybe the first time.

At the school I'd even made some friends. Sure, they were crazy, drugged-up friends. But they were friends nonetheless. Dr. Chang had a staff of young doctors working with him, most of whom rotated out each semester. But they were all bright, and had the energy of camp counselors. I remember a lanky young man in his twenties, and a girl with red hair who smiled a lot. But there were so many of them over the years and they stayed for such a short time, I can't recall many faces or names. I think you try to forget a place like that.

I lost touch with all my nutty friends, too. No one wants to remember crazy school. Once you're out, you don't admit you were ever there, and you think about it as little as possible. But for some reason, as I was crouching there at the attic access, it was coming back.

It was something about Luke's hideaway, his bags of candy and weirdly inappropriate reading material. Something Rachel had said about how he manipulated the other kids with candy. Something buried deep inside me was crawling its way back up through those layers.

My brilliant plan: as soon as I saw the figure come up, I would go down. I would race down the stairs, grab my bag, and flee out the back door into the woods. That was one advantage to being small. I was fast as lightning when I wanted to be. I was going to go straight to Dr. Cooper. I needed to talk to her. I was going to tell her everything. I was going to ask for her help. I could tell Jones Cooper everything I'd figured out; he'd get the police to go into the woods. Maybe they'd find Beck. But the minutes ticked by, and no one came. I waited, and waited, then finally I decided to go for it.

I pushed the hatch down hard and the ladder crashed to the landing with a bang. And I scrambled down quickly. I landed lightly on the floor and ran. I was already downstairs by the time I heard the reaction, a crash, a sudden storm of footfalls.

I ducked to grab my bag as I passed the kitchen counter in one lithe maneuver, but on an upturned corner of the area rug, I lost my footing. I fell, sprawled, spilling the contents of my bag. The footfalls were on the stairs now as I gathered up my things—a notebook, my cell phone … *leave the pens. Let's go. Let's go. Let's go.* As I hit the back door, I realized it was locked. The dead bolt, the one I had locked myself. I needed the key.

I fished in my pocket, panic rising up my throat, adrenaline making me clumsy, butterfingers. Fumbling with the lock. Then I was bursting out into the cold, racing for the woods. I dared to look behind, where a dark form lurked in the doorway.

I froze at the edge of the woods, staring. For a moment, just a moment, I thought I was looking at my father.

26

Dear Diary,

I'm here again. Even though I promised myself that I wouldn't visit with you anymore. But I honestly don't have anywhere else to turn. I can't stand to burden my mother. I know she worries about me so much already. And my sister? Well, the ugly truth is that she's just so goddamn perfect, I can't handle the idea of losing face in front of her again.

I mean, I look at her, and envy just curdles all the love I have for her inside. She seems to grow ever dewier and more youthful, even as the years drain me of whatever beauty I once possessed. Her marriage is strong and healthy. Sure, she and her husband argue all the time, she insists. He's a slob, thinks she's a micromanager of everything in the house. He's too lenient with the girls, says she's too strict. She doesn't like to cook; he feels they eat out too much. Really, I think, that's what you argue about? I would love to argue about things like that, normal, meaningless things that only prove your foundation is rock solid.

Meanwhile, she's a natural mother, never seeming beleaguered or overwhelmed by it all. Even when the girls were small, there was none of that wild-haired, stained shirt, exasperated impatience that seems to characterize motherhood for so many. She was the one milling baby food and breast-feeding for years. She was carrying her girls around in slings, quitting her job, making gingerbread cookies. (Sure, they tasted like shit. She really *was* a terrible cook—her one personal flaw. But still, she *baked*.) She was the kind of woman who said she was grateful for her life and her children and her husband. And she meant it. And she had really great taste. I mean she always looked amazing and her house could have been in a magazine. Seriously.

How could I tell her that I thought my husband wanted to kill me? That he was perhaps *plotting* to kill me? I could imagine the look on her face. Open at first. Then wondering if perhaps I'd lost my mind. Then, stern. She'd have an action plan, and would hover until it was implemented. She'd save my life probably, and still get home in time to order Thai takeout. And all the while she and I would both be aware of her vast superiority, how well she ran her life. How she had recovered after "what Daddy did" and how I never really did. How I floundered after that and never quite found my footing, not really. And she'd have to take a certain kind of pleasure in it. Because for a time it seemed like things would be quite the opposite. While she grieved and was nearly crushed beneath the weight of our shame and tragedy, I ran wild.

She disappeared into school and books, spent years in therapy. I lived it up, skating through school, enjoying my role as the pretty one, the popular one, the one that boys liked.

And my husband was rich and handsome. While hers— well, everyone agreed that John was a good guy, stable and reliable, everything her own father wasn't. But he was a bit of a geek, wasn't he? A computer nerd. He wasn't dark and mysterious, not one to whisk her off to Paris. And her ring was lovely, but well within his means. No one really got that he was a fucking genius and that he'd invent some piece of hardware that would revolutionize computers. No one expected him to get crazy rich. I didn't anyway.

So—really. How could I call her up and say, *Sis, I'm in trouble*? *Again.* I couldn't; that's how. I won't. From all outside appearances, things have normalized. Our son is doing well in school, has some friends. If he's a bit bookish, a bit girlish— well, he goes to an artsy, progressive private school that is well supervised, so there is no playground torturing. And the kids seem to accept him. So that's a big deal and I'm happy for him.

My husband has finished his novel and he's found an agent. It's gone out to publishers, and it looks like he might actually sell it. So the surface picture of us looks fine to my family, and I'd like to keep it that way. And to think I was actually feeling pretty good about things.

And then I realized that my husband was having an affair. It was not a fling or a one-night stand, but a relationship that

323

had spanned the better part of the last five years. He tried to call it off when we moved to Florida. When I told him I needed him and we thought we were in love again. But it started up again soon after. I wonder: Did we not make it because he loved someone else? Or did he go back to her because we couldn't make our marriage work?

His flaming, torrid e-mail correspondence (of which he has studiously saved every single miserable missive) with her is pathetic and full of all the old clichés. *You deserve so much better than this. But I can't leave them. My son can't handle it.* Or: *Just be patient, my love. We'll find a way to be together.* Or: *A love like ours that has survived so much, will survive. We'll have our day.* I know: Barf. It doesn't bode well for his novel.

The worst part is that there's a child, a boy. My husband steals visits for birthdays, sends gifts charged on a card he doesn't think I know about. He sends money. The child is small, just five now, I think. I feel bad for that kid. I really do.

I can't really fault my husband, though. Our love is dead and buried. We are together only for the sake of our boy, and we *did* agree to live separate lives. And I think I wouldn't mind the affair so much except that recently the tenor of the correspondence has changed.

I know he's been to see a lawyer. He is careless with his computer, doesn't realize that I know his password. He wanted to know how much I would get in a divorce. Here's the worst-case scenario: half of everything (including his family money and inheritance because we were too in love to get a prenup—ha ha), child support (for our special-needs boy), and alimony until I married again (which, trust me, I *never* will). Marriage sucks, by the way, diary. It's like a mirage in a desert. Tired, travel-worn, and dying of thirst, we all stagger toward it looking for water and shelter. But when the shimmering image fades, we find only what we brought with us. Which in my and my husband's case was simply selfishness and vanity.

Suddenly their e-mails are short and cryptic. He's been away every third weekend, meeting with his agent, he claims, visiting with publishers. But I know they're together. She sends pictures. And there he is, holding hands with his other son in Central Park, pushing him on the swings. He looks happy, free from the grim frown he always wears at home. I hate him for it. The last time we fought, he called me a succubus. *All you do, both of you, is drain and drain and drain. You give nothing.*

I wonder if that's true. Maybe it is. I haven't been the wife I wanted to be. Motherhood has dominated me for the last sixteen years. But it's too late to look back in regret. At least that's what my therapist says. There is only moving forward.

I'm weak. I'd let the whole thing slide. But the violence has escalated. And I can feel his frustration mounting. We have constructed a trap for ourselves. Yesterday, I stumbled upon (while I was snooping in his office, which I clearly do a lot of) a term life-insurance policy that he has taken out on me.

I know, another cliché. But there you have it; I've built a life out of them, as most of us do.

When I think of uprooting our son, ending my marriage, and opening whatever Pandora's box of neurosis and breakdowns such acts would inspire, I can't. I just can't. I have no real proof that he's actually planning to kill me. He hasn't threatened me. It's possible that I'm being paranoid.

If I'm right, I wonder how he'd do it. Would he hire someone to break in? Would he find an evidence-free way to poison me? The stairs would be a good plan—most accidents happen in the home. There might be an investigation. He'd be expecting that, I'm sure. He's a man who knows how things work; he's canny and wise. He'd have a plan, a good one. He is charming and semi-well-known, a B-list celebrity journalist—or he was once upon a time. He'd walk away from my demise richer than ever and free to be with his new family. And what would happen to our son? How would he fit into my husband's new life?

He's so fragile, our boy. Even in his newfound happiness, what passes for us as wonderfully normal. He has friends, a group of funny, funky, artsy, alternative kids. I think he's been smoking. He's adopted a kind of Gothic androgynous look, with spiky, wild black hair. And I think I saw just the hint of black eyeliner under his eye the other night when I picked him up from the movies. Like he'd had it on and washed it off. He's had both his ears pierced, which is apparently the style among a certain set. I didn't say anything. I honestly don't care. It's only recently that I've seen him smile, and heard him really laugh. Whoever he has to be to make himself happy? It's okay with me.

Am I making a mistake? Staying here in this dead and loveless marriage? Am I being paranoid, thinking my husband might kill me? Maybe I'm just creating drama, as he has so often accused me of doing. Should I ask him to leave, tell him that he can keep his money, that we'll be fine? Maybe that's all it would take.

Even so, I worry about my son all the time. The other night, when I picked him up from the movies and his friends were calling after him, waving, I think I heard one of them call him by a name that wasn't his. I can't be sure, and I certainly didn't ask about it. But I have been turning it over in my mind. How the name sounded on the air, and how he smiled a little at the sound of it. Then, again, maybe I misheard. But I could have sworn that one of the girls (who I thought might be his little girlfriend) waved her arm wide and yelled, "Good night, Lana."

PART TWO: lane

27

Why is God so unfair in His distribution of gifts? Why does He give so much beauty and love and wealth and ease to some? Why does He ask others of us to toil, to struggle, to grieve? This is something that has always bothered me. How could He create the monarch butterfly, and the pit viper? Why is the world so twisted, so dark and complicated, so impossible to understand? I was thinking all of this as I trekked, wretched and exhausted, through the woods. I expected helicopters to come swooping in overhead. But, no, there was nothing.

They'll think I killed her, my father said to me. *I'll go to prison. And you'll go to a group home. You have to help me.*

There was so much blood. When I had knelt down to her, I got it on my palm and I thought about preschool and how they used to brush our hands with finger paint and press our palms into paper, write our name and the year.

Mom? Mom? What's wrong? She was so still and white. Her head was misshapen, flattened on one side. Her arm was twisted so horribly, it looked as if it were rubber tubing. I stood staring, the world around me reeling, and me falling through space and time.

You have to help me, he said again. He stood in the kitchen weeping.

I ran, keening, up the stairs to my room. There had been so many day-mares, so many ugly visions and imaginings, surely this was just another of them. *My mom, my mom, mom, mom.* I dove under my bed and stayed there. I listened to all the strange noises downstairs, the afternoon light fading, the room growing dark.

Onetwothreefourfivesixseveneightnineteneleventwelve.

Later, after her body was discovered, after he finally admitted to burying her, he said she fell from the landing, down to the marble floor below. She must have—or someone else pushed her. But not him.

He hid her body because he'd been having an affair, he said. She'd discovered it, and knew he wanted to leave her. He knew how it would look. He was a journalist, had reported the story a million times. It's always the husband. He panicked, he claimed. He hid her body and made me help, but he didn't kill her. Of course, no one believed him.

I helped him carry her body, wrapped in the Oriental carpet she had so loved, out to the car, heft it into the trunk. And we drove and drove, endless miles into endless night. Why? That's what the police would want to know when I finally, with the help of my aunt and grandmother, screwed up the courage to tell the truth. I've done a lot of thinking about this. Why would I help the man I believed had killed my mother? And the truth is as simple as the fact that I loved my father, too. It was my mother who put the stars in the sky, but I loved him, too. Absent, short-tempered, sometimes distant—he was *still* my father. I couldn't lose them both. I knew neither my aunt nor my grandmother would want me. I didn't think they'd take me in after all the things I'd done. I didn't want to go back to crazy school or a group home like the place where my mother worked. I would rather have slept in my own bed down the hall from my mother's killer. But of course, I was in shock, too. And I wasn't the most stable kid on the block to begin with.

Our parents hold an awesome power over us, Dr. Cooper said. *The child of abuse will do almost anything to protect the injuring parent.*

I jumped to his defense (sad, pathetic): *He didn't abuse me.*

He was absent and often angry with you, by your own account, all your life. He was violent with your mother. You and a jury of twelve believe that he killed her. That's abuse, my dear, even if he never laid a hand on you.

They came to get me on the third afternoon, Aunt Bridgette and my grandmother. My father had been taken in for questioning, and I was under my bed again. Because that was the only place in the house that I could stand to be.

They helped me pack a bag and took me back to my grandmother's house. And there, in her old-lady living room complete with floral-patterned furniture, varnished dark wood, and doilies and a baby grand piano, I told them everything I had seen. I told them how we drove and drove, and finally I helped him carry the dining room carpet through a swampy, treed area until we came to a small clearing. And I wept and moaned as he started digging in the moonlight.

She wouldn't want me to go to prison. Thud. *You know that. She'd want me to take care of you.* Thud. *Whatever happened,* he said. He paused, breathless and sweating in the blanket of humidity that hung in the air. *It was an accident. You have to believe me.*

And, oh, I so very badly wanted to believe him. I wanted to believe him so bad that I saw my mother's ghost hovering in the air, blue and saintly. She was nodding her agreement, and I knew that she wanted me to protect myself since she couldn't protect me anymore. She'd want me to go along with him until I figured out what the hell to do now that my whole universe had broken into a million little pieces.

Mom, don't leave me, I called to her. *Don't go.* And my voice rang out, as young and desperate and terrified as I was.

Shut up, he said. *Stop saying that.*

And I did stop. Because, from the look on his face, I had to wonder: if I didn't do what he asked, would he be digging a grave for me, too?

For three days I kept his secret, told the police that I had come home to an empty house that day. And no, I had no idea where my mother was. But I was a shaking, miserable wreck, and that detective never let up. She saw my fear, my pain. She knew that I was playing a game I didn't want to play. It was her idea to bring my father in for questioning again, to let my grandmother and aunt take me away with them. With my mother's people, in their safe and normal camp, I could tell the truth.

When I finally told my grandmother and aunt, we went straight to the police. And the second phase of our nightmare kicked in. *But at least we'll have her body*, my grandmother kept saying. She clearly derived some comfort from this. *At least we'll be able to lay her to rest.* I don't have to tell you that it killed her. My grandmother never recovered from her grief. I'm not a parent, but I don't think you can lose a child like that and go on with your day-to-day. It's hard enough already, as it is.

No one blames me for what happened to my mother. No one blamed me for being afraid, for keeping my father's secret, for lying. No, no one could blame the disturbed child, the mentally ill, gender-confused young person that I was.

*

Back in the woods, I needed to think, but I couldn't think. Panic was running the show. So I found the hollow of a tree and sank into its moist embrace. I let the silence wash over me, the wind in the leaves. Who was that man in the door? I kept seeing him there, just a shadow. Not my father, of course. He was on death row in Florida. News of his release would have reached me by now. Or had there been anyone there at all? I fished around in my bag for my medication and the bottle of water I always carried. I took my pills right there. Better late than never.

I felt better after a minute of just sitting and catching my breath. I had the book I'd found in Luke's attic, and I had the GPS on my cell phone which I knew might not get a signal. But really, who has a compass? I fished the envelope out of the bag, removed Beck's necklace. I was going to find her. That had to be where she was, right? The location I had found in the book? That was the next clue that he hadn't had a chance to leave me. It had to be.

How Luke could have gotten her out there, I didn't even consider. But I was sure that she was there, and I was going to rescue her. That's where I was in my mind. I'd hurt her. I was responsible for this. I would save her. Obviously, I wasn't operating at top capacity.

Then I heard a sound. At first I thought it was the calling of a bird, distant and strange. Then I realized, it was the sound of someone calling my name. It was far off in the distance. I strapped my bag around my body and looked up the location of the site on my phone. I studied the aerial map, the bird's-eye view of The Hollows Wood. It wasn't that far, maybe three miles. If I could find the state-maintained trail, I could get there faster.

I was used to this kind of terrain, comfortable in the silence of the trees. I heard the voice again, faint and distant, so I started to hoof it. Man, woman, or child, I couldn't tell. Was it the police? My aunt? Luke? I had no idea. I just started to run.

There's murder in my blood. A twisting rope of psychosis from my father and maternal grandfather, and probably others before them. From father to son, from father to son, it travels down the chain, a poison in the blood. Only it doesn't kill you. I have often wished it did. I hate the thought of who I am. I despise my origins. I have done everything in my power to shed that person. And yet that person is with me always.

It was after my grandmother died and my father was convicted that I informed my aunt of my desire to be called Lana. I took my grandmother's maiden name, Granger, as my own. I had a thought that I could bury myself this way, by taking my grandmother's name before she was touched by my grandfather's evil. The gene for violence, for murder, is one that travels through only the male DNA, as far as they know at this time. If I could hide from that, too, maybe I could escape my father and my grandfather's legacy.

Beck was the first person to make me feel like a man. I had been hiding among women, dwelling in the persona of my female self. Living as Lana Granger allowed me to hide from my past, cloister myself from any sexual contact. But since my night with Beck, I was coming alive in ways I'd never experienced.

Still, I'm not sure I feel what others feel. I see people laugh and cry. I see Beck with all her rampaging emotions—her passion, her anger, her joy. I am aware of distant stirrings that might approximate what I see in other people. But have I been swept away in love, overcome by joy? No. I have felt sorrow, remorse, and fear. That's how I know I am not a monster.

Does the psychopath know himself? I have often wondered this. Do you know if you are evil, devoid of normal human emotion? There are people, doctors at Fieldcrest and at the crazy school I attended in Florida, who believe that a child psychopath (for lack of a better term—no one wants to diagnose a child that way) can be taught to display empathy, or to understand feeling.

Because above all else, the psychopath is a mimic. He learns to display emotions he doesn't feel. He seeks to blend into his group, whatever that is. He will shape-shift and mold himself into whatever he needs to be to survive and thrive. The United States is excellent at breeding psychopaths—a country where we reward the individual with a hyperfocus on success at any cost. We reward narcissism—with our social networks and hideous reality television programs. We laud business leaders, even as they abuse workers, rape the environment. In other cultures, where the individual subordinates himself more freely to the needs of family and society, we see fewer psychopaths. So some forward-thinking doctors believe that if you interfere early in the budding psyche of a disturbed individual, he can be taught to think of others. He can be taught to see others not only as instruments of his desires.

What am I? The truth is that I don't know. I know that I have truly loved and cared for people—my mother, my father, my aunt, Beck. I have regretted things that I have done, hurting people that I hurt when I was a child. So I do have feelings. It's just that they're muted and strange. Dr. Cooper thinks it's a kind of arrested development, partly hormonal, partly psychological, partly related to the traumas of my life. Some of it has to do with the cocktail of medications I take, a antipsychotic, antidepressant cocktail. She thinks I will grow into myself someday. She doesn't think I'm evil, or a monster, or a bad seed. She doesn't believe in those things. And neither do I. I am buried beneath layers and layers of genetic and pharmaceutical debris. But I can feel myself, ever since my night with Beck. I can feel myself breaking through.

The miles were hard and the cold winter sun was high

in the sky by the time I finally found the trail. It must have been going on noon. But the light was dimming. A thick gray cloud cover was blanketing the sky and I could smell snow. I glanced at my phone; the compass app showed that I was headed in the right direction, due north. Another mile and I'd be at the site marked in Luke's book. But I started to slow my pace, wondering if I was making a mistake. Maybe it would be better for Beck if I went to the police and told them what I knew. Maybe this was just wasting time. What if I got to the site and there was nothing there?

My phone was constantly buzzing. I'd turned the ringer off, but I could feel it vibrating in my pocket. My aunt, Sky, Dr. Cooper, another number I didn't recognize.

I decided I should listen to the messages:

"This is a bad move," Sky warned. "Just come back and we'll figure all of this out. That lawyer, whom you obviously are going to need, is on her way. Come back, meet with her, and we'll go talk to the police. They don't know you're gone yet, but it won't be long before they figure it out. I can't hold them off forever."

"Please, sweetie," begged my aunt. I could hear the tears in her voice. "I promised your mom that I would take care of you if she couldn't. You need to let me do that. I know you. I know you wouldn't hurt anyone."

"Running away might seem like a good choice," said Dr. Cooper. "It might seem like the only choice. But we have lots of options that we can explore together. Call me. Or just come to my office. I'm here for you."

Why couldn't I ever let anyone help me?

There was one more message.

"You don't know me," he said. "But I know you. My name is Peter Jacobs, and you might be familiar with me as the man who has been leading the initiative for your father's release. Some new information has come to light and I want to discuss it with you. Give me five minutes of your time."

All famous killers have their followers, and my father was no exception. And this guy was his number one fan boy, the journalist who always believed that there was another man at the scene of the crime, my mother's lover. It was my initial testimony that encouraged this idea. I said that I had seen a strange pair of shoes at the door. But I wasn't sure of that anymore. I couldn't swear to it now. In my memory, there is a pair of simple black walking shoes. But was it that afternoon, or another afternoon—I couldn't be sure. Even so, it had been enough on which to hang years of defense, appeals, and investigations. Who is *S*? This initial that was scrawled into my mother's calendar with a little heart beside it that everyone seemed to think was evidence of an affair. Personally, I had no idea who it was. My mother, as far as I saw, only worked and cared for me.

As I came into the clearing, I saw it: a mine-shaft

entrance, built into the swell of a small hill. The splintered wood frame was bent and sagging, and the hole was boarded shut. It looked like something out of a fairy tale, the hole in which a troll or hobbit might live, and I stood looking at it for a second. Was she in there? The sky had grown darker, and the air ever colder. I was so far from everything now, a three-mile trek in either direction to safety. It was then that I realized how stupid I was. I needed to call the police, or someone, and I was going to do that right away. I took the phone from my pocket and was about to dial when I heard something that I was sure came from inside the mine.

I dropped my bag, moved in close, and listened. I laid my head against the wood for a moment. The boards were nailed in tight, no amount of prying with my bare fingers was going to pull them out. And the nails were rusty, as if they'd been there for a hundred years. A big red sign warned people away—DANGER: CAVERS, SPELUNKERS, HIKERS AND ALL, DO NOT ENTER THIS MINE SHAFT. IT IS TREACHEROUS AND UNSTABLE AND NOT FIT FOR ENTRY!

I tried to pull at the boards anyway, and then started yelling: "Beck, Beck, it's me. Are you in there? Answer me! I'm sorry!"

My voice rang out, strident and panicked. A flock of blackbirds fluttered away, squawking into the sky.

"Have you completely lost your mind?"

The voice rocketed through me, a blast of adrenaline

nearly shot me into the air. I turned around to see Langdon standing there. He was red-faced and sweating from exertion, in spite of the cold. I leaned against the wood and slid down to the ground, wrapping up and burying my head in my arms.

"How many times am I going to have to ask you this question?" he said. "What are you doing?"

"I thought she was out here," I said.

I fished the book from my bag and tossed it over to him. He was bent over, leaning on his knees. He was still trying to catch his breath. But he picked it up and looked at the page I had marked.

"Was that you calling me?" I asked. "All those miles ago."

"Who else?" he asked.

He walked over and inspected the shaft. He ran his fingers over the rough surface, touched the nail heads. "No one's been in this mine for a hundred years," he said. "These nails are so rusted they're practically fused to the wood."

"I heard something," I said. I was still listening, but there was nothing. It could have been that all I'd heard was Langdon's approach. I was so confused and so tired now, I couldn't trust any of my perceptions. *She's dead,* a voice whispered in my head. *She's dead because you left her alone in the woods. It's your fault.*

Langdon put his head to the wood. "No," he said. "I don't hear anything."

I was spent, completely and utterly done. I felt myself shutting down, going blank, all feeling draining down that hole in my center.

Langdon reached down a hand and lifted me to my feet.

"We have to get you back, Lana," he said. "This doesn't look good. Everyone's going crazy. Your aunt ... she's a wreck."

"That's not my name."

The gray daylight seemed to deepen, and the whispering of the leaves all around us swelled to a chorus of voices.

"I know," he said. All the color had left his face, and his features had fallen slack. He was a black tower against the gray behind him. And something in my body was responding—a hollow in my gut, a tightness in my throat.

"I know that," he said again.

A universe of understanding passed between us. I ticked back through the last few months, remembered him pulling Rachel's ad from the board, turning up places he had no reason being, climbing down into that grave after the last scavenger hunt clue. Impossibly, he was part of this. But how? *Why?* I couldn't even think of the right things to ask.

"Was that you in the house today?" I asked. There were a million other, more important questions. But that's the only one that came to mind.

He smiled, but it was not the warm and reassuring smile that I expected and needed from him. He offered a slow nod, and he didn't seem like the person I knew at all.

Run, said the voice in my head. *Get away from him.*

But I was frozen where I stood. I couldn't get my head around the idea that this man … my mentor, my adviser, my professor … was anything other than my trusted friend.

This was always my Waterloo, that I'd stand around trying to figure out the things that confused me—like that day on the playground after I pushed the boy who'd been bullying me off the jungle gym. The world was so impossibly complicated, so many factors at play in any circumstance—physics, psychology, chemistry. That boy and I hadn't liked each other, that was the first thing. Bad blood. He'd teased me, so I pushed him. Cause and effect. He was too close to the edge to save himself with a step back, too heavy to stop his own backward momentum. Physics.

Such a delicate interplay of forces; and I had always been fascinated by how things wove together. I got lost in contemplating it. It always unsettled people, made me seem like a freak—just standing there and thinking like I did.

I saw Langdon bend down and pick something up.

"What are you doing here?" I asked him. "What do you want?"

"I'm here for you," he said. "Just like I've always been."

345

He moved closer, reaching out a hand for mine. I let him take it and realized how little physical contact we'd had over the years. His palm was cool and soft.

"I've been waiting for you to tell me who you are," he said. "To let me in."

His nearness unsettled me; he didn't even look like himself. There was a strange yearning gleam to his gaze. He kept moving toward me and I realized too late that he was leaning in to kiss me. I pulled back quickly, shrank from him, really. It might have seemed like disgust, but it wasn't that. I don't know what I was feeling, other than a desire to get away. Certainly, under other circumstances I'd have been more gentle with him. I watched that yearning turn to anger, dark and petulant.

"No," I said. "I'm not like that. It's not like that with us."

It was a realization for me, too. I started backing away from him. Again, that voice in my head: *Run.* This time I nearly listened, but it was too late.

"I have to go," I said. I still thought he might let me. "Okay?"

He didn't answer, just drew his arm back. Then slowly but inexorably, his fist was flying in my direction. But I was already on the ground, my head filled with the twin sirens of fear and pain, when I realized that he had hit me.

I stared up at him, feeling small and helpless. He stood over me, a rock in his hand. I tried to ask him why he was doing this. It was crazy . . . and what did he want? But none of those words made it out into the world. His face, as blank as my own, was the last thing I saw before everything went from bright white, to fuzzy gray, to black.

28

When I came back to myself, I was lying on the cold, hard earth and night had fallen. The cloud cover must have hung thick and low, because I couldn't see the stars, and the moon was just a silvery glow in the sky. I squeezed my eyes closed, assessing the pain in my head, the hard place where my hip connected with the earth, the bindings on my wrists and ankles. There was a rhythmic sound that echoed off the trees around me. It was a sound I recognized immediately. And for a second I thought I'd lost my mind or that I was stuck in some kind of nightmare loop in my life.

The night I helped to carry my mother's body out to the place where my father buried her, I kept thinking I was dreaming. Several times I was sure of it. Because such things didn't really happen, and my daydreams and nightmares were often much more vivid than my waking life.

And, certainly, even with all I'd suffered, nothing had prepared me for a reality like this.

The truth was that I often knew my visions weren't real. I knew there wasn't an old woman in my room that told me my mother didn't love me anymore. I said things like that to upset my mother when I was feeling jealous or insecure. And I had overheard my mother and grandmother talking about my child-murdering grandfather. That time I was trying to comfort my mother. Maybe if she thought my grandfather was sorry, she wouldn't think he was so bad. And if she didn't think he was so bad, maybe she wouldn't be so worried about me. It all makes a sick, twisted child's kind of sense, doesn't it? My poor mom. I wonder if she's at peace now. I hope she is.

The digging continued, and I listened to its echo in the night.

This is the right thing. I know you'll see that someday, my father said. I sat weeping against the tree. *Otherwise, what will happen to you? Stop crying. You're too old to be crying like a girl.*

Yet another gender inequality: Boys and men are not allowed to feel. They're not allowed to accept and express their emotions in the same way that women are. It's weakness. Only pansies and little faggots cry. Everyone always talks about how bad women have it, how systematically they have been abused, maligned, hated, and discriminated against throughout history. And, of course, it's true. But no one ever talks about how that misogyny has had its backlash on men.

When you hate women, you hate all the female elements of your own psychology. Jung believed that there were two primary anthropomorphic archetypes of the unconscious mind. The animus is the unconscious male, and the anima is the unconscious female. Because a man's anima, his more sensitive, feeling side, must so often be repressed, it forms the ultimate shadow self—a dark side that is hated and buried. Jung was a big believer in accepting the shadow, embracing it … or suffering the consequences in psychic pain.

I didn't want to stop crying then. My father himself had been weeping just minutes earlier. The pain inside me was a living thing, a beast of fear and grief and horror. If I didn't weep, I might have imploded.

But I didn't cry this time. I lay very still, listening to the sound, wondering what the hell was happening to me and what I was going to do. No one knew where I was. I was not experiencing normal levels of terror for the situation I was in. Part of that had to do with the beta-blockers in the medication I was taking. They dulled the chemical fear response, hence my flat affect, which people were always so put off by. Tonight, I had a feeling my emotional flatness was going to work in my favor. Then the sound stopped and there was only silence.

I waited.

*

I have thought long and hard about those shoes I saw. I remember they were smallish and that I thought they might have been my mother's. They were sensible, leather lace-ups—not like anything my mother would ever wear because she was all about style. She'd tell the girls at the group home that when we put on clothes, we're telling ourselves something, and we're communicating that something to every person we meet. *If your clothes are dirty, or wrinkled, or ill-fitting, you're telling people that you don't care enough about yourself to put yourself together. It speaks volumes to teachers, to prospective employers, and to men. If you don't care about yourself, why should they?*

Those shoes belonged to someone who was practical, who cared little about form or style over function. But if they had been lying by the door when I came in, which I couldn't swear to anymore, they were gone when my father and I left. I think. See? It's hard. When you're crazy to begin with, and deeply traumatized to boot, your so-called eyewitness testimony is next to useless. There were voices, too. I remembered hearing voices from my hiding place under the bed. But I couldn't be sure of that either. Male or female, I didn't know. And over the sound of my own frantic screaming, I certainly didn't hear any words.

"What was it like that night?"

Langdon was standing over me. He, too, was wearing very sensible shoes, those all-terrain Merrells—the perfect choice for hiking, climbing, and digging graves. Whose grave *was* it that he was digging? I wondered. Mine?

"It was Florida," I answered. "So it was warm and humid. And it was more of a swamp."

"But tonight is the night, right? Seven years ago tonight?" There was an unpleasant eagerness in his voice.

"Yes," I said. I had forgotten. I didn't mark the calendar with my personal tragedies anymore. I thought I was moving beyond it all, in the ways that you can. When you begin to heal, you can tell because you start living your life again. You start living in the present moment, in the here and now. You look toward the future. You're not always looking back, wishing, always wishing, that things had been different.

"Why did you let her touch you?" he asked.

I dared to look up at him, and I swear, he didn't even seem like the same person I knew. The angry, hateful expression on his face so transformed him that he looked like a ghoul. I wondered, would there be a stop on the Haunted Hollows tour for this site in a few years?

"Why do you care?" I asked.

I tried to push myself up, but he pushed me back down with his foot. It didn't take much; the whole universe was wobbly. I could feel something in my pocket, something hard pressing against my hip. It was the Mace; I finally remembered that I was carrying it. I couldn't have picked a better day. Too bad I couldn't get to it with my hands bound.

"What does it have to do with you?" I said.

There was some kind of battle taking place on his face

then—a battle between despair and rage. I realized then that he always knew who I was, what I was. I thought about Beck's gossipy little dig: *I heard he has a boyfriend in the city.* Maybe there had been some kind of weird undercurrent between us. But Beck showed me something about myself that I hadn't really understood. I'd been so wrapped up, so repressed in that way, I didn't know what the hell I wanted. Now I did. I wanted Beck.

"Where is she?" I asked. "Where is she, Langdon? Did you hurt her?"

An ugly smile broke across his face and he walked away from me. I pushed myself up to sitting with my elbows, despite the binding around my wrists. I started trying to rub them free. And that's when I saw Beck lying in a fetal position near the grave he'd dug. She was pale, and bound, just as I was. She was wearing what she'd been wearing the night I left her. I'd done this to her. It was my fault.

"Beck!" I yelled, but she was still, too still.

He put his foot on her shoulder. And I saw her move, I thought. Did she shift? Did she give a weak, frightened moan? He gave her a hard push and she rolled into the hole in the earth, landing with an ugly thud.

I need you to believe that I didn't kill her, my father said in the car on the way home. *I need you to understand that.*

I believe you, I said. Even though I didn't believe him at all.

I mean, what are you going to say? And a numbness settled over me. I was comfortably sleepy.

I'm doing this for you, okay?

Okay.

Son, are you all right?

I'm fine.

Dr. Cooper and I have been over and over this conversation, how wrong the whole thing was, how manipulative and insane.

Now, this is how we're going to handle it. We might have been talking about a particularly challenging school project. And he went on to tell me how tomorrow—after he cleaned up—he was going to report her missing. All I had to do was say that the last time I saw her was in the morning before I left for school that day. That I came home to an empty house, and assumed that she was working. And he said other stuff, too, but I don't really remember what he wanted me to say to the police. Still, it was a fairly extensive coaching session on how to act and what not to say. Use as few words as possible when talking to them. Don't answer any questions they haven't asked. Don't rush to fill silences.

I do remember when the police came the next morning, that detective gave me one look and knew. Later she would tell me that I was vibrating, giving off a terrified and grief-stricken energy that she picked up on right away.

But the question remains. Did my father kill her? The truth is that I just don't know. I know they hated each other and that they stayed together just because of me. I know that he was having an affair—another woman, another child, another life that was better than the one he had with us. This information came out early in the list of things that damned him with me and everyone else. Beyond that: the police had visited our various homes several times, the neighbors having called to complain about raised voices and the sounds of violence. My father had been to a divorce attorney who would testify that he reacted badly when he learned how much a divorce was going to cut into his personal fortune. It was a lengthy and ugly list of damning activities. But there was no physical evidence, nothing that placed my father on the landing, nothing to show that he had pushed her. But how else might she have fallen? A thousand freak ways, the defense argued. Most accidents happened in the home. Or the missing lover had done it. Maybe he had pushed her.

But my father was convicted, and appeal after appeal was denied. And now the clock was ticking, his life winding down. For the first time, now that my own life was hanging in the balance, I began to wonder. Did I owe him something more? Was he on death row because he was a poor husband and worse father? Had someone else been there that day?

"Why are you doing this?" I asked Langdon. I am not sure he understood what I was saying, because it came out like a wail as I struggled to get to my feet.

"It's where dirty little sluts like Beck—and your mother—belong, isn't it?" Langdon said. "In an unmarked grave, deep in the middle of nowhere."

His words, his tone, shut me down cold. A shudder moved through me and I let myself fall back.

"I've read every word ever written about you," he said. "I know you helped him bury her body."

"I was a kid," I said. "I was a scared, confused kid."

"Sure. I get that. But still. You helped him."

I had heard this before, or rather read it. On those crime Web sites, where freaks gather to analyze various cases, people come to speculate and analyze media coverage, use pop psychology and knowledge gleaned from the myriad police procedure shows that dominate prime time to come up with their own personal theories. Much was made of this element of that case, of my supposed complicity. I always hated those people who tried to make me guilty, even as I pitied them. How sad, how pathetic and dull must their stupid lives be. Plenty of people believed that I killed my mother, and that my father went to jail to protect me.

In fact, even the private investigator who continues to lobby for my father's release suspected my guilt at one time, though by this point he seemed to have dropped me from his list of suspects, for whatever reason. But it makes for a pretty story, doesn't it, for my father's fan club? He's not a murderer, after all! He's a hero! He went to jail to protect his crazy son. That's why I wasn't eager to return the calls

I received from my father's team. They'd been wrong about everything for years.

"You know my history," I said to Langdon. "You know I was taking an antipsychotic, antidepressant cocktail, not to mention what they gave me to sleep."

"I know, with the whole suite of side effects—sedation, blunted awareness and feeling, inability to feel pleasure, asexuality," he said, bored. "They really fucked with your brain chemistry. They're still fucking with it."

"So they are."

I was deeply screwed up and had been for as long as I could remember.

"So how do you even know who you are or what you want? You can't want *her*." He glanced toward Beck's motionless form.

"Maybe I don't."

I saw his expression change, and somewhere inside I smiled. I was a fuckup, to be sure, but I was also extremely smart. Did I know what I was and what I wanted? I wasn't gay. I understood that now. My feelings of affection, my closeness to Langdon … I think, looking back now, I saw him as a father figure—someone to advise me and direct me, someone I could trust. And I had become so divorced from my feelings, had so little idea of what good, healthy feelings *were*, that I confused my feelings for something else. Maybe he'd picked up on my confusion and mistaken it for repressed desire.

He moved a step closer to me. I lifted up my wrists. "Untie me," I said softly. "This is crazy."

I realized then how little I knew about Langdon. He'd been my professor and adviser since my freshman year. We'd arrived at Sacred Heart College at almost the same time, but all we ever talked about was me. He'd never told me anything much about himself, just that he'd grown up in the Northeast. His parents were both dead; he had a married sister in Poughkeepsie, two nieces. I only knew that because he kept their picture on his desk. Who was he? What had formed him? What were his appetites?

He moved closer to me, seemed to consider me a moment, and then he undid my bindings. Everything in my body wanted to run to the grave. Was Beck dead? Could I still help her?

"Anhedonia," he said.

"What does that mean?" I asked, even though I already knew.

"It's the inability to feel pleasure," he said. "It's a common side effect of antipsychotic drugs."

"Yes," I said.

"You didn't seem to be experiencing that with her," he said, nodding toward Beck. There was anger, bitterness in his tone, and I found myself repulsed by him. But I held my ground as he moved closer.

"So you wrote that last poem?" I asked.

He nodded.

"And the one before it?"

"I wrote them all."

"You used him?" I asked. He had access to Luke at Fieldcrest. He'd pulled that ad from the board and handed it right to me. "You used Luke to get to me?"

"He was easy to use," he said. He offered a slow shrug. "The kid's a wreck. So desperate for male attention, he'll do just about anything."

I felt a deep twist inside—sadness and sorrow for Luke. We pick our own predators. The flower gives off the scent that attracts the insect that nature designed specifically for the task. Had he picked Langdon? Had I? We draw them to us, sending out messages we often don't even know we're sending. Luke and I were both easy victims. In other circumstances, we might have been the predators, especially Luke, if he were older. Instead we were prey.

He took a step closer, approaching me tentatively. He'd only undone the bindings on my wrists. My legs were still tied. He didn't want me to run. I tried to smile, but it felt tight and insincere on my face. My hand was itching to reach into my pocket. But still I held my ground.

"Just let her go," I said.

It was a mistake. His face became a cold, hard mask. He reached for me, and as he did I shoved my hand deep in my pocket and brought out the tube, spraying.

He roared, stumbling, clawing at his eyes. And I dove my way out of his path. As he doubled over, screaming, I quickly undid my bindings and bolted for the grave where he'd dumped Beck. He was after me, but slowly—one hand rubbing at his eyes, one arm outstretched, feeling his way.

I jumped down, and landed beside her, nearly on top of her. Then I bent and lifted her shoulders, and nearly died with relief when she lolled her head and opened her eyes. They were glassy, and staring. She was heavily drugged. Shit. She was *heavy*. How was I going to get her out of this place? I had jumped into the grave without any notion of how to get us out.

"You left me," she said. Her words were slurred and slow. "You asshole. You left me."

"I know," I said. "I'm sorry. Beck, I'm sorry."

"Fuck you, Lane." She reached up to hit me, but her arm fell heavily on my shoulder.

"Okay," I said. Yes, that was my name: Lane. My real name. "Fine. We'll fight about it later."

That's when Langdon started raining dirt down on the grave we were sharing.

29

For all the talk in our culture about how important it is to find ourselves, we don't have a lot of patience for the task, do we? It's kind of a joke, a mode of light derision, to say that someone is still finding himself. Most people, it seems, have a pretty good idea of who they are. At least that's how it appears to someone as lost as I have been. The big things usually seem to be in line for other people anyway, like gender for example.

We have more patience for girls who act like boys than boys who act like girls. A tomboy is considered cute. One day she'll shuck her muddy jeans and put on a dress, and everyone will gasp at her beauty. They'll all laugh about her tree-climbing, frog-catching days.

But there's no such tolerance for the boy who puts on a dress, who wants a toy kitchen or a baby doll to love. Jung would say that this is because, even culturally, our anima is repressed, hated, derided. We hate our female selves. A boyish girl is perfectly acceptable. A girlish boy? Not so much. In certain places, you'd get your ass kicked, find yourself "gay-bashed." You might even get yourself killed. That's how much we hate our anima.

Beck was fully unconscious, and I was trying to keep the falling dirt off her face, away from her nose and mouth.

"Why are you doing this?" I yelled at Langdon.

He walked to the rim of the grave.

"Why?" he asked. He seemed incredulous, as if he couldn't believe I'd ask such a stupid question. I could see the sweat pouring down his flushed face in spite of the cold. The walls around me seemed high, but they were crumbling and I started clawing at them, trying to create a foothold to lift myself out.

"I came here for you," he said. He swept an arm to the trees. "I followed you to this dump in the middle of nowhere."

I didn't know what he was talking about. He must have seen it on my face.

"Don't you know me?" he asked.

Now he looked hurt, as though I'd let him down terribly. He was a different person than the man I'd known all these years. There was nothing of the mellow, kindhearted adviser and professor that I had grown to rely upon.

"Dr. Chang was my mentor," he said.

It took a few seconds for the name to register. I thought about those years so little. The space between then and now was a dark and chaotic parade of horrible events. I didn't think about Dr. Chang and his crazy school, even though I suppose I owed him a debt of gratitude.

It had been a place much like Fieldcrest. But my memories of my old school, my teachers, the day-to-day, were somewhat fuzzy and vague. Did I remember Langdon? It would have been more than ten years ago. He would have been one of the young doctors that rotated through for a semester.

For a medicated, mentally ill person such as myself, ten years might as well have been a million years. I could hardly remember my mother's face, if I closed my eyes. She'd been slipping further and further away from me.

What should I do? I thought. Pretend that I remember him? Tell him the truth? Instead, I did what I always did, stared blankly at him, trying to figure out what he wanted.

"I'm sorry," I said. "I don't remember much from that time."

"I assisted in your group therapy sessions," he said. "You were a standout. Sensitive and gifted in a room of maniacs."

I was struggling to place him. But I really only remembered Dr. Chang, and some of the others—Dr. Rain, who taught science; Dr. Abigail, who did art therapy. There was a music teacher, young and very pretty. I remembered her, but not her name. I had no memory of Langdon at all. Really, in all the years we'd spent together at Sacred Heart, wouldn't I have remembered before now? But was there something? Something deep within me that remembered

365

him and had been drawn to him because of the memories? I don't know.

"I'm sorry," I said again.

Now it was his turn to stare, the shovel in his hand. I waited for him to say something else. But he walked away from the grave then. As scared as I was, part of me was grieving, too. I'd trusted him and cared about him. *Why is it that no one you love ever seems to stay?*

When he came back, he had a gun. It didn't look right in his hand. He was the kind of guy to carry a book, a laptop, a pen, not a semiautomatic.

"You killed her because she discovered your secret," he said flatly. "You dug her grave. Then, in despair, you killed yourself and fell in with her. That's how I found you. That's what I'll tell the police, and they'll believe me. I'll tell them that I've been watching you, following you for days, because I've been so worried."

It would work. It really would. It was a perfectly logical story, fit right together when all my lies were revealed. It would make a fitting end to a tragic, titillating tale. Everyone loves a good murder-suicide.

"Don't do this," I said. "Please. We can both walk away from this, all of us can. Nothing has happened yet that can't be fixed."

"You confided in me that you had killed your mother," he went on, blankly, almost trancelike. "That you let your father go to jail to protect you."

"Is that what this is about?"

"Your father is a friend of mine," he said haughtily. "We're close."

Was that true? I had no way to know. Was my father pulling strings from behind bars?

"This is not going to work," I said. "It's almost impossible to get away with a crime these days. The forensic science is too advanced. They'll see the trajectory of the bullet. You'll get caught and go to jail. You might even get the electric chair."

I know I sounded rambling and desperate. And I saw with despair that he was beyond listening.

"If my father has anything to do with this," I said, "he's using you. Just like you used Luke. Just like you're using me. We collude with our predators, Professor. Wasn't it you who taught me that?"

He lifted the gun on me, and I closed my eyes. When the shot rang out, I wondered what it would be like to die, how long it would take, if it would hurt, what was waiting for me on the other side ...

It was silent then for a long time, and finally I opened my eyes. I saw Langdon's arm dangling over the side of the grave. Inspecting myself, I realized that I hadn't been shot at all. Then a small white face, as pale and round as a moon, was floating above me.

Luke looked down at me and smiled. I could see that he held Langdon's shovel.

"I hit him," he said. He held up the heavy shovel. "With this. He was going to kill you."

"Good job," I said, for lack of anything better to say.

As glad as I was to see Luke, as glad as I was to see anyone, there was something unsettling about him standing so high above me, holding a shovel.

"Are you okay?" he asked. He dropped the shovel and started rummaging in his pack.

I shook my head and said, "Can you get us out of here?"

He looked up from his pack, and he gave me a grim little nod. "I'll get you out. I brought a rope."

"Do you see my pack up there?" I asked. "I need my phone."

He didn't answer me.

"Did you bring anyone with you, Luke? Did you call the police?"

"No," he said. "I came alone."

"Luke," I said. "Where's the gun?"

He looked over the side at me. "Who's that?"

"That's my friend," I said. "She needs help. I need you to find that phone before you get me out of here."

"Okay," he said, and he walked off.

"How did you get here?" I called, just to keep him talking. The cold air was starting to feel painful now that I didn't have adrenaline pumping through my blood.

"Same as always," he said. He was still out of sight, and it was making me nervous. I got to work on that foothold again. "I rode my bike," he was saying. He sounded far away. I looked up to see Langdon's lifeless arm still dangling over the side.

"You've been here before?"

"You know I have," he said. He was closer now. The sky was clearing and I could see a few stars. Beck was moaning, muttering something I couldn't understand. I put my hand on her head, offered her some soothing words … "It's okay … we're okay … we're going home."

Then Luke was looming again, this time holding my phone. "You were in my room today, in my crawl space."

I didn't say anything. This was not the time for a tantrum.

"Right?" he said, when I stayed silent.

"We have a lot to talk about," I said. I put on my best Dr. Cooper voice, soothing but firm. She always has such a clear idea about the right things to do and the right order in which to do them. I always admired that about her. "And we'll do that. But right now we need to get me out of this hole, and call the police."

"But I want to talk now," he said.

He knelt down and I saw that he was binding Langdon, which probably wasn't a bad idea. But I *needed* that rope, or the phone. And he obviously wasn't in any hurry to deliver on either one.

"How about we play a game?" asked Luke.

Oh my God, really? I struggled to keep my composure, but the stress was starting to mount. I looked up to see that the gun lay on the edge of the grave and he had his hand on it. *For fuck's sake.* I leaned against the wall and drew in a deep breath as I dug my toe into the hole I'd made, and started, as subtly as possible, pushing it in deeper. The dirt was cold and hard, and my progress felt painfully slow.

"What kind of game?" I tried to keep my voice steady. I didn't want him to know how close to the edge of my endurance I was. Or that I was scared. So far, I'd never beaten him at any game we played.

"Twenty questions," he said.

"And if I win?"

"Then I'll help you and your friend out of the hole. And you can call the police."

"And if *you* win?"

He smiled a little, and his eyes were shiny and dark with mischief.

"Maybe I'll kill you all and fill in this hole, then go home and climb back into my bed. They'll think I was locked in my room all night. The only two people who know I can get out are right here."

I didn't answer, just kept pressing my foot in, scraping and pushing, scraping and pushing.

"They'll figure it out, Luke."

He shrugged. "Or maybe I'll help you anyway. If I win, I get to do whatever I want. Because you know what? I *never* get to do what I want. Do you know that? Kids *never* get to do what they want. It sucks."

He was as sullen and whiny as any eleven-year-old. But he was fucking nuts, and that's what made him dangerous—like those little African kids, high on drugs, carrying machine guns. Crazy, drugged, and violent as sin; it was a nasty, terrifying combination. I felt the rise of bile—it might have been anger or it might have been fear. So divorced from my emotions was I that I couldn't tell which. But even so, there was an undercurrent of empathy for him. I understood him. I *was* him—if no longer, then once a long time ago.

"That's cool," I said. "I get it. I'm not that much older than you, you know. I've been through all the same shit."

"I know," he said. "Believe me. I know everything about you, *Lana*."

And here I thought I was so good at keeping secrets, at hiding myself away from the world. Beck, Luke, Langdon … they had all figured me out.

"You can call me Lane," I said.

"Lane," he said, as though he were testing it out on the air. "That's a really gay name."

"So," I said. "How do you want to play? You think of something and I guess what it is?"

"Don't you know how to play twenty questions?" he asked.

"It's been a while," I said. No, I'd never played twenty questions.

"I'll change the rules a little," he said. "You can ask any question. It doesn't have to be just yes-or-no answers. We don't have all night."

He sat on the edge of the grave, dangling his legs over the edge, kicking his heels against the dirt. He gazed up at the sky and seemed to be thinking. In the moonlight, he was an angel in a parka. If he'd sprouted wings and flown away, I wouldn't have been surprised. "Okay. I'm thinking of something."

I watched his face. It was perfectly still, carved from stone. But there was a flicker of something. I knew how lonely he was. I knew because I had been lonely like that, too, all my life.

"Just get me out of here," I said.

"No," he said. He was cool and certain. "Play with me."

30

"Is it a person, place, or thing?"

"It's a person," he said. "But it's also a state of being."

"Male or female?"

He gave me a look. How ironic that I would ask, his face seemed to say. "Male. That's two questions," he said.

Beck said something unintelligible, and I looked down at her.

"Shut up!" he barked at her.

I don't think Luke saw me jump. I knelt down to Beck, and she suddenly seemed so much paler, weaker. She was drugged, probably starved, dehydrated. I put a hand on her and her skin felt cool—that couldn't be good, right? Shock or something like that? She opened her eyes at my touch and all I saw on her face was fear; it opened something up in me. I realized how deeply fucked we were, and bit back panic. The brain seizes in panic, and I was already out of my league. She reached for me and whispered something, but I could barely hear her.

"That's cheating!" he said. He held the gun now and I could see that he was getting angry.

"She doesn't even know what's happening."

"Yes," he said petulantly. "She does."

I stood to face him, and I could feel Beck's hand on my leg. "Young or old?" I asked.

"All ages," he said.

"Look," I said. "Can we just end this? Why are you doing this?"

"Three, four, and five," he said. His kicking grew rhythmic, and he was biting on the edge of his thumb. I began pressing my toe into the earth again. It felt like I was getting deeper. A few more inches, I thought, and I might be able to lift myself out of the grave. I thought I heard something on the air then. Was it a siren? The wind picked up and a light snow started to fall. I could feel Beck shivering. Were we going to die out here tonight?

"Do I know someone like this?" I asked.

"Quite a few, I'd say."

"Am I like this?" A little deeper.

"You are, but you don't know it."

"Are you?"

"Yes."

Honestly? I had no idea what he was getting at. I mean, really, I was intellectually shut down. All I could think about was getting Beck and myself out of the hell we were in. Luke cocked his head, seemed to be listening to the night.

I used his diverted attention to kick harder at the foothold and my toe slipped in deeper to the frozen ground. My hands were shaking from cold and fear.

"Where do men like this live?"

"Everywhere," he said. "Anywhere."

Beck was tugging at my jean leg but I was ignoring her. If I looked at her again, I was going to fall apart and risk Luke's anger.

"Don't look at her," he said. "Look at me."

His ankle was well within my reach. But if I pulled him into the grave, we'd all be stuck. The flakes falling from the sky were sharp and cold. The snow had already started to stick to the ground. If I was going to make my move, it would have to be one motion. I'd have to step up hard, grab his ankle, and push myself up and pull myself out at the same time. Maybe he'd be too surprised to shoot. How much experience could Luke have with guns?

I couldn't even think of another question to ask. Luke and I locked eyes.

"Do you give up?" he asked.

"No," I said.

I heard a moan from up above, and Luke looked toward the sound. Then he bounced up out of sight. Langdon's arm slowly disappeared as he was dragged away from the edge.

"Luke," I called, but he didn't answer.

After a second I heard an ugly *thwack*. Then again. The sound of it made my stomach turn, but Beck was pulling at me harder. I bent down to her. This time I heard her. Her breath was hot in my ear as she whispered the answer.

I felt myself reel back from her. But even in my utter disbelief, I knew that what she said was the truth. Part of me had known it all along.

When I looked back, Luke was standing above me. He held the shovel in his hand, and there was a fine spray of red across his face and jacket.

"Next question," he said.

I pretended not to notice that he looked like a horror-movie killer standing there, blank, empty, covered with blood. I tried to offer him a loving smile. Isn't that what we all want, really, deep inside? Just to love and be loved? Well, maybe not everyone.

"You don't have to do this," I said. "Langdon used you. I get that none of this is your fault."

He made a little noise somewhere deep inside his throat, and for a moment I thought he'd break down with relief. His face did a little wiggle, the corners of his mouth twitching. But then I realized he was laughing.

"Is that what you think?" he asked. "That *he* used *me*? That pathetic gay pedophile? No."

I did it in one motion. I dug my foot in hard and lifted myself up high enough to grasp the edge and pull myself up. Luke already had the shovel lifted by the time I landed on the slick ground, but I rolled away before he could bring it down.

It landed with a thud, spraying dirt and sharp cold flakes of snow inches from my head. But I was up quickly. And in the next second, I was diving at him, throwing all my weight in his direction. I caught him by the waist and we both fell hard to the ground, Luke issuing a thick groan when my body hit his.

I had his wrists. The shovel had fallen out of reach, and the gun sat uselessly on the edge of the grave. He struggled at first, writhing beneath me, issuing a strangled yell of rage. But I held him down, and after a while he started to sob. Big, gulping, pathetic sobs.

"You're right," he said. "He did use me. He molested me and used me to get to you."

"I know the answer," I said, still pinning him.

"No, you don't," he wailed.

"I do. The answer is 'brother.' You're my brother."

He drew in a little gasp, all his fake wailing drying up instantly.

"She told you," he said. He narrowed his eyes at me. "You cheated. You didn't win."

"No," I lied. "I knew it all along."

"I'm your *half* brother," he said. He almost spat it at me. The tears left his voice and it was suddenly flat as glass. "We don't have the same mother. Your mother is *dead*. He killed her because he wanted to be with *my* mother. But instead he went to jail—because of *you*."

I felt like he was slashing me with razors. Every word out

of his mouth had sliced me, too deep to hurt but not too deep to bleed.

"You little fucker," I hissed at him.

Then he started to sob again, wailing something about wanting to know his father, wanting to go home to his mother, and how he hated me, hated me, hated me. And I saw that he was just a little boy. And then, because I'm a weakling and a fool, I started to feel bad for him.

Then, "If you'd kept your mouth shut, we'd all have been together. That was the plan."

Another slash across my heart. I started to feel myself weaken—physically, emotionally. That drain opened up inside and everything started to pour out of me—my strength, my fight, my will to live. My world was too ugly. Why would anyone want to live there? When Luke twisted his hands away from my grip, I had no inner resources to marshal. Even the sound of Beck calling weakly from her grave wasn't enough to put the fight back in me. It took nothing for him to flip me over and straddle my chest. Then he closed his hands around my neck and started to squeeze.

Was it true? Had my father killed my mother so that he could be with Rachel and Luke? If he'd gotten away with it, what had he planned for me?

Luke wasn't very strong, so he wasn't completely cutting off my air. But it still hurt, and that biological imperative to survive kicked in. I was gasping, seeing stars, and finally the lack of oxygen motivated me to start prying his little fingers from my throat. But he had a death grip.

"Luke, that's enough."

I wasn't sure where the voice was coming from. But then it rang out again, louder, more stern.

"That's enough!" It was Rachel, her voice a shout that echoed off the trees. "Let your brother go."

He released me and I sucked in air, felt the blessed filling of my lungs, and rolled over to start coughing and coughing.

He rose to face his mother, who approached us slowly. She looked around the scene, her jaw open in naked awe. "What have you done?"

She reached for his shoulders and gave him a little shake. *"What have you done?"* Her voice was a shriek, an absolute wail of horror and despair.

But Luke didn't have a chance to answer, because those distant sounds grew suddenly louder. There were voices and lights in the trees, the whopping blades of a helicopter overhead, and suddenly our clearing was filled with a bright light from above. I crawled my way over to the grave where Beck lay, and she was so still and so white at its bottom. And Langdon was lying in a dark circle of blood.

My father would have said that boys don't cry. But I did. For the first time since my mother died, I cried my heart out.

31

Cold still clung to the region as I left my building and climbed on my bike. Even as the end of February approached, the frigid temperatures held on tight. There was no sign of warmth. The groundhog saw his shadow and quickly retreated to his burrow. There were no crocuses pushing their way up through the persistent cover of white. It was frigid and gray as I rode my bike the short distance from my new condo in town to the Coopers' house.

I was headed to the first of three sessions we would have before the Skype conversation I'd agreed to have with my father. Dr. Cooper wanted to prepare me, to get my head straight, my questions in order. She didn't want me to be blindsided. I'd asked her to be present for the actual conversation and she'd agreed. Isn't it amazing how much power our parents have over us? I was afraid even of his image on a screen.

I didn't want to go to Florida to see my father. And Dr. Cooper said I didn't have to, that it wasn't my responsibility to give him what he wanted. But I had questions, a lot of them. And I needed answers. So I agreed to a Skype conversation that would take place in Jones Cooper's office, a place I would never have cause to visit again. I didn't want to do it in my new apartment, the one I shared now with Beck, or in Dr. Cooper's space. These were both safe havens where I was free, finally, to be myself and I wasn't willing to give either of them over to the man who killed my mother, even if he was my father.

News interest in Beck and me had faded, though for a while we were mobbed by reporters when we left our new apartment. So I was grateful for the quiet street as I sailed down the hill. You can imagine the coverage: BAD SEED AND PSYCHO PROFESSOR KIDNAP COED! MISSING GIRL RESCUED BY CROSS-DRESSING BOYFRIEND! It was endless—we couldn't turn on a television or pick up a newspaper without reading more of the story that was gripping the area and the country. Beck was constantly Googling us, and reading all the insane things people were writing and saying. Naturally, she thought it was a gas—or she pretended to think that, just to feel like her old self again.

But until the trials started, if they ever did, interest in us had died down. I never gave an interview, never reacted to the mob, kept my head down. I wore the same boring outfit every day, my androgyny uniform: jeans, white shirt, black peacoat, ski hat, Doc Martens. There was never an interesting picture of me to publish. And Beck behaved herself, too. Which surprised me, because I expected her to lap it up. But she was too shattered to have fun yet. She still had nightmares, was taking an antidepressant. She'd started sessions with Dr. Cooper.

I'd left her behind, wrapped in a blanket on my couch, sulking. She didn't want me to talk to my father, wasn't happy with Dr. Cooper's prep sessions either.

"What can he say to you?" she asked. "It can only set you back."

"I'm fine," I lied. "I'll be fine."

But the truth was, neither of us was exactly fine. We were getting there, maybe, but it would be a while. Lynne, Beck's mother, was staying with us until Beck seemed "more like herself." She and Frank totally accepted us, which surprised me. But they were those type of hippie parents who tried to get behind whatever was going on. Frank was a bit aloof with me, but polite and respectful. Honestly, it's the most you can ask of men sometimes. They're so wound up, so buried beneath layers of "boys don't cry," and "pussy," and "man up," that they don't even know how to feel about anything. I should know.

Me and Beck? I don't know. It's weird. But it's definitely love.

"I always knew you were a boy," she told me. "Maybe at first I thought you were a lesbian. But I never thought you were just a regular girl."

"I never thought you were a regular girl either," I told her. And she found that funny.

"I wanted you right away," she'd said.

She was a little angry that I couldn't say the same. So bound up, wound up, repressed, confused was I that I didn't even know what I wanted, if I wanted anything at all. I was a twenty-two-year-old, mentally unstable virgin, with gender confusion. I didn't want anyone to touch me. I didn't even want anyone to stand too close to me. If anything, Beck's physical presence had made me extremely uncomfortable. But, for me, maybe that ranks as attraction.

What I could tell her was that I'd always loved her, which made her happier. And it was true.

"I'd still have loved you if you were a girl," she said. "All I see is you."

I don't know if that's true for me, but I love the way Beck loves. If everyone loved like she did, the world would be a better place.

As I rode my bike through town, I was thinking about Luke, as I had every day since I learned he was my brother. They carted him off screaming that night, and I could still hear him at night after I fell asleep. *IhateyouIhateyouIhateyouIhateyou*, he'd yelled into the night. I didn't know if he meant me or his mother or the world. Maybe he meant all of us.

That night, as the cavalry arrived, I was the only one who could explain what had happened when Detective Ferrigno came on the scene. So I told him—everything. I told him who I was (he didn't seem too surprised—either he already knew, or he was one of those guys that had seen everything).

I told him about my panicked flight to Luke's and why, what I had found there, and why I had come to this place in the woods.

I told him about Langdon, and how I thought he might either be obsessed with or associated with my father. That he had been obsessed with me. Finally, I told him and the other officers about Luke. It all sounded totally crazy, of course. And the look on Detective Ferrigno's face, a kind of mystified, angry frown, told me that he wasn't quite buying the story. They took Beck and me to the hospital, but a police officer was stationed outside my door. It was a few days before they decided that I was victim and not perpetrator.

"Don't tell them anything without a lawyer," said Rachel as I was being led away. Which I thought was a strange thing to say. I couldn't answer her; I couldn't even look at her. Were the things Luke said true? "Your father wouldn't want you to do that."

She stood watching me as the paramedics walked me down the path toward the ambulance that waited. Beck had been airlifted away from me. And I just remember feeling nothing but that familiar numbness. I turned to look at Rachel one last time, and I had a strange thought. *What does she know?*

I passed the Kahns' house on the way to Dr. Cooper's. There was a "For Sale" sign in the yard, and the place had a strange air of desertion. I knew that Luke had disappeared into a kind of catatonic state. (Yeah, right. Everyone else seemed to believe that, but I knew that little freak better.) He had been committed to a mental health facility about forty minutes from The Hollows. Langdon was in a coma, having suffered catastrophic brain injury from Luke's blows with the shovel. A full recovery was not expected. How do I feel about this? It sucks. I hate Langdon; I miss him. I wish he was here to talk all this through with. I hope he lives so that he can be punished, and to answer all the million questions that I have.

So Beck and I were the only ones able to tell the tale. And neither of us really knew the whole story, just our pieces. And Rachel was playing the suffering mother, completely innocent in the whole matter. She was, she claimed, as mystified as everyone else about how Langdon and Luke connected and conspired to torture me, and why. Her decision to move to The Hollows was just for Fieldcrest; neither she nor Luke had any idea I was here, hiding from my ugly past. Yeah, sure. I don't believe her. Jung didn't believe in coincidence, and neither do I. What he believed in was synchronicity: the experience of two or more events that are causally unrelated or unlikely to occur together by chance, and yet are experienced as occurring together in some meaningful way. In other words, the universe conspires—our minds, ideas are linked, suggesting a larger framework, a kind of neural web where we are all connected. I'm not so sure about that. But people conspire, that I know. Especially people like Luke.

The Kahn home was now behind me. And even though I was just a few blocks from Dr. Cooper's, I found myself turning around.

After I left her alone in the woods that night she disappeared, Beck sat crying. (Would she ever forgive me? I really don't know.) Eventually, she grew cold, calmed down, and started to pull herself together. *I hated you,* she said. *I was going back to tell everyone that you were a boy. I was going to set your whole life on fire.* Would she have done it? Probably not. Beck burns hot but cools down fast.

She heard Luke approach and she thought that I had come back for her.

"He was small, just a kid," she said. "But he looked so much like you, it was stunning. How could you not have seen it?"

She knew so much about the case—everything really. She said that she'd suspected all along that there was something strange about me. That's why she liked me. Once she knew about my aunt, it was just a quick Google search to find her blog. And once she knew who Bridgette was, it was pretty easy to figure out who I was. She read all the books, the articles. She'd seen all the news documentaries, the made-for-television movies. She knew immediately who Luke was when she saw him. She knew that he was my father's other son.

"But he's not like you," she said. "He's heartless; I saw that right away. He's evil."

But he had approached her sweetly. "Are you okay?" he asked. "You're upset?"

"What do you want?" she'd said. "Who are you?"

She tried to walk past him when he didn't answer her. But he followed her. When she started to run, he gave chase. "He was laughing," she said. "It was just this little-boy giggle in the dark night. It was nightmarish." In her mounting panic, she lost her footing and fell hard.

"When I pulled myself up," she said, "Langdon was ahead of me. And Luke was behind."

"He doesn't love you," Langdon said. "He can't. He belongs to me."

He caught up to her fast, and hit her with something she didn't see. After that, things came back only in her nightmares—dark, fairy-tale memories of being carried through the woods, Langdon sticking a needle in her arm, Luke sitting inside the mine shaft, staring at her. He brought her candy and water; she remembered that. She lived on mini Mars bars. Why did they keep her like that?

"I think they were enjoying it," she said. "Like a kid keeps a lizard or a frog."

Dr. Cooper thinks I should worry less about the how and why of things. How did Rachel and Luke find me? How were they connected to Langdon? What kind of an agenda were they running? What did it have to do with my father?

Who was manipulating who? She says, for my purposes, it doesn't matter. But it does. Between Beck's nightmares and my obsessive thinking, neither one of us may ever sleep again. I felt myself getting more ragged. It was killing me. I had to know the answers; it was part of the reason I needed to talk to my father.

I stopped my bike in the street in front of the Kahns' house. Rachel's car wasn't in the driveway. And I was thinking about that journal. Surely, Rachel had changed the locks. Still, I just happened to have that key in my pocket. What if it still worked?

Dr. Cooper and Sky had both asked me for different reasons to stay away from Rachel Kahn. *She can't give you what you need,* Dr. Cooper warned. *Everything you need is inside you. Her reasons, her answers, whatever they are … they matter to your psychological wellness not at all. It is only the here and now that matters. You've come through tremendous trials, internal and external. And you've survived. You're on the road to healing yourself. Stay focused on the present and the future.*

But the past, the present, and the future are not a straight line. They're all woven together, the strands twisting and turning through each other. How can you walk into the future without understanding your past? I said as much. *Your past is important to process, yes,* she said. *Not Rachel's. Not Luke's. Yours.*

That desire I had on first meeting Rachel and Luke—I so badly wanted to help, to be there for them. Did something deep inside draw me into their lives? Was there some psychic and/or biological link that attracted me to Luke? When I thought of my time in the Kahns' home, at their table, it was the most comfortable, most happy I had been in my adult life. I fit into their little union. However twisted and strange that is, it's true.

I felt my phone vibrating, and I pulled it out and answered without checking the caller ID. Only a few people had the number of this new phone: Beck, my aunt, Dr. Cooper, Detective Ferrigno, and Sky.

"Is this Lane? Lane Crowe?"

It was strange to hear my real name, so long had I hidden behind Lana Granger. It was everywhere now, my real name. I was Lane Crowe, hero, freak, lady boy, transgender poster boy for the bullied, for the gender dysmorphic. I was derided by the gay and lesbian community, the feminists, the Republican pundits. I was the number one most-wanted guest on all the major talk shows—I'd be the biggest hit since the pregnant man was making the rounds. The new cell phone I had was the third I'd had in a month.

"Who's calling?" I asked, ready to hang up and get a new phone.

"It's Paul Rodriguez," he said. "I worked for your father."

It was the private eye who had been calling for some time.

"Don't hang up," he said quickly. "I think you'll want to hear what I have to say. The cops won't listen. They're sick of me."

I held the phone to my ear, kept my eyes on the house. "I'm listening."

"Your dad fired me because I finally figured out who killed your mom. I'm sorry to be so blunt with you. You've been through a lot. But it was what happened to you, with that kid, that made me realize. I can't believe I didn't see it years ago. She was investigated and cleared. She had an alibi."

"Okay," I said. He was dragging it out. "Tell me."

"I know you're going to talk to him in a couple of days, right? I want you to know the truth. Maybe you can convince him to save his own life."

It didn't take him long when he finally got to the point. As he spoke, I saw Rachel move into the living room window. She lifted a hand to me, gave me a weak smile. My breath was coming out in clouds.

"Thank you, Mr. Rodriguez," I said.

"Can you talk to him, kid?" he said. "I think he wants to die."

No, that's not what he wanted. I finally understood it after all this time. What he wanted was to take care of his children.

"I'll talk to him," I said. "Hey, Mr. Rodriguez, can you do me a favor?"

"Sure," he said. He sounded like the kind of guy who would do you a favor and never ask for anything in return.

"Can you call Detective Ferrigno at The Hollows PD, and tell him what you told me?"

"Hey, wait a second," he said. He must have heard something in my tone that he didn't like. "Don't do anything stupid, okay?"

But I ended the call and stuck the phone into my pocket, then I walked up the path to Luke's house.

32

I remembered the shoes. The small pair of practical walking shoes I saw the day my mother died. Not shoes that belonged to a man, but to a woman. The voices downstairs, as I had hid under my bed, were panicked and arguing voices. I had heard my father and a woman. Rachel. It must have been her.

Now, years later, she opened the door wide for me, and I stepped inside. I'd always felt welcomed here, as though I belonged. And that's because I did belong among the murderous and psychotic. They were my peeps.

She walked into the kitchen and brewed me a cup of tea—peppermint with honey, just the way I liked it.

I sat at the table, in the same place where I sat on the day of my interview. It seemed like a lifetime ago. But it was just a little over a month. I was literally a different person then. I had sat there, presenting myself as a girl. Today, I was fully dwelling in my male self.

I felt real and right for the first time in my life. I had

dwelled among women to hide myself, to heal myself. It was so much easier to be a girl, so much sweeter, and truer and closer to the heart and the spirit. I had embraced and accepted that part of my psyche, my anima. And I had let it go. And I was a stronger person for it.

"I just wanted to talk to her," she said. She knew why I had come and she got straight to the point. "Your mother."

She looked down at her neatly manicured nails. "It was so crazy for her to keep him, your father, just because of you. They stopped loving each other years earlier. And I had a troubled child, too."

My mother could not have been more different from Rachel. She was fiery—big emotions, big temper, big love. (Like someone else we know.) How would she have reacted to Rachel's visit? To her pleas? Not well, I'm guessing. She'd have lost it. In her fights with my father, she was by far the one that blew the hottest, the one who might resort to violence first.

"But she didn't see it that way," Rachel said.

My mother let Rachel into the house. She was civil at first, but things got ugly quickly.

"We started to argue," Rachel said. "We were both angry; he'd made promises to both of us. We each had a child with him. She called me a whore, and I'll admit that I slapped her."

I could envision the scene, see my mother reeling back from the blow. What would she do? She'd strike back. Of course, she did. Then she ran upstairs to get away, to lock herself in the bedroom to call the police.

"But I got to her first. We struggled for the phone she had in her hand, and she ran with it out into the hallway. Your father was supposed to be there. We were planning on talking to her together. But he was late. He was chronically, forever late for everything when it came to us. Because he was always with you and her."

There it was, the bitterness.

"You act like my mother was the other woman," I said. "She wasn't."

We were none of us innocent in this. We all had our roles to play. But of all of us, my mother was the most wronged. If I'd been normal, if my father had been faithful, none of this ever would have happened. I wouldn't hear her maligned.

"It was an accident," said Rachel. "In our battle, she tripped over the runner in the hall. The corner slipped from beneath her, and she fell over the railing."

She took in a little gasp and began to cry. Silently, stoically, the tears fell.

"It was an accident, Lane. Please believe me. It has haunted me. Not a day goes by that I don't look back in regret."

And I could see that it was true. Looking at her, I saw how hollowed out she was. I thought it was Luke who had turned her into the small, careful, joyless woman she seemed to be. And surely he played his part, but it was so

395

much more than that. Guilt, if you live to carry it, is a terrible burden. It weighs you down, stoops your shoulders, pushes you right into the ground.

But her sorrow, her regret? It didn't mean much. Her actions had led directly to my mother's death. She had let my father go to prison, was clearly willing to let him die for a crime he didn't commit. She wasn't that sorry. Not sorry enough to own up.

"Your father came home then," she said. She reached her hand over the table to me. But I didn't move a muscle. "But you weren't supposed to come home. You were supposed to be late at school."

I didn't answer her. She nodded and kept her hand where it was, an open invitation.

"I wanted to call the police, to face the consequences. But I couldn't. What would happen to my special-needs son. I had no family, no husband. No, we decided that he'd hide the body, act as though she'd run off with her lover. She was having an affair, too, you know?"

"Sure, trash the victim," I said. "That's always a good defense. The slut got what she deserved, right? Meanwhile, nothing was ever proved."

She bowed her head. "I'm sorry. I shouldn't have said that."

I heard the clock ticking in the kitchen. She was an analog girl in a digital age. I had really liked her a lot.

"I had to take care of Luke, and your father had to take

care of you. We were thinking of both of you. I know she would have wanted your father to take care of you, Lane. Our plan was to wait until things blew over. Then we were going to be together, all of us. We were going to be a family."

"Right," I said. "The world's most fucked-up family."

"No family is perfect," she said stiffly. "We all have our problems."

There was more, so I waited.

"Luke struggled even more after his father went away," she said. "The older he got, I've told you, the worse he was. We went from school to school, from doctor to doctor. He'd been diagnosed and dosed for several different disorders. Nothing ever helped. You know the drill; you've lived it. I was literally at the end of my rope when I got a call from Langdon Hewes."

She leaned back a little, looked up at the ceiling. Then she wiped the tears from her face.

"He said he'd met your father when you were boarding at the school in Florida. They'd maintained a correspondence, he said, and he'd been keeping an eye on you at Sacred Heart College—unbeknownst to you, of course. He told me what you'd done, how you were hiding from the events of your past. He asked me to bring Luke to Fieldcrest. Langdon thought it could help Luke."

"But Luke is beyond helping," I said.

And Rachel nodded. "It wasn't long, I don't think, before

Langdon was in his thrall. Luke sniffed out his obsession with you almost immediately."

It was true that Langdon had an ongoing correspondence with my father. Detective Ferrigno had told me as much. But he'd said it seemed fairly benign. He said the notes from my father simply asked about my progress, expressed his hope that Langdon would look out for me and for Luke, if he could. It was a normal correspondence between a concerned parent and his child's college adviser, someone who is a recognized expert in cases like Luke's and mine.

Except that it wasn't normal at all, was it? Langdon had used my father's disconnection from Luke and me to worm his way into our lives. He had sought to bring us together, for reasons I didn't quite understand. Maybe he did, in some twisted way, think he was trying to help us. But only so far as it served his desire to be "there for me," to get me to "let him in"—what he said he wanted in the woods. And Rachel, probably also acting out of desperation, had let him use us all. But I didn't feel the need to say any of this. I was just there to listen.

"Over the years, Luke had grown to hate you," said Rachel. "He blamed you for your father going to jail. Of course, I tried to shield him from all of it. But as he grew older, he found things out on his own.

"We thought—Langdon and I—if he could get to know you, we could work through that. I thought it would be good for both of you to get to know each other. I thought it might help him and you. Hence the ad and Langdon's putting it in your hands."

She made it all sound so innocent and benign. It was anything but that. Langdon never had Luke's best interest or mine at heart, just the fulfillment of his own desires. Why didn't she seem to realize that, even now? And was she underplaying her part in all of this? She couldn't have thought any of this was good or right or healthy.

"It was Langdon's idea," I said. Of course, it was. He was the one pulling the strings—at first.

"I don't know how quickly Luke figured it all out. I didn't realize how complicated things had gotten. They were running a whole other agenda that I had nothing to do with. Luke was raging all the time; I had no idea why. I was locking him in his room every night just because I had no idea what he would do after I fell asleep. It wasn't until that night that I realized he'd been sneaking out."

"And what about Beck? Why did they take her?" I asked because it was something I'd been puzzling over. I was really just thinking aloud, not imagining she had an answer. But what she said was surprisingly insightful.

"I think Luke would have done anything to hurt you. And Langdon just saw her as a threat to his relationship with you. Ultimately, neither one of them saw her even as a person. For Langdon, she was an obstacle. For Luke, she was just a game piece."

With Langdon in a coma and Luke supposedly catatonic,

the details of who was using who and why were elusive. I asked her what she thought.

"I honestly just don't know," she said. She was the embodiment of exhaustion. Just looking at her made me want to lie down and go to sleep for a thousand years.

I couldn't help but think about my father. Two sons, by two different women, both with mental illness. My mother and Rachel were physically and energetically so different. What was it about each of them that drew him?

I remembered what she had told me about the mental illness in her family—her father's battles with depression, her brother's suicide.

Was it the damage in each of these women that attracted him? My father was a man who liked to solve a problem, to fix the damaged things. He liked to feel needed. Maybe Rachel and my mother exuded a kind of scent that attracted him. They needed his stability, and he needed their chaos. Yin and yang.

"Why are you telling me this?" I asked her. "Why are you telling me this now?"

So many years had passed, and my father was so close to the lethal injection. Rachel was just about to get away with murder. I always knew that part of my father's money would go to the other child. He'd told me himself long ago. It was something that I had pushed away. I didn't want to know about them. Rachel was around the corner from a big payday.

She sagged across the table, dropped her head in her hand.

"Because I'm tired, Lane. I can't do this anymore. I don't want your father to die because of something for which I am ultimately responsible. I can't lie my way through another day. I can't help Luke. I thought I could, that's why I kept this secret so long. But I see now. This incident has proven to me that he has grown beyond me. One day he'll be bigger than me. One day, when it's the most advantageous for him, he'll kill me."

I didn't say anything. It was true. Part of me wanted to comfort her, but I held myself back. There was a hard knock on the door then.

"Hollows PD," came a booming voice. "Open up."

She looked up. "You already knew," she said. "You called them."

"Are you ready to tell your truth?" I asked.

She gave a faint nod, had the pale, trembling look of fear. She grabbed my hand. This time I held hers tight, gave her a comforting squeeze. I know how soul wrenching it is to face the truth, the past, everything you've sought to hide. It's vertigo, standing on the edge and looking over, imagining the fall, the impact. But at first, it feels like flying.

"Will you take care of him, Lane?"

"I will," I said. "I'll take care of him. I promise."

33

Langdon Hewes died. It was written in the headlines of *The Hollows Journal*: HEWES DIES FROM ANEURYSM. The words, so stark on the page, so devoid of all the layers of incident that led to them, made me angry. I folded the paper and tossed it to the floor, where it lay soft and harmless in the morning sunlight.

And even though I have no reason to wonder, I do. Langdon's injuries were extensive, but the last I'd heard he was showing some improvement—some movement, some speech. Then, suddenly, he died. Some would say that his death was a blessing. That's what people say when something has gone on too long for their comfort. *It was a blessing. He's at peace now. It's for the best.* Of course, none of us knows if that's really true. What awaits Langdon on the other side? Who can say?

It is September now, autumn in The Hollows. It's still warm outside, and the days still seem long and lazy. Beck and I are back at school. She's redoing her last semester.

And I am beginning my master's work in abnormal child psychology in the graduate program at Sacred Heart, working at Fieldcrest as part of my study. My mother wanted me to help people, and I want that, too.

It's the work you were born to do, Beck always quips. *Psycho.*

It had been an Indian summer day like this when Elizabeth went missing. I still think about her and how her life was cut short. Her case was never reopened, and the ruling of accidental death still stands. Once it was understood that I had nothing to do with Beck's disappearance, there was less reason to take a fresh look at the events of that night. Another loss for the world, another beautiful girl gone. But was she a victim of fate or a victim of violence? I have tried to remember that night. Did we fight? Did she somehow know about me? Did she run away from me that night and not her boyfriend, as some witnesses claim? I pray that my dreams of her crying are just that, and not memories. I do know I never would have hurt her, not on purpose. Which doesn't make anyone feel better, does it? Death by accident is as cruel as murder would have been, just as merciless.

Speaking of bad intentions: Luke still resides at a mental health facility about forty minutes from The Hollows where I visit him every other week. And today is visiting day.

Beck has already left for class. So I shower and get dressed. She was angry with me this morning, picked a fight over who was supposed to stop at the store yesterday and get the coffee. We were forced to drink the dregs from yesterday, because *whoever* it was (Beck) forgot to run the errand. She's always mad at me on visiting day, consistently creates some kind of drama. She doesn't want me to visit with Luke, and she hates that I consider it an obligation.

He's my brother, Beck. Who is left to care for him?

Um, his father.

My father can't even care for himself.

Why is any of this your problem? Your brother tried to kill you. Your father might as well have murdered your mother even if he wasn't the one to push her. This is nuts. How are we ever going to have a normal life?

We're not, I told her. *Nothing about our life will be normal. Ever. If you wanted normal, you picked the wrong guy.*

She left in anger, which she had promised before that she would never do again. But we break our promises, don't we? All the time.

I head downstairs, hop into my new hybrid, and putt-putt out of town. I wanted a muscle car, one of those new Chargers, to connect with my newfound *maleness*. But I guess, ultimately, I'm too crunchy, too concerned about the planet. Beck and I shopped for a hybrid and wound up with a Prius, which looks more like an orthopedic shoe than a car. But, fine. *See,* I told her as I signed the paperwork. *This is normal. We're buying a car.*

Fuck off, she said. But she smiled. Who knew that beneath all the tats and piercings and bad attitudes, my girl just wanted the things all girls are supposed to want. She wants to be loved, to be safe, to have a home and a car. And she wants those things with me. I can give her some of it.

I cross the town limits and wind through the outlying suburban developments. Eventually, those give way to farmland. Then I'm heading through a thick, wooded region. And the trees around me are starting their show of gold, orange, red, and brown.

I wish I could say that the sight of it fills me with joy, a sense of peace or renewal. But that's not how I feel. Let's face it, not that much has changed. I am still in therapy, still need medication to control my various problems. Beck and I . . . well, our relationship is exactly what it has always been. It's intensely loving, but we still have the same degree of heat, the same arguments that escalate instead of wind down. My coldness sometimes makes her cry.

I think of her parents' relationship, stormy, on-again, off-again. I think of my parents, often resorting to violence. How will Beck and I learn to love each other differently? We both know we have to try, and we *are* trying. But it's not all hot sex and hybrids.

At least I'm whole, fully realized, as Dr. Cooper is quick to remind me. I'm not hiding. I'm not lying. And I have made my home in The Hollows. I feel like it has closed around me, ensconced and protected me. I feel like I can live a real life here. Untethered from the past, I can walk into the future.

I approach the grounds of the juvenile facility that houses

Luke. It tries hard not to look like what it is. The land-scaping is lovely. The gates manage to seem ornately decorative, even though I know them to be electrified—like a mansion (for maniacs) or a country club (for nutcases). And the man who greets me at the gate is armed. He knows me, this aging guard with his slick gray hair and formidable paunch. He waves me in, and I feel a familiar lurch in my stomach. I hate this place. And I have grown to hate my brother.

My father is ill. He has liver cancer and very little time to live. I have taken the trip to Florida to see him after he was released from prison and admitted to a hospital not far from where he spent the last seven years. The visit, without my going into too many details, was awkward. He apologized for all of his mistakes.

I'm sorry, son. I can't count the ways I failed you and your mother.

Dr. Cooper urges a journey toward forgiveness. It's a concept that I don't really understand. What does it mean to forgive someone? *It only means that you release the anger, the hatred. It doesn't mean that you're saying it's all right now, or that you've forgotten the wrong. It just means that you've drained the boil. When you touch it, it doesn't hurt as much. That's all.*

But I am not angry. I do not hate my father. I miss my mother, every day. I wish everything about our life together had been different. But I do not blame him, or her, or even

Rachel. Really, I blame myself. Maybe if I had been a different kind of child, they would have had a different kind of life. Dr. Cooper says we need to work on my thinking.

It's all right, Dad, I told him. *I failed her, too.*

He tried to argue with me, but he was just too physically weak. We made peace, I think. We are bound by blood, but we are strangers of circumstance. We are so far apart that we cannot come together now. If I could feel more, I imagine I'd feel deeply sad about that.

I had one request for him, and he was happy to comply. A couple of weeks later, the paperwork came in the mail from Sky. It has been signed by all parties.

They always have Luke and me meet in this comfortable, sunny room. They call it "The Morning Room." There's a fireplace and some plush couches. Fresh flowers in plastic vases are placed artfully on end tables, books are arranged carefully on shelves. It is a soft and comforting place, pretty even. Except for the armed guard that sits just outside the door.

Today, Luke is sitting by the window when I arrive. His twelfth birthday has just passed, and it's interesting how he seems to change every time I visit. He is growing up, getting bigger. It fills me with dread.

Usually, we just sit. I talk about innocuous things—the weather, events in The Hollows. I avoid anything loaded. I don't talk about our father, or his mother. I don't talk about Beck. I talk about television shows, movies, and video games. He stares blankly out the window. He hasn't uttered a word since the night he was admitted.

But today, there's an electricity in the air, something palpable that I can feel. When the door closes behind me, the hair on my arms stands on end, and someone walks over my grave.

I take my usual seat as far away from Luke as the room will allow.

"Hey, Luke," I say. "How are you feeling?"

How can you live with it? Sitting there and talking to him after what he did to you? To me? Beck asked me this morning, tears in her eyes.

"It's still pretty warm out," I go on. "But a cold front is moving in."

He's a monster.

"Did you hear the news?" he says.

I practically jump out of my skin. I haven't heard his voice in over a year. It sounds strange, a crackly high and low to it. I try not to show my surprise.

"What news?"

"The nutty professor bit it." He is still looking out the window.

"Where did you hear that?"

"I know people," he says. "People tell me things. I think you know what I mean."

"I have no idea what you mean," I say. But I do. I know exactly what he means. He means that he is manipulating the staff.

"And it sounds like dear old Dad's not far behind." He has a young boy's voice, but an old man's cadence and phrasing. Very unsettling.

"He's not well, no," I say.

"Ironic, isn't it?" he says. "You can take the man out of death row . . ." He lets his voice trail off.

"I have a friend here," he says when I remain silent. "A nurse. She's a sad person. She lost a son about my age a couple years back. I don't think she's over it."

What is he trying to tell me? I feel myself go very still. The air in the room grows thick and overwarm. Again, I think silence might be the best answer.

Eventually, he turns to look at me. His eyes are glassy, probably from the medications they are giving him. I know the list, since I consult with his doctor every week. I disagree with his being medicated. There is no medication for someone like Luke. He is a psychopath, a ruthless, calculating machine with no empathy or feeling for other people. Whatever window might have existed to teach him something that approached empathy, as Dr. Chang insists is possible, has closed. Luke is a tiger cub in a cage. He will only grow and become a stronger, more efficient predator. He will never be anything other than what he is. He can only be managed.

He shifts in his seat, keeps his eyes on me as if waiting for me to speak. He wants me to ask the questions he knows I have. But I don't say anything. I want him to start, know he will.

Then, "You know they lied to me? My mother and Hewes—they tried to trick me. But I knew right away who you were."

"How?"

He wrinkles his nose at me. "I recognized you. Ever heard of Google?"

I think of the searches I have seen on his computer. There are no secrets anymore, not really—not even from an eleven-year-old.

"And I made sure he knew I figured it out during our private sessions."

"Your private sessions?" The thought of that is creepy on so many different levels. I can just imagine the two of them, each of them running a separate agenda, manipulating and using each other. Who was the predator and who was the prey?

"Once I figured it out, he told me that he'd been talking to our father, that he wanted to help us reunite as brothers. But I knew he was in love with you—which is sick. And weird. I mean who could love you?"

I smile a little at that. He can't hurt me but he still wants to.

"So you talked about me? In your private sessions?"

Luke shifts again, as if physically uncomfortable. He is growing more agitated, more restless.

"He never cared about me at all," he says. "He never wanted to help me get better."

411

He seems upset about it, which takes me aback. Does Luke know that there is something wrong with him? Has he hoped to get better? I keep reminding myself that he is just a child. I had been no less ill at his age. We aren't the same, of course. I'm not a sociopath. I have problems, but I can feel, love, have empathy. I don't see others as pieces in a game I play. That's why therapy and guidance and medication help me. Can he be helped? I don't know.

I still keep silent. There is so much I want to know, but I won't give him the satisfaction of asking.

"I followed you; I was always following you. Do you know that?"

I shrug. I'd guessed as much, thinking back on the dirt on his tires. The form I saw in the woods that night at the graveyard.

"And that night I saw you go into the woods; I could tell you were upset and then that girl followed you. I called Hewes on my mom's cell phone, which I'd lifted, and we went together. We saw you. We saw you with her. It was gross."

"Why did you follow?"

"Why not? It was an opportunity. He wanted to know you. I wanted to hurt you. We both got what we wanted. Only, he didn't get what he expected. And he went a little crazy after that. I wanted to kill her. He wanted to wait until the anniversary of the night your mother died. Which I had to admit was pretty good."

The crazy leading the crazy. Wow. It is amazing any of us has survived. But because I'm not as crazy I still have to ask.

"So what was it all about?" I ask finally. "What was the point?"

It is part of the reason I keep coming here week after week, not to take care of him, or to let him know he isn't alone. I know one day he is going to have to crack and tell me all the things he must be dying to tell me. The corners of his mouth turn up in an ugly facsimile of a smile.

"Langdon, the scavenger hunt, kidnapping Beck," I say, just for clarification.

"The point?" he says. He seems annoyed. "I thought you knew."

"Enlighten me."

"The point was to win." His lips are dry, chapped white. His skin has an unhealthy gray pallor. But he undeniably looks like me, except he will be much bigger than I am when he finishes growing.

"It was a game," I say, just to clarify.

"You know it was," he says. "You agreed to play. You *wanted* to play."

I almost laugh. "And who won?"

"I did, of course."

I sweep my arm around the room. "How do you figure?"

"I exposed your secrets," he says. "That was the first thing. You were a liar and a poser and I wanted the whole world to know it."

He looks at me, waiting for a reaction like any little boy. I don't give him one. "P.S.," he adds. "I think you looked better as a girl."

I offer him a wan smile, which he doesn't seem to like. He shifts uncomfortably and leans forward in his seat.

"Langdon is dead," he goes on. "He'll never be able to tell anyone how I used and manipulated him, teased him into helping me. Not that anyone would have believed him. No one ever believes a pedophile."

"Was he that?"

"He was if I say he was," Luke snaps. He is getting wobbly, not enjoying my flat affect. Rachel was emotional; she'd admitted as much. She responded to Luke, gave him a lot of energy when he acted out. He liked that, because it fueled him. But he will get nothing from me.

Maybe Langdon had been a pedophile. He was obsessed with me, that was clear. I was a girlish boy, or a boyish man—in either case, pretty much a freak. So maybe that's what he liked—not men, not women exactly. Or maybe he *was* trying to help me at first. But he was unstable, and Luke pushed him over the edge. Now that Langdon was dead, there was no way to know. Okay, Luke, you won that one.

"He got me the key to the caretaker's building, by the way," he says. "The Hollows Historical Society has an office on your campus. It was nothing for him to take the key."

He is true to his word: I'll give him that. He'd promised to tell me everything when the game was done.

"My mother is in prison," he says, ticking off another win. "So I'm out from under her."

Here, I smile a little. I can't help it.

"And soon our father will be dead."

"So?"

"So, I'll be an orphan more or less," he says. "A filthy-rich orphan. And our good friend Sky Lawrence will make all the arrangements for me to be well cared for. Once I'm well, of course. And I have been feeling better."

Of course, Rachel and Luke knew Sky. He managed my father's money and Luke was one of the beneficiaries of his will.

"So all of this was about the money?" I say, playing dumb.

"No, *stupid*," he says. His voice goes up an octave. "This was about me being able to do whatever I want. Kids never *ever* get to do what they want. I told you that already. Weren't you listening to me? I'm free. I'm rich. I get to do anything I want to do from now on." He is actually gritting his teeth, sticking his jaw out at me. It isn't pretty.

I stand up from my chair and put on my coat.

"Well," I say, "congrats, kiddo. You win again. I'm not a sore loser and you played a good game. The long con, right? Nice one."

I move toward the door, and I can feel the daggers of his gaze on my back. I rest my hand on the handle and turn around.

"There's just one thing," I say. "I went down to Florida to

see our father. Man, it's hot down there. I don't know how people do it."

His face goes slack.

"He signed over your guardianship to me," I say. I love the feel of those words on my tongue. "Your mom? She knows she's not going to be in a position to care for you for a while. So she signed, too. I'm your primary guardian. And the guardian of your trust."

His whole body goes rigid, and what little color he has drains from his face.

"You'll be a legal adult at the age of eighteen," I say. "But I'll control the money until you're thirty. And there are lots of conditions built into the trust, which we will discuss when you're feeling better. Nothing big—do well in school, stay out of trouble, community service, therapy—stuff like that."

He makes a move toward me, but I hold up a hand and he freezes. "Before you get any ideas," I go on. "If anything suspicious happens to me, to your mother, to Beck, or to anyone or anything I care about—all of that money will be divided equally between Fieldcrest and Dr. Chang's school in Florida. You won't get a dime."

He is a quivering statue of rage, his mouth hanging open in a silent scream.

"Do you understand me, brother?" I ask.

He comes racing toward me then, issuing a kind of stran-gled warrior's cry, but I am already out the door and close it quickly behind me. He crashes against the glass, his face a red mask of fury. The guard, who had been dozing, rises quickly to his feet.

Our faces, mine and Luke's, are inches from each other, separated by thick glass. I look him right in the eyes and mouth the word I have been dying to say since our first afternoon together.

"Checkmate."

acknowledgments

My deepest thanks to:

My husband Jeffrey and daughter Ocean Rae for their tireless enthusiasm and support and abiding love. Words are never enough, but hopefully I show you every day.

My brilliant editor Sally Kim for knowing that I needed to write this book even before I did and for helping me make it everything it needed to be.

My amazing agent Elaine Markson has been a guiding hand, a loving and supportive friend, and the champion of my career. I'd be lost without her.

The stellar team at Touchstone, including: Carolyn Reidy, Susan Moldow, Michael Selleck, Liz Perl, Louise Burke, Stacy Creamer, David Falk, Brian Belfiglio, Cherlynne Li, Wendy Sheanin, Paula Amendolara, Tracy Nelson, Colin Shields, Chrissy Festa, Charlotte Gill, Gary Urda, Gregory Hruska, Louise Burke, Michelle Fadlalla, Bryony Weiss, Teresa Brumm, Meredith Vilarello, Ana Paula De Lima, Paul O'Halloran, Alanna Ramirez, and Allegra Ben-Amotz. All of these people have made me feel welcome in my new home and bring their own particular style and talent to the table. And I can never heap enough praise on the sales team, out there on the front lines in this super-competitive business, getting books into as many hands as possible. It's everything; thank you.

My amazing network of family and friends who cheer me through the good days and carry me through the challenging ones. My parents, Joseph and Virginia Miscione, my brother Joe, and his wife Tara are my unflagging supporters. It means so much. Heather Mikesell and Shaye Areheart are two dear, dear friends and early readers whose advice and input I rely on too heavily. Marion Chartoff and Tara Popick, my two oldest friends, have been with me every step of the way.

about the author

Lisa Unger is an award-winning *New York Times* and internationally bestselling author. Her novels have sold more than 1.5 million copies and have been translated into twenty-six different languages. She lives in Florida with her husband and daughter and is at work on her next novel. Visit her at www.lisaunger.com.